# Motor City Justice

Tony Aued

ISBN: 13-978-1517323882
ISBN-10-1517323886

# DEDICATION

Special thanks to my family for all their support. To fans of both the Blair Adams Series and my new Murder Mystery series, I appreciate your loyalty and continued support.

# OTHER NOVELS BY TONY AUED

**FBI Thrillers**

Blair Adams, The Package

Blair Adams, Abduction

The Vegas Connection

The Blame Game

**Murder Mysteries**

Murder in Greektown

Greektown Conspiracy

Motor City Justice

# ACKNOWLEDGMENTS

Special thanks to Beverly Styles for her editing. The work you performed is excellent.

To my friend, Carl Virgilio, your cover again jumps off the shelf. I cannot tell you how much you and our friendship has meant, thanks for everything.

# CHAPTER ONE

**Interstate 94 had turned into total chaos; cars were piled up** in all lanes. Emergency crews were having trouble getting to people that were trapped in their vehicles. Michigan State Police helped divert cars off the road as entrances and exits on the Interstate from I-96 to past Mt. Elliott were all closed. Gawkers pointed to a garbage truck that teetered over the center guard rail on top of a white and blue Dodge Charger. It was just past the Woodward underpass that was under construction for the new M1 Light Rail Project. Local NBC television dispatched their Sky 4 chopper with Iraq veteran Dirk Stanfield at the controls. He hovered over the scene but couldn't get confirmation on the vehicles at the center of the action. Dirk turned to the reporter on-board, "Aaron, I'm going to move further east to get you a better angle on the action." Once he banked the chopper, they were in a better position for Aaron to get the details. The reporter was surprised, but confirmed, that it was a Dodge Charger under the garbage truck; it indeed appeared to be a police vehicle. He focused on the blue and white lettering on the side door helping make the identification. Stanfield watched the action below; *it brought back so many memories of action he saw during his time in the Afghan war. Dirk thought about the rescue missions he flew over Kabul and often suffered flashbacks to those events.* He held the controls tight and turned back to the reporter, "Aaron, hold on; I'm going to go a little lower to see if we can get a better view of that garbage truck." Aaron continued to film the scene below as it was being streamed live to the Channel 4 television station.

Cars were now backed up on both sides of the freeway and emergency vehicles were trying to clear the crash. Just as Dirk brought the chopper lower, he pointed out two speeding vehicles on the freeway, "Aaron, quick, look on the other side." A yellow Mustang suddenly lost control and collided with the fuel tanker that was stopped. The chopper was too low just above the new crash and bystanders heard the loud noise of sheet metal crunching below. Dirk yelled out, "We've got a small flame coming from under the tanker that was just hit by that speeding car."

Aaron panned the camera around, "Yeah, I see flames coming from under that car." He started reporting back to the station, shouting into the mike. "We've got emergency crews helping those stranded on the freeway, I saw what had just happened and police started to get everyone back out of danger." Dirk quickly tried to pull the chopper back up and out of danger. People below were grabbing their children trying to carry them to safety and chilling screams could be heard from those close to the rising blaze.

The tanker carrying eight thousand gallons of fuel exploded, erupting into a ball of fire that rose over fifty feet in the air. Dirk did everything possible to escape the flying metal and debris when a large chunk of metal sheared the front of the chopper sending glass fragments onto both him and Aaron. Stanfield's face was bloody and he turned yelling to Aaron, "Grab on!" Holding the levers tightly he fought to gain control. He was losing the battle, "We're going down!" Struggling to hold onto the controls with blood gushing from the right side of his face, he tried to pull them out of their fall. Aaron was grabbing onto anything he could and screamed, "Oh God, help!" They spun out of control with metal fragments and flames battering the chopper as the war veteran fought to hold on. Thoughts flashed through Dirk's mind, *how could this happen here? After so many close calls during the war, why?* Onlookers gasped as the chopper came crashing to earth.

This was the second explosion in less than a minute. Black plumes of smoke rose high over the area filling the sky and could be seen for miles, sending more fuel over vehicles on the ground, igniting vehicles that now went up in flames.

Fire Departments from downtown to Woodward North Station working the accident charged in to help. Trucks positioned on the service drive were now sending streams of water and foam retardant onto the blaze below. Firefighters knew there was no way anyone could get closer with so many cars and trucks now engulfed in the inferno. The combination of automotive and diesel fuel, and now aviation fuel, was a recipe for a major disaster. One explosion after another could be heard as vehicles stranded in the melee were exploding like a string of firecrackers.

Stunned reporters were watching from station headquarters when Dirk and the helicopter spun out of control crashing to earth. Screams of 'No, no,' were heard in the control room. A young reporter collapsed on the floor and the news director stood, tears streaming from his eyes, not knowing what to do. People rushed around the station in a panic and the video editor slumped at the control board. The station's anchor was shocked and tears streamed down his face as footage from the scene was still broadcasted from crews on the ground. The news producer had to decide how to proceed. He barked out orders to his staff as people tried to help those that had fainted or passed out.

People along the freeway were capturing the events on their cell phones. Some could be seen trying to help those escaping the inferno by climbing the grassy hills and scaling over the fence. They helped pull some of them over the fence but the intense heat began to push those helping away. Channel 4, WDIV Action News, had dispatched reporter Lauren Podell to the scene when the initial accident was reported. She captured the chopper falling from the sky and the explosion that took place when it hit the ground. She was yelling into the mike while her camera man filmed the flames erupting from behind her. Holding the microphone in her right hand, she was almost inaudible due to the loud sound of engines below bursting into flames below. She continued speaking into the mike that she held in one hand, with her other hand over her left ear and shouting out what she was witnessing, as tears streamed down her cheeks.

Police and fire departments from all over the city were dispatched to the scene, all hoping to help. There had to be over fifty vehicles now on fire and the flames climbed up the grass on the sides of the freeway threatening businesses and homes. A team of firefighters continued to fight the blaze from the service drive hosing the freeway, as well as the vehicles below. NBC national news teams broke into television coverage picking up the action filmed by the WDIV reporter on the scene. Natalie Morales, from the Today Show, covered the action for the nation as she picked up the information from Lauren Podell. Herds of people in bars and restaurants hovered around televisions not believing the events taking place in their city.

\*\*\*

Chief Mathews had been alerted about the initial accident and now was being informed by Lieutenant Jackson of the new situation on the freeway. They both watched the television reports as he waited for news from his Captain on the scene. He turned to his assistant, "Lieutenant, call Captain James, he needs to fill me in now!"

As she reached for the phone, it rang. "Chief, Captain Williams is on the line, he just arrived at the freeway, do you what to talk to him?"

Mathews nodded and grabbed the phone, "Captain, what do you know?"

Williams was out of breath, "So far we're just trying to put it all together. From initial reports it appears that a garbage truck and a police car may have caused the initial crash."

The Chief wasn't sure why a police car would be involved, but feared the worse, "How in the hell could this happen?"

Williams continued, "Chief, Captain James and I checked, none of our cars from the command post had reported police action or a possible chase on the freeway. There hasn't been any other contact from an officer on the scene. My Lieutenant was first on the scene but couldn't get close enough to confirm the number on the car involved. Once the cars burst into flames everyone had to pull back."

"Captain, could our officer in the police car have gotten out before it all went up in flames?"

"We're checking with the EMT squads but none have records of a police officer being transported to the hospital."

"Thanks, Captain, keep me informed." The Chief told Lieutenant Jackson, "Place calls to every Captain in the Eastern District, I want all officers available to the scene." The Police Department stationed on Woodward had already dispatched six squad cars to the scene and another five cars from the Seven Mile Department were en route. "Lieutenant, put a call out to every precinct to check on all personnel. Someone has to know who might have been in that car. Lieutenant, it might just be a process of elimination."

She could see the worried look on her Chief's face. Trying to reassure him, "Sir, we don't know that an officer was involved. If so, maybe he got out before the vehicle caught fire."

"Thanks, Lieutenant." Mathews knew she was trying to ease his mind. "Regardless, we've got to find out who's assigned to that car and where are they. God, I hope our officer wasn't the cause of this."

She hadn't thought about that. "Why would you think that, sir?"

"What if the officer was involved in pursuing a driver on the freeway?" Mathews paced around his office, grabbing his phone he called upstairs to the SIU team. Detective Harper answered.

"Harper, this is Chief Mathews." She was surprised that he was calling upstairs instead of Lieutenant Jackson.

"Chief, what can I do for you?"

"Harper, I'm sure you've seen the horrendous accident on I-94."

"Yes sir, the team wants to help any way you need us."

"Thanks, we've got officers on the scene. Right now I need to talk to Detective Frederickson, is he up there?"

Harper cleared her throat, wondering if her boss was supposed to be in the office. "Um, no, I'm pretty sure he left after the press conference. I think he said he was going home. Detectives Spano and Adams are here."

"Thanks, detective, I was just hoping to follow up with Detective Frederickson on another subject. I'll call him on his cell."

Once the Chief hung up, Harper turned, walking toward where Detectives Spano and Adams stood. "Chief Mathews just called asking for Don."

"You mean Lieutenant Jackson called for the Chief."

"No, the Chief made the call. Do you think something is wrong?'

The two men looked at each other. "What did he say?"

"Just that he was looking for Detective Frederickson. When I told him Frederickson left for home, the Chief told me he'd call Don's cell."

Spano nodded, "I guess until Don fills us in, there's nothing we can do." Pointing to the TV, "Adams and I are still watching the action on I-94. Christ, there must be a hundred cars on fire. Did the Chief want us to help out on the freeway action?"

Harper had been watching the crash with them until the Chief called. "No, I asked but was told they have enough officers on the scene. I still feel we should be doing something."

Spano understood her concern, "Nothing for us to do if they have every available emergency vehicle called into action. Unless the Chief wants us involved, we need to continue what we're working on."

The three detectives moved back to the Conference Room continuing to watch the events happening on the Interstate.

Chief Mathews again dialed Detective Frederickson's cell phone. Waiting for an answer, the detective's voice mail message came on. Once he listened, the Chief left a message, "Don, Call me. I want to run something by you." Mathews turned his attention back to the events on the Interstate.

Lieutenant Jackson informed the Chief that his city Captain was on the line. He grabbed the phone, the man was talking extremely fast, "Chief, we're running out of options. The fire department said that their only hope is to contain the blaze to the vehicles currently involved. No hope to save any of them, although, they've been able to push many of the cars stuck on the freeway back away from the fire. They're moving special foam trucks en route from the airport to the freeway."

"Okay, Captain, do we have any idea about the officer who was in that car under the garbage truck?"

"I've been in touch with the rescue squad that was first on the scene. They have seven people that were pulled from the early wreckage and all of them were transported to the Detroit Medical Center. One of them was the suspected garbage truck driver but no one said anything about a police officer. I've sent two of my men to the DMC to get the identification of the people that were taken in."

Mathews understood, "I hope one of those survivors is our officer."

The Captain answered, "Us too, sir,"

"Captain, keep me informed." Once the Captain hung up, the Chief turned to Lieutenant Jackson, "Have we heard back from any of the officers at the Medical Center?" She shook her head.

The Captain followed the Chief's orders and contacted one of the officers dispatched to the DMC. The officer answered, clearly out of breath. He asked, "Officer, the Chief wants to know if you've been able to discover the identity of the injured persons transported to the hospital?"

"Some of them, but Captain, the place is a zoo. There are firefighters and EMS personnel all over bringing survivors in. We're having trouble separating those who came in first from all the people being brought in later."

"Officer, we need to know if any of those brought in were police personnel."

"I understand, sir. I've got information on four people so far, but none of them is a police officer."

"How do you know that?"

"The ER team said none of the people brought in were wearing a police uniform or had the identification of a police officer."

"Officer, get us the names of everyone that has been brought in. I didn't ask what they were wearing. Understand!"

"Yes!" The next thing the officer heard was the dial tone.

# CHAPTER TWO

**The tall, man grey haired man sitting behind the large** mahogany desk had a broad smile on his face as he watched the television news reporter standing in front of the inferno on the freeway. Coverage from NBC filled the television screen as Dominic Parma, who was sitting across from the man, pounded his fist into his left hand. "Boss, this is just what you planned."

The distinguished grey haired man looked back at him. "Dom, it's not only what we planned, it's what we needed." The man sitting behind the desk was Vinnie La Russo, the owner of the largest trucking company at the Eastern Market. He continued watching as the reporter on the scene was trying to be heard over the noise behind her. She was covering the horrendous accident on the interstate. Vinnie leaned forward as the reporter related details from witnesses on the scene.

Lauren Podell repeated details, "Initial reports we're getting from witnesses on the scene are that a garbage truck, driving erratically, slammed into the back of a police cruiser causing it to spin out. We're all still in the state of shock with the loss of our news team when the helicopter crashed moments ago." The reporter was visibly upset as she was giving the details but kept on going. La Russo slid to the edge of his chair, listening to her intently.

Vinnie watched the flames continue to leap in the air as cameras panned down the freeway, cluttered with mangled cars and a huge blaze engulfed the stretch of the highway. Firefighters were in the background trying to get control of the flames that climbed up the embankment of the highway while concentrating on the vehicle below. Every station was covering the action and

National News interrupted prime time shows covering the events in Detroit.

Dominic watched his boss and wanted to say something, anything, but knew Vinnie was enjoying what he was watching. He cleared his throat, "Boss, what's next?"

Vinnie turned away from the news coverage, "Dominic, we still have some things to take care of. We've got to get those three trucks from Castellanos' lot. I can't have the Fed's or local cops finding what's inside. Go across the street and get Oscar and handle it like we talked about earlier."

Dominic stood, "We'll take care of it."

Vinnie trusted the man. Dominic Parma was Vinnie's enforcer. He had moved up in the organization with a reputation for being ruthless. If you wanted someone to disappear, Vinnie would say, "Dominic's your man." Parma stood six foot-five and weighed close to two-hundred thirty pounds. A deep scar ran along the right side of his face from his ear to just below the chin. His head was clean shaven and he wore the scar as a trophy. One never asked about it, but when he wasn't around, people would comment that Dominic was a scary looking dude. Dom left Vinnie's office and crossed the street taking large strides toward the display shed that was near the end of the Eastern Market's wholesale area. Trucks were parked in the stalls with men unloading fresh vegetables and plants. Once he entered, Dominic looked around and saw Oscar talking to a small group that was unloading a truck. Dominic stood off to the side where he knew Oscar would see him. After close to two minutes he tilted his head to the side and pointed at Oscar.

Oscar had seen him arrive but ignored him. Finally he had to go see what the man wanted. Oscar turned toward his men, "Okay guys, finish getting this truck unloaded and everything put up; I'll be back." Oscar walked over to where Dominic stood, he wasn't happy that he was being interrupted. There were trucks lined up with fresh fruits and vegetables that had to be unloaded. "What in the hell do you want?"

Parma put his finger in Oscar's chest. "The boss wants you, and he wants you now."

Oscar pushed his hand away. With that Dominic turned, walking away. Oscar looked back at his men who were watching what was happening. "Get back to work!" He slowly followed Dominic, not sure what the man wanted, but Vinnie La Russo put Oscar in business and always made sure that he had plenty of customers. Oscar White had been a truck driver for Vinnie back in the day. He was once taken in by the police and, although fifteen years ago he spent time in Jackson State Prison, Oscar had proven to be a capable and trusted person, never giving up the information the police wanted. When he was released, La Russo realized that Oscar could be important to his organization. Vinnie put Oscar in charge of assigning vendors spots in the important Market's sheds. Oscar also handled men that loaded and unloaded the trucks. This was normally a position help by a member of the Teamsters Union; but Vinnie was a powerful man and the Union let him handle his operation. Oscar White was a smart guy who knew what La Russo could do and always made sure that he did anything the man wanted.

The two men crossed the street and made their way into the large grey warehouse that sat across from one of the large buildings. They walked up the staircase that ran along the front entrance next to the Coney Island restaurant on the street level. They passed one of the famous corned beef restaurants that was across the street from the building and a group of truck drivers were gathered outside. Parma looked back, "I got some guys that were lined up there." Oscar hadn't any idea what he was talking about.

They reached the top of the stairs and Dominic pushed open the large outer brass door. In the outer office there were three men sitting at a round table who appeared to be waiting for instructions of some sort. One of them, a short guy with a dark complexion stood. "Are you the guy that's supposed to give us a job?"

Dominic looked over at the guy with a sneer, "Sit back down, I'll let you know when you're needed." The other two men averted their face away from the short guy. He slid back into the chair and put his head down, pulling his cap a little further down covering his face. Oscar laughed, that made the three men even more nervous.

Once they turned toward the interior office door, Oscar nodded at the pretty blond sitting at the desk outside of Vinnie's office. Gloria was a real looker, tall and thin, all the men enjoyed saying hello to her; Oscar wasn't any different. "Good morning gorgeous."

She smiled back at him, "Hello Oscar, haven't seen you in a while."

"That's my loss, always nice to see you."

Dominic looked at him, "Come on, this ain't a dating site." Looking back at the group sitting at the round table, he pointed to them, "Stay here till I get back." With that Dominic and Oscar entered the door at the end of the room.

Vinnie was seated behind the big desk and his nephew, Mario, was sitting in the corner of the room. "Oscar, thanks for coming right up. I asked Dominic to ask you in because we have to move some trucks tonight."

Oscar raised his eyebrows at the mention of being asked to come up to the office. He quickly answered, "No problem, Mr. La Russo, I'll be happy to take care of anything you need."

"I knew that Oscar, have a seat." Oscar pulled a chair from in front of the desk and sat down; Dominic sat down next to him. "You know we've been working to get our trucks released from Castellanos' trucking yard. The DEA is still screwing with me, but I gotta get the trucks out of there. Dominic went there this morning and the gate is padlocked but there wasn't any sign of the place being guarded. This is important to me, Oscar."

Oscar nodded as he listened, knowing that Mr. La Russo wanted the trucks and although he was asking for help, this wasn't optional. They'd get them one way or another. "How can I help, Mr. La Russo?"

"Tonight, I want you to take some men to the trucking company and get our three trucks. Dom's got it worked out. He'll give you the numbers of the trucks I want."

"Do you want me to use my men?"

"No, Dominic has that handled. Can't have anyone around telling what we did."

Oscar understood, "The place got any guards at night?"

"Our people were out there last night for three hours, they didn't see anyone around."

Dominic moved from where he was seated and brought over a map. He laid it on Vinnie's desk in front of both him and Oscar. "My man was positioned right here," pointing to the gated area along the front entrance. "After about thirty minutes he got out of the car and walked around the place. He said he even climbed the side fence, no one was around."

Vinnie added, "You see Oscar, we did a lot of the work for you. Like I said, I didn't want you to get your men involved, so we got three guys outside that will drive the trucks away once you get them inside."

Oscar laughed, "Guess that's Larry, Moe and Curly sitting in the outer office."

Vinnie let out a big laugh and Mario chuckled. "Better these knuckleheads than taking a chance with a couple of your guys. I picked them up on Gratiot, in front of the warehouse where so many guys wait hoping to get a day job. Most of them are just looking for cash to buy drugs."

"I like that idea, thanks for not using my guys. What trucks do you want and where do we take them to?"

Dominic wrote down the three truck numbers on the corner of the map. "Oscar, I bought a new padlock, the same kind that's on the gate. Once you cut the lock and get the trucks, we'll put the new padlock on the front gate."

"Good, what do those guys outside know?"

"They just want to have a chance to make a few bucks. They don't know anything about the three trucks or what we have planned. We told them it's a trial run for a future job. Once we get them out of the area all they need to do is take their truck to the location I've written down. Each one of them will be going in a different direction and leave the trucks where they are instructed. You pick them up and handle whatever is needed after that."

Oscar reviewed the map that Dominic had given him and the three pieces of paper, one for each driver. The papers had a small map and directions where they were to drop off the trucks. Oscar was curious as to why the trucks were being dispatched to different locations but he wasn't going to ask why. "What do I tell the three stooges out there what's going down?"

Dominic looked at Oscar, "Mario and I are going with you. We'll give them the job details but they only need to know that we'll pick them up and take them for a trial run. They will think that the object is to get the right truck and get it safely to the destination, nothing more."

Oscar knew that this wasn't a request but an order, one that he didn't have an option on. "Thanks Mr. La Russo, we'll get everything done that you need."

With that Vinnie stood up, he reached out and shook Oscar's hand. "You're a good man, Oscar. There's a little extra in this envelope for you." Handing it to Oscar, he tucked it into his front jacket pocket. "Now you and Dominic take the crew outside and maybe buy them lunch. I suggest you take them away from the Market area. You can go over the details with them."

Oscar got up and headed to the door followed by Dominic. When they left Vinnie turned to Mario, "Everything's okay, I want you to go with Oscar."

"Okay, I know what to do."

"Once you get back here let's go over the details from the freeway. I know Dominic can handle this but if he needs back-up you'd be there."

\*\*\*

The two men sat in the black Lincoln MKX outside the gated truck lot as Mario talked on the phone to his boss. The driver, a gruff looking man in his early forties, turned to the big man that sat in the passenger seat. His voice was gravely and deep, "Where to next?"

"Mr. La Russo knows that Dom and Oscar have the guys to pull it off tonight. We need to get back and let them know we confirmed that the lot isn't guarded."

The driver asked, "Wasn't Dom handling this?"

"Yeah, but it's too important not to check it out one more time. Let's head back downtown to the office; I have to go over this with the boss." The driver pulled away from the curb and turned right onto Twelve Mile Road and headed east to Jefferson. Once they were on Jefferson they'd take it west all the way downtown. They knew the crash on I-94 had everything closed and planned to avoid the freeway. It would only take a little over half an hour to get back to the Eastern Market.

Vinnie La Russo was pleased with how things were progressing. La Russo built his trucking company after his father left him a fleet of small vegetable trucks that delivered produce to neighborhoods and then small grocery stores. He moved his operations to the bustling Eastern Market area twenty years ago. Vinnie knew Detroit's Eastern Market, located on the city's central east side, about two miles from downtown, was a great spot for his organization. The history of the market wasn't lost on the man; it originally opened in 1841 as the Farmers Market and operated out of Cadillac Square in the downtown area. With the distribution of fresh produce to local restaurants, he saw that his organization had the opportunity for underworld activities. He planned to be a king pin in the drug business under the cover of a legitimate business. The FBI was well aware of the gangsters that had opened both trucking and distribution offices in the market but hadn't had success in bringing them to justice. They had kept a watchful eye on the Mob who now set up corporate businesses and eateries along the corridor. Vinnie La Russo was soon at the top of the FBI watch list.

The black Lincoln made its way along Gratiot and took a right turn on Riopelle Street. Mario told the driver to drop him off in front of the Coney Island. "I'll wait for you upstairs." Mario La Russo was Vinnie's nephew and worked for his uncle at the Eastern Market location for ten years. Mario was a strong business man and was the one who organized Castellanos Trucking in St Clair Shores into their operation. He convinced his uncle it was a good idea to partner with a firm that was located outside of the downtown area. It would be harder for the Feds to link us together, he'd say. Once the trucking company fell under the suspicious eye of the FBI and Castellanos went missing, the Bureau put the operation under lock and key. Mario and his uncle knew they had to get their three trucks, and get them before the Bureau started going through all of them. Entering the office upstairs, Mario was pleased to see Dominic with his uncle. "I've got everything under control at the lot, how's it going here?"

Dominic answered, "Oscar's in. He and I got three dumb shits from the street to handle the trucks tonight."

Vinnie listened as Dominic and Mario went over the plans. "I don't want to see any of these three guys back around here."

"We'll take care of them once we've got all the trucks out."

"Dominic, make sure this doesn't come back to us."

"I'll personally handle it, boss."

# CHAPTER THREE

**It was dark and Oscar leaned back in the passenger seat as** Mario went over the details one more time. "Once we pick these guys up at Seven Mile and Gratiot, we'll head to the trucking lot. All three of them were told to get to the meeting spot. We're supposed to pick them up along the side of the Charter One Bank. The bank will be closed so no one will be able to connect us to them." Oscar knew the plan; he also knew that Vinnie wasn't the type to use strangers and then send them on their way. He just hoped that this wasn't his last job for Mr. La Russo.

The Cadillac Escalade moved slowly to the curb along the side of the bank and the three men were standing around the corner, away from any street surveillance, just as instructed. Oscar rolled his window down and ordered them to get in the back. Once they were all in, Mario pulled away down Seven Mile toward I-94. The short guy immediately started asking questions. This didn't sit well with Mario. "We gave all three of you the assignment, and told you that this was a dry run, sort of a job interview for a truck driver job. That's what you applied for, right?"

"Yes sir. I just was wondering…"

Mario pulled into a vacant lot, "One more question and you can get out right now!"

The short guy, the one they called Moe, put his head down, "Sorry, I've got it."

Looking over at Oscar, "What do you think, do we give Moe here one more chance?"

"My name's not Moe, its John."

"Okay, John, but we're calling you Moe from now on."

Oscar smiled at the reference to the Three Stooges, turning

19

around, "Listen we only need two drivers but decided to give all three of you a chance. The two that do the best job tonight get the job." One of the other men in the back, Andy Jones, nodded his understanding. "How about you?" Oscar asked pointing to the third guy. He nervously nodded too. "Okay, we're going to continue but without one more word from any of you."

The ride along I-94 was very quiet. Mario pulled off the freeway onto Little Mack and turned south. He headed past the Meijer superstore and down to Twelve Mile Road where he turned right. Oscar wondered why he just didn't get off there. Once they were heading west on Twelve Mile, Mario turned to Oscar. He quietly said, "Tell them what they need to do one more time." As they each read the papers that Oscar handed them, Oscar repeated the details. "Okay, you've each got a set of keys; once you're out of the trucking lot and take your truck to the assigned area, we will pick you up. You are to leave the truck, with the keys under the driver's side mat. We will be there in less than fifteen minutes; any questions?" All three men nodded that they understood. "Good, this is not a race, don't get a ticket or you'll be out of consideration for any position. The trucks must be in good condition, we inspected them earlier." Everything was in place; the cover for men to think this was a driving test for future employment was set.

Mario pulled off of Twelve Mile onto a dark lit street lined with warehouses and a cement company on the right side. He pulled to the front of the trucking company lot and saw that Dominic had already arrived. He nodded to Dominic, knowing that the coast was clear and proceeded to cut the lock. Oscar was supposed to install the new lock once the trucks had pulled out. Dominic was driving a black Chevrolet Avalanche pick-up truck. It had the rear cargo covered and he planned to follow Mario and Oscar to the pick-up spots.

The three drivers moved into the gated lot looking at the numbers on the back of each truck and checking their assigned vehicle list. One guy jogged to a white refrigerated vehicle that was parked near the office. He tried the keys and was pretty happy when it started. He pulled through the lot and out of the gate, waving at the other guys. The second man, the short guy, Moe, who asked too many questions also found his unit and started it with ease. He pulled out of the lot and headed to his assigned delivery area. Oscar turned to Mario, "How long have these trucks been sitting?"

"A couple of months. When I was out here yesterday I made sure each one had new batteries so they'd start." Oscar should have known, *this operation was too polished to leave it up to trucks that had dead batteries.*

The third truck was also on the move, although the driver, Andy, seemed to be looking around the lot at the other vehicles parked there, before pulling out of the gated lot. He seemed out of place to Oscar, but once the trucks were on the move, he didn't say anything to Mario. Oscar pulled the gate shut, slowly looking behind him. He inserted the new lock and walked back to the Cadillac. Mario was pleased things were going as planned, but he asked Oscar, "Why was that last guy so far behind the others?"

"Not sure but at least we're out of here. They all have assigned drop-off spots a few miles away, we'll head to the first spot." Oscar wanted to ask about Dominic, who planned to follow them, but knew better. He knew his reputation and preferred not to be counted in the number of men that Dom made disappear. He turned toward Mario and asked, "Are we coming back to get the trucks?"

Mario looked over at him, "I've got a team on the way, they should be minutes behind us. They'll take all the trucks to a storage lot."

Oscar smiled, "Nice plan," looking back toward the gated lot he wondered what else the follow-up team was assigned to do. As they drove away, Oscar decided to ask, "Mario, that taller guy, I think his name is Andy, seemed out of place with the other two we brought out here."

"What do you mean?"

"Not sure, but he handled himself differently than the other two. Never asked questions but seem to pay special attention to everything we were doing."

"You think he's a plant or something?"

"I'm not sure but I think we need to keep an eye on him; it's probably nothing but let's keep our eyes on him."

Mario nodded as he drove to the first pick-up spot. The first man was waiting exactly where he was assigned. The Cadillac pulled up next to him and he climbed into the back. "I put the key under the mat; the truck is parked right where you told me to."

Mario turned around, "Good job." They pulled away heading to meet the second driver. They spotted Andy walking up to the corner right where they were supposed to meet. Mario stopped the Cadillac and then he got in the back seat.

Andy sat back in the rear saying, "I put the key under the mat, just like you wanted. The truck is parked where you told me to. It's kind of strange to just leave it on the street."

Mario looked over at Oscar; this was the guy that Oscar earlier said just didn't fit in. "The job was to see how you all followed the plan. You got a problem with that?"

"No, no problem." He put his head down.

Oscar turned to the two guys in the back; he was hoping to change the tone. "We're going to want both of you to come to the office tomorrow; we'll have the final decision for you then." He handed them both an envelope that he had put together.

The two guys in the back fumbled with the envelopes and the first guy started to open it. He broke out in a huge smile. His had three one-hundred dollar bills inside. "Yes," punching the air, smiling he looked over at Andy. "What did you get?"

He hadn't opened his envelope yet. He saw that Oscar was watching. Tearing the top of the envelope he nodded, "Yeah, you're right, three-hundred bucks."

"Cool, me too!" The guy was smiling as he fingered the three large bills. "Going to be a good time tonight." Andy just nodded.

Mario knew the third driver should be just a mile up the road. He continued to the last pick-up point. As they pulled down the deserted street the short man wasn't there. Looking over at Oscar, "Where in the hell could he be?"

Oscar was concerned, "Okay, let's wait a minute; maybe he caught a couple of lights." He turned to the two men in the back asking, "Did Moe say anything to either of you?"

One of them shook his head, "That guy isn't too bright, maybe he got lost." He chuckled, knowing that the short guy just lost any chance of getting a job.

"How about you?" pointing to Andy, "He say anything to you?"

"No, can't say I've even talked to him. He seemed a little slow."

Mario got out of the car, moving to the back of his vehicle he grabbed his cell phone and called Dominic. "We've got a problem, Moe isn't here."

"You mean the short guy?"

"Yeah, we've got the other two guys and the keys are in the trucks but that short dude isn't at the pickup spot."

Dominic assured him, "I'll find him; the truck had a GPS in it. You clean up and I'll find Moe."

Mario was sure he knew what clean-up meant. "No problem, Oscar and I will take care of things here." Mario got back into the Cadillac, "Okay guys, our partner will wait for that other guy, and we're supposed to take you both back." Oscar figured what he and Mario were going to do; he was originally hoping that Dominic was going to handle all of that.

Andy sitting in the back asked, "Are you going to take us back to where you picked us up on Gratiot?"

Mario quickly answered, "Yeah, that's the plan, but first we've got to handle one more thing. It won't take long."

The other guy in the back nodded and whispered to Andy,

who seemed pre-occupied with watching where they were heading to. "I didn't know we'd get three-hundred bucks for the trial run." With the money in his pocket he seemed pretty happy. However Andy appeared a little nervous, maybe a twitch or something that he showed. Oscar wondered if he was hooked on drugs. He decided to keep an eye on him. Mario pulled away from the curb, heading east. He had gone about three miles when Andy, the taller guy, in the back asked, "How long before you take us back?"

Mario turned toward the two guys. "Maybe you both want to give us those envelopes back?"

"No," the other one of them quickly said.

"Okay, then just be quiet until we finish this thing." He continued driving slowly along the dark street. Giving Oscar a wink, Mario said, "Oscar, tell them what we'll need them to do tomorrow morning."

Both men looked back toward Oscar, as he turned explaining the directions for the next day; they intently listened to the new instructions. Oscar started to give them the details and had both of them listening when Mario pressed his gun against the back of the front seat, and fired; two blasts. "Guess this is your stop boys." The two bodies slumped, blood pouring out from their chest. Turning toward Oscar, Mario said, "We'll drop them off, got a spot on the lower east side, a vacant lot. We will make it look like a drug deal gone bad. I've got a small packet of coke to put on the bodies. Leave one of the envelopes in their pocket; that will insure the cops write it off as drugs."

Oscar looked over at Mario, "Got it." He leaned back just glad that he wasn't one of the bodies in the back seat. "The car's going to be a mess to clean."

"That's okay; not my car," He let out an eerie laugh, "We'll dump the car too."

\*\*\*

Dominic continued driving, following the GPS signal he was getting from the last truck that the short man was driving. He was closing in, just a few blocks from the signal. Making a turn onto Lancaster he saw it, just three vehicles ahead of him. Dominic pulled in behind a high cube truck, keeping about thirty feet away. *Wonder what this guy is up to.* The truck slowed, pulling into a large empty lot. Keeping his eyes on the truck, as he moved up along the side of a large warehouse, he spotted the short man climb out of the truck. The little guy walked around the back and was checking the handle on the tailgate. It had a large padlock. Dominic thought that the short guy seemed frustrated. *Hell, he had to know it would be locked, this guy is really dumb.* Just then a dark grey Ford pick-up headed into the lot and parked next to the short guy. Now there were two more men joining Shorty. *They had this planned out; maybe he's not so dumb.* Dominic reached under the seat, pulling two hand guns out, tucking one into his waist band; he kept the other one to his side. *Okay guys; let's see what you've got.* Dominic got out of his vehicle and moved along the side of the warehouse. The men were working on trying to get into the back of the truck. None of them saw him approaching. Lifting the gun, Dominic let out a volley of bullets, dropping the two men that just arrived in a puddle of blood. Shorty ran around the front of the truck, "Okay little man, your next." Dominic checked the two bodies on the pavement first, and put another bullet in each one of them for good measure, than he moved slowly to the side of the truck. He stooped down; looking under the truck and saw the little guy's legs near the front of the truck. "Last chance, asshole, come out or you'll join your friends."

The guy was sobbing, "No, please don't. This wasn't my idea; I was forced into doing it." The short man slid around the side of the truck and looked at the gun pointed at him, he started talking real fast. "I didn't have a choice, and they made me do it."

"What are you talking about, who made you do it?" *Could this guy be a plant of some kind?*

He stuttered, "My brother-in-law, it was all his idea. When I told him that I might get a driving job and he heard that it was for La Russo's he thought we could make a big haul."

Dominic was still pointing the weapon at the man, "Who's your brother-in-law?"

"What?"

"Your brother-in-law, what does he do? Who is he?"

"What does he do?"

"Listen, little man, either you answer my questions or I'm blowing your ass away."

Shorty was trembling. "He's a small time con man; always looking for a quick score; never worked a day in his life. My sister begged me to help him."

"That's the thing about brother-in-laws, they always have plans." Dominic kept the gun pointed at him and slid around the side of the truck. He figured the guy didn't have a weapon or he would have fired back. Still hoping to get answers, Dominic tried to get him to stop whimpering. "What's it going to be, buddy?"

"Promise you won't kill me too?"

Why would I kill you now, I want answers about your dumb shit brother-in-law."

The little guy stuttered, "Okay, I'll do anything you want. Please don't kill me."

Dominic stood tall, keeping his weapon aimed at the guy's chest. "What's your brother-in-law's name?"

"His name, its Sammy, Sammy Franklin. You already killed him, he's lying back there on the ground."

"Who else knew what you both were up to? He's got another guy back there with him."

"Just Sammy and his buddy, I don't know his name, he's dead too, no one else, I promise." The little guy was shaking and broke down in tears. "I don't want to die, please don't shoot."

"Okay, move over here with your hands up." Dominic frisked the man." Putting his hand on the man's back he shoved him toward the back of the truck. Once they were standing over the two bodies that Dominic had shot; the little guy looked down at his brother-in-law and the other body and he begged again. "I'm sorry, please let me go."

"You should have thought about that before trying to steal our truck. Here's the key. Unlock the back and put these bodies in."

The little man did as he was told. Climbing over the two bodies, he tried lifting the first one. "I need help, he's heavy." Dominic shook his head and kept the gun pointed at him. He turned back toward the first body and lifted it, then pushed it in the back of the truck. Then he lifted Sammy and repeated sliding the body and putting him in the truck.

"Okay, climb in!"

"Please no."

Pointing the gun at him, "Get in!"

He got into the back of the truck. Once he was inside, he turned toward Dominic. "Please!" was his last words.

Dominic fired his weapon into the man sending him flying into the truck and crashing into the back wall. The little man's brother-in-law's body was right next to him. Dominic walked around the side of the truck and looked in. The keys were still in the ignition. Looking back inside at the bodies, he sneered and slammed the tailgate shut.

# CHAPTER FOUR

**The SIU team was still huddled together in the Conference**
Room going over the details the FBI had sent over from their
previous case. Their task was to finalize the drug bust that took
place last week. The detectives kept tabs on the action that was
happening on the freeway, watching what was being broadcasted
to the nation. Detective Spano watched the firefighters and police
who were battling the blaze, "I feel we should be doing something
to help," he said aloud. The rest of the team nodded in approval.
"Guess the Chief has it all under control," one of the team was
heard mumbling. Spano knew what the Chief had said earlier, "*If
we need your team, I'll call.*"

Detective Harper was separating documents when she looked
up and saw Mindy, the team's secretary, waving. Harper turned to
Detective Spano, "I'll be back in a second, guys." She walked over
to Mindy's desk and asked, "What is it?"

Mindy was holding a piece of paper, "Detective, you got a call
from a Detective in the Eastern District; he said you would want to
talk to him."

"Who was it?"

Looking down at her notepad, "His name is Tom Baker."

Mindy thought that Harper had a strange expression on her
face when she told her who had called, "Did he say what it was
about?"

"No, just that it was important, and he'd only talk to you. I
took down the number and some information." Mindy handed
Harper the note, and watched the detective's expression as she read
the message. "So, who's this guy?"

Harper was staring at the note, looking up; she seemed to
stutter, "What?"

"That detective that called; who is Tom Baker?"

"Oh sorry, Mindy, I just hadn't talked to him in years; we were in the Academy together." Harper turned and started walking away, still staring at the note.

Mindy stood at her desk, "Oh no you're not; you're not getting away that easy. I want to know more, especially after he said it's critical that you meet him as soon as possible."

Harper turned back, "Mindy, promise, I'll tell you later." Amy Harper folded the paper and pushed it into her pocket. Mindy watched her enter the Conference Room and then quickly walk back out. Harper walked back to her desk and grabbed her jacket and headed toward the door. "Mindy, I'll be back in a little bit; let Detective Frederickson know that I had to take care of something personal." As the door closed to the SIU office, Mindy sat wondering what that was all about. She ran the message back in her mind, nothing jumped out as suspicious. Just a friend from the past Harper said, or was it?

Detective Harper looked again at the note that Mindy gave her as she drove to the meeting spot. Driving up Woodward she spotted the sign for the entrance to Palmer Park. Her mind flashed back to her senior year in high school when she was on a field trip to the area. Pulling off of Woodward and Seven Mile Road, she was amazed how nothing seemed to change. The golf course and tennis courts were still pristine and the huge homes that surrounded the park stood out like a beacon from the glory days of Detroit's past. She pulled to the end of the parking lot past the golf course club house. Grabbing her cell phone she tried calling Tom Baker. When he answered, she asked, "How far are you from here?"

"Amy, glad you agreed to meet. I'm about five minutes away."

"Okay, I'm parked at the end of the club house parking lot. Tom, I don't know why you're being so mysterious but you better have something I need or I'll be leaving."

"I promise this is important; I'm pulling in now."

As she waited, her thoughts went back to her Police Academy days. She hadn't thought about Tom Baker or many of the other cadets in a long time. They were both in the Police Academy as rookies trying to make the police force. Amy, like most of the female cadets, thought Tom was interested in more than being a fellow officer. Tom made a move on her one night when the team was out celebrating near the end of the training. Amy quickly made sure he knew that she wasn't interested. Once she turned him down, he never made another attempt to push their relationship further. Tom was outgoing and many of the female cadets shared Amy's opinion of him, *good looking but superficial*. She remembered what one of the other ladies said, "We all know what Tom wants." Amy really only had one friend from the Academy, and she hadn't seen him in a long time. Now hearing from Tom Baker brought back many memories, the ones of Baker had her thinking that she didn't care if she'd ever heard from him again. Watching the entrance to Palmer Park, she wondered, what could Tom want? What kind of important information does he have that she would want to know? It had been ten years since they were in the Academy. His black Ford pulled up next to Amy's vehicle and she watched him climbing out. He headed toward her car. Tom Baker was tall, close to six-foot two and slender. He was a nice looking guy with a pleasant smile; it was that smile that he tossed around at all the women during training. This was the same smile that Amy made disappear when she turned his advances down. She figured they'd never see each other again after that.

Baker stood near the front of her vehicle as he watched her climb out of the driver's side. He had a broad smile and quickly said, "Wow, you never change, still beautiful."

"You haven't changed either, Tom, still full of shit." He smiled; a nervous sort smile. "So tell me, Tom, what's this all about?"

"The same old Harper, right to the point; Amy I wouldn't have called if it wasn't important." She watched as Tom looked around, maybe making sure they weren't being watched. He turned back to her, "Amy, last night my Captain got a call that two bodies were found in a vacant lot just off of Lenox and Jefferson on the lower east side. It appeared like so many other killings in the city. Once my partner and I investigated we confirmed that it was likely a drug deal gone bad; both men shot point blank. One of the guys had an empty envelope, maybe it had money in it and there were a few designer pills and a packet of coke still in there."

Amy shifted from one foot to the other, obviously appearing impatient. "Okay Tom, what does this have to do with me?"

Tom hesitated for a second, taking a deep breath, "Amy, I hate to tell you but I'm sure one of the dead guys is Andy Jones."

Amy was visibly stunned. Tom watched as she leaned back on the hood of her car. She muffled out the name, "Andy, are you sure?" Her hands were shaking, and her voice cracked as she again sighed the name, "Andy?"

"Sorry, Amy, I knew you'd want to know right away." Tom moved a little closer, "It wasn't good, Amy. Looks like whoever dumped his body didn't want us to be able to identify them right away. It was a real mess."

He wanted to place his hand on her shoulder, but knew that would be the wrong move. She stood shaking her head in disbelief, "Tom, it can't be Andy, the last time I talked to him he was getting clean. He was trying to get back on the force. Why are you sure it's him?"

"When was that?"

"Maybe two or three years ago. He was kind of secretive about it all."

How he wished he wasn't the one giving her the news. "Amy I recognized that tattoo that Andy had on his right arm. Can't be too many of those; I remember asking him about it in training. Andy was proud of his service in Iraq, and putting the names of fellow fallen soldiers from his unit tattooed on his arm meant a lot to him." Tom watched Amy, and although she hadn't said anything for a minute, she seemed to stumble a little. "Amy, what can I do for you?" She turned away from him, and he thought she was crying. Her shoulders shook and Tom wanted to say something but didn't know exactly what.

Turning around, her voice still cracking; she looked over at him, steely eyed, "Tom, I want to know more details. I hadn't talked to Andy in a couple of years. The last time we talked he promised that he was getting help." She stopped talking, wiping away a few tears. Tom saw that tough glare, the one that other cadets talked about, even though she was visibly moved with the information he delivered.

"Amy, I never knew what happened with you and Andy after the Academy. I only knew that you both seemed close. I'm not assuming anything, but I knew you'd want to know right away."

Trying to gain composure, she took a few steps, pacing back and forth, "Tom, you're right I needed to know. Has anyone contacted his mother?"

He was surprised by her question. "Not yet, the official identification from the Medical Examiner hasn't been made. I'm the only one who knows who it is. I kept it that way so it wouldn't be released to the media. Amy, I'll do anything you want to help."

She didn't answer, still pacing and nodding her head. Tom watched her look up to the sky and he was sure she was wiping tears from her cheek. Amy Harper turned back toward him, "I'm sorry, Tom, once you know for sure that it's Andy; and the Medical Examiner confirms the identification, call me. I want to be the one to contact Andy's mom before it hits the news."

Tom knew she was in denial. "Amy, I'll keep you in the loop on the investigation. But you can't tell anyone that I gave you this information."

Amy reached out shaking Tom's hand. "No problem, I'll keep your name out of this. Tom, thanks for telling me in person. Let me know as soon as possible when you find anything else out."

Tom Baker nodded and headed back to his squad car. Looking

back at Amy Harper one more time, he watched her as she still leaned against her car. He wished he could do more but he would tell her when the M.E. made the final identification. It was typical Amy Harper, he thought, worried about Andy's mom. Tom Baker wished he wasn't such a jerk in the Academy. He knew Amy Harper was a special person, someone he would have wanted to be better friends with. Maybe he could change that.

# CHAPTER FIVE

**The fire departments continued spraying chemical foam from** water cannons hoping to contain the freeway blaze. With the mixture of fuels, fears now grew about fluids flowing into the sewer system that lined the freeway. The fire department had the Department of Public Works bringing sand to backfill the sewers so that the fuels wouldn't contaminate the system. There was a river of fire running down the sides of the freeway and nothing was stopping it. Television news teams continued sending pictures of the blaze and televisions across the city beamed them into living rooms. It was just the start of rush hour when this all happened and the freeway was packed with cars that would be stuck for a long time. No one could imagine how bad the damage to the roads and infrastructure would be; however, the main concern now was the loss of life in the action on the freeway.

The State Police along with local officers, the fire department and city officials conferred on the next step. The Mayor and his team were now on the scene, and along with Chief Mathews, were being updated on the action. The Captain on the scene updated them, "Sir, the EMS units have rescued over a dozen people from the freeway before the explosion, most with cuts and bruises from colliding into each other. After the explosion we've had fatalities and people critically injured that have been transported to the hospitals in the area. The fire department has their hands full with the blaze and my men are trying to support the State Troopers who are taking charge of the action below."

The Mayor shook his head, "How many fatalities, Captain?"

"We've got seven so far, but no one has been able to get to the garbage truck or tanker since the chopper crashed. They're both engulfed in the blaze. I've got two officers at the hospital where the initial seven people with serious injuries had been transported."

"Do they have any identifications?"

"No, not on all of them yet."

"We need to know if one of those is our officer that was possibly in the car found under that garbage truck."

"We're making that top priority, Sir. My team at the hospital is checking with the staff on the identification of everyone that has been brought in."

Chief Mathews looked at his local Captain, "I know you have your hands full down there, let me know how I can help."

"Thank you, sir. Our men, along with the fire department and EMS, are working together on this. We'll get it handled." The Captain's phone rang and he looked at the screen. "It's my officer at the DMC." Everyone stoodby as he answered. "Yes officer, give me that name one more time." He held the phone to his side, looking over at Chief Mathews he stuttered, "Chief, it's one of your guys in the crash with the garbage truck.

"What? One of my guys! Who is it?"

"Detective Don Frederickson." The Captain thought that Chief Mathews looked pale as he continued listening to the information from the officer at the hospital. "Chief, Frederickson is still in the Trauma Unit. They are working on him and my officer is having difficulty getting an update on his condition."

"That's not enough, Captain. Tell your guy that I need to know everything and know it as soon as possible. Have him keep in touch and call me as soon as you know more." Walking away from the group, Mathews knew he had to call the SIU squad.

Detectives Spano and Adams were updating Detective Harper on the material that they had been going through. Harper had just returned to the office and Spano wanted to ask her where she had been, but figured he'd wait. She seemed to be a bit distant since returning. The group continued to watch the action being beamed on the television from the freeway. Spano looked up and saw Mindy walking toward the group, "Detective Spano, Chief Mathews is on line three and he wants to talk to all of you from the

Conference Room phone."

They looked back at her somewhat confused, "You mean he wants all of us on a conference call?"

"Yes, he sounds pretty serious."

"Okay Mindy, patch him through. We'll all head right in." Once they entered the room Detective Harper hit the speaker button on the phone. "Chief Mathews, we're all in here, sir."

"Detectives, I just got confirmation from our officer at the Detroit Medical Center. I'm sorry to tell you but it looks like it was Detective Frederickson who was involved in the incident on I-94." The team all had a shocked look on their face. The Chief continued, "The information we've received from witnesses is that it appears that Don's vehicle was hit by the garbage truck on the freeway. We're not sure if he was in pursuit of another vehicle or that he was a target. Right now our only concern is for him."

Spano looked over at Harper first, then to Adams. Both were just as stunned as he was. He took a deep breath, "Chief, what can we do?"

"I'm going to call his wife, Nancy; she needs to be at the hospital. Spano, I want you to head to their house and take her to the DMC. I don't want her alone right now. I'll tell her you're on your way."

"Yes sir, I'm leaving now."

The Chief handed out more orders, "Harper, I want you and Adams getting everything on that damn garbage truck that hit Frederickson's vehicle. We need to know what the hell happened."

Detective Harper answered, "I'm on it, sir."

He added, "Harper, call Captain Williams, here's his number. He's on the scene; he can give you all the information they have so far. Detective, I want you taking charge of the unit for now. Once you know something, anything, call me!"

Harper and Adams were still standing looking back at each other in total disbelief. Harper wasn't sure if she heard him right, *did he put her in charge?* The Chief had hung up and they turned to see Mindy standing behind them in the doorway, tears running down her cheeks.

\*\*\*

Vinnie La Russo listened as Mario filled him in on the action at Castellanos Trucking.

Mario told him, "We got all three of the trucks, Boss. They're on the way to the warehouse and my men will call when they are put away safely."

"How about Oscar, everything go okay?"

"Boss, he was great; actually helped me with the two guys when we dumped them off."

Vinnie thought for a second, *two guys*, "I thought you took three men out there."

Mario hadn't planned on telling him about the short guy trying to steal one of the trucks. He figured he'd leave that to Dominic. "Boss, we had two of the guys and Dominic was taking care of the last guy. I think he had some problems; but he called and said everything had been handled. Like I said, we moved all three vehicles to the storage building and our guys are unloading everything into the warehouse. Once they finish we'll get rid of the trucks."

"Where's Dominic now?"

Mario knew Dominic had to get rid of the bodies he had in the Avalanche. "Boss, he's handling dumping his guy somewhere. I'm sure he'll call and fill you in."

"So, you took care of your two guys but Dominic has the other guy?"

"It's all handled, Oscar and I dumped our two in a field; we made it look like a drug deal gone bad."

Vinnie didn't like that his team was handling things separately, he again asked, "Okay, but what about that third guy?"

"Dom's handling it." Mario preferred to have Dominic

explain the details to the boss. "He called when he took the other truck to the warehouse, he said that he had to dump a couple of bodies." Mario waited, hoping Vinnie was okay with the explanation.

"Now it's a couple of bodies? Dominic better call me soon and fill me in. Make sure those trucks won't be found."

"I'll handle it." Once Mario hung-up he turned to Oscar. "We need to dump this Cadillac and get out of here."

Oscar was still concerned about his own safety but happy that he was with Mario and not Dominic. "I know a spot. It's north of here close to Port Huron. There's a gravel pit that has been abandoned. We can dump the car in there. It'll never be found."

Mario appreciated the suggestion. "I like that. We'll get a couple of my guys after they empty the trucks to take them up there too."

Oscar knew that Mario was Vinnie's nephew, and keeping in tight with him was critical to his well-being. "Mario, let me handle this for you. You probably need to get back downtown."

"Thanks, Oscar." Mario walked away and grabbed his cell phone. He was speaking to someone quietly. Oscar wished he knew what that was about, but knew better than to ask.

***

The call was one that the wife of every police officer always dreaded. When Nancy Frederickson heard Chief Mathews' voice on the other end of the line, her heart sank. She was in the kitchen and dropped the glass of water she was holding. The sound of broken glass echoed through the phone and the Chief knew how difficult this was. "Nancy, I'm sorry to be making this call but I just got off the phone and Don was in one of the vehicles involved in the crash on I-94. He's at the Detroit Medical Center right now but I don't know much more. Detective Spano is on his way to your house to take you down there."

Although her hands were shaking and she was terrified at this news, Nancy answered, "Chief, I can drive myself."

"I'm sure you can, however, Detective Spano wanted to do this. He said that's what Don would do for one of his team members. Nancy, he can get you there faster than if you drove. He should be there in just a few minutes."

She leaned against the kitchen counter to steady herself, "Chief, what aren't you telling me?"

"Nancy, you know everything right now that we do. I just found out a few minutes ago myself that his car was involved. The good news is he wasn't near that tanker that's on fire. His vehicle must have been rear-ended or something like that. If I hear anything else before you and Spano get to the hospital, I promise that I'll call you."

Once she heard that, Nancy broke down, sobbing. "I should have let him retire."

"Nancy, you can't think about that, I know Don's going to be okay. He's a tough guy."

Trying to gain her composure, she answered, "Thank you Chief."

"Nancy, anything you need, just ask. I told Detective Spano to call me when he has more details."

Once she hung up she paced around the kitchen. It was almost impossible to process what she had just been told and what might have happened. She had been watching the incident on I-94 on the television while making dinner. It looked terrible. She remembered saying to herself, *hope we don't know anyone that's involved in that.* She was going over everything in her mind, *what had her husband said in their last conversation.* She remembered, he told her he was going to grab a car from the motor pool and head home when the Chief finished his news conference. *Did he say which way he was going to be driving? Maybe they're wrong, maybe he wasn't in that car.* Nancy was doing what everyone in this situation would be doing, second guessing everything. She jumped when the doorbell rang. Heading to the door, she spotted Detective Spano through the leaded glass window, opening the door, Joe stepped in.

He didn't quite know what to say, "Sorry Nancy, the Chief thought it would be a good idea if I drove you to the hospital."

"Joe, what do you know?"

"Not much, the Chief called upstairs and said they were pretty sure Don was involved in the crash on I-94."

"Joe, what aren't you all telling me?"

"Nothing, Nancy, I promise. The only thing I know is Don is at the DMC and the Chief was trying to get more information from the officers that were down there."

She wasn't satisfied with that, "I'm going to call the hospital."

"They won't tell you anything over the phone. I've tried calling. Grab your coat. I'll try calling again for you. They might tell us something because you're here with me."

Nancy thought that made sense. Grabbing her jacket she followed him to his car.

"Nancy, don't panic, but I'm going to be using my siren."

"I appreciate that, Joe." He looked over at her; Nancy's hands were still shaking and tears welled in the corner of her eyes. "Joe, the sooner I get more information the better off I'll be."

He placed his arms around her shoulders, "Me too, Nancy, me too."

# CHAPTER SIX

**Events in Detroit over the past two years had cast a dark** shadow over the city. Although the Police Chief, Barry Mathews, had successfully cleaned up many areas of the police department, the city was still struggling. The Mayor formed an alliance with the Chief, and together promised a new era of cooperation and respect. They all knew that Detroit had indeed suffered from years of neglect and corruption. The Mayor hoped that since the city had now solved their bankruptcy issue and the Federal Government had pledged support for revitalization, that people were starting to see positive signs of recovery. His election focused on a brighter future.

National news teams in the past had focused on all the negatives but recently the news coming from the city had been brighter. This horrible crash brought back the negative attention to the city, attention that it didn't need. NBC and ABC were carrying live feeds from the local affiliates and sending the crash scene to the nation. CBS, along with their local reporters, were also running footage of the crash and the blaze from the tanker. Representatives from the NTSB were studying the footage of the crash, hoping to determine why the chopper came down so fast.

Chief Mathews and the Mayor were still on the scene supporting the teams of firefighters and officers trying to get the situation under control. Mathews paced in the Command Center waiting for a call from the Detroit Medical Center, hoping to get news on the condition of Detective Frederickson. Spano called the Chief confirming that he had picked up Detective Frederickson's wife and was en route to the hospital.

Joe Spano sped through traffic as Nancy Frederickson was still on hold with the hospital hoping to get some details on her husband's condition. The nurse kept telling her that she couldn't give her that information over the phone. Nancy wouldn't accept that. She immediately told the nurse, "I'm riding in a police car with a Detroit detective and we need to know now what's going on." After what seemed to be an eternity to her, a voice came back on the line.

"This is Doctor Chavey, who am I talking to?"

"This is Nancy Frederickson, wife of Detective Don Frederickson. I know he's in your Trauma Unit. I need to know his condition, and need to know it now!"

"Mrs. Frederickson, I hope you understand, but we've gotten so many calls from news teams and people claiming to be relatives of those brought in, we have to be extremely careful."

Taking a deep breath, Nancy slowly answered, "I understand, however I need to know the condition of my husband."

"Mrs. Frederickson, could you provide me with a few details."

"Sure, whatever you need."

"What is your husband's badge number?"

"Absolutely, his is a gold shield with the numbers 1326 right under the Detroit Police insignia."

"Thank you, Mrs. Frederickson. Just one more thing?"

Although she was becoming very impatient, she said, "Sure, but after this I better get some details!"

"What is his birth date and middle name?" Nancy quickly gave him the information. "Thanks, I'm sorry to have had to ask you those things but we have to be careful. Your husband is about to come out of the Trauma Unit. We confirmed he suffered a broken leg and he also has a cracked breast bone."

Before the doctor could continue, Nancy said, "Cracked breast bone?"

"When he was brought in he was exhibiting major chest pains and trouble breathing. We didn't want to take any chances and our team called in a thoracic surgeon to evaluate his condition. Mrs. Frederickson, he may have hit the steering wheel in the collision causing this injury. His leg has been set and we're taking him for more X-rays to make sure he doesn't have any other issues."

Nancy was repeating everything the doctor told her aloud so Spano knew what was going on. "Thank you, thank you. We're just a few minutes away. Where should I head to?"

"If you come to the Emergency Room, they will direct you from there."

"You've been great, Doctor Chavey. Will I see you when I get there?"

"Probably not, our team has been working to help the people that are being brought in from the accident. However if I get a chance, I'd be happy to talk to you."

"Thanks again, doctor." Nancy turned to Spano, "Joe pull into the emergency area and drop me off."

Spano negotiated the last few streets that had been re-routed because of the problems on the Interstate. As he turned onto John R. Street and into the hospital complex, Nancy almost jumped out of the car before he came to a full stop in front of the Emergency Room doors. He watched her trot into the hospital and pulled out of the drive to a spot for official vehicles. He also jogged into the emergency entrance, hoping to catch up with Frederickson's wife. Joe saw Nancy talking to a doctor in the hallway. He moved to her side and listened.

"Mrs. Frederickson, I'm sure he'll be okay." The doctor turned and made his way back down the hall as Joe waited for her to hopefully update him.

"Nancy, what did he say?" He thought she looked flushed, maybe because of the panic of the situation or the news that the doctor delivered. "Nancy, are you okay?"

"Yeah, I'm okay. The doctor said Don's going to be okay, that's what we've got to go on now."

"Thank God, where is he now?"

Nancy turned back to Joe, "Let's head to the second floor. The doctor's confirmed that Don has a broken leg and fractured ribs.

Also his breast bone is cracked, but not broken. They were afraid that it had damaged his heart, hopefully the test will show that everything will be okay."

"Why are we headed to the second floor?"

"They took Don for more X-rays. He's being moved upstairs to room 244. The doctor suggested we could sit in the waiting room on that wing. We'll be in good position to see when they bring him down the hallway." Spano didn't know exactly why but he gave Nancy a hug. She patted his back and whispered in his ear. "You're a good friend, Joe." The two smiled, maybe for the first time in a while.

"I better call the team and then the Chief to let them know that he's going to be okay."

Nancy knew that was a good idea. She found a couple of nice chairs near the bank of windows in the waiting room as Joe talked to Amy Harper on his cell phone. Once he finished updating the team, then the Chief, he sat down next to her. "Joe, I know you must have important police business to take care of. I'll understand if you have to head back to the office."

He looked back at her, "I'm not going anywhere until I see that gruff look on his face for myself."

She laughed, "I know he'll be just as happy to see you too."

\*\*\*

Chief Mathews updated the Commanders and Captains on the scene. "We've confirmed that it was Detective Frederickson in the police car. My SIU team is working on who owns that garbage truck that appears to have rammed his vehicle." He looked at both of them, "Witnesses stated that the truck crashed into the police car sending it over the center guard rail. Make this a top priority, we need to know why."

The Commander asked, "Chief, was Frederickson involved in a case that leads us to think there was more to this than an accident?"

"Yes, we're sure this was much more than an accident. The SIU team has history to check on and your help will be utilized. Right now I know you've got your hands full; keep me informed on the action on the freeway. I'll let you know how you can help with the investigation."

Mathews walked over to the Command Center to update the Mayor on the progress that the police department was making on the Interstate. "Mayor, our teams have pushed all the vehicles back as far as possible so the fire won't spread further. I talked to the Fire Chief, he said they've got two more foam trucks coming from the airport and they're getting the blaze under control. It's going to take at least five or six more hours."

"Thanks Chief, I talked to the DOT head. They're concerned that the damage is so great that we're going to have to close the section of the freeway for at least four days, maybe more." Mathews shook his head. The Mayor knew this would be a problem for every department in the city. "This is going to be a real problem for all of us. We're going to have to make sure we get the best routes to avoid for all the news networks outside."

"I'll have my Lieutenant put something together to release to the media."

"Thanks, Chief. Have her forward a copy to my information secretary."

# CHAPTER SEVEN

**The SIU was happy to get the good news that Detective** Frederickson was being moved to a room and should be recovering at the hospital. Detective Harper had been consoling Mindy, making sure she was okay. The news that Frederickson was involved in the massive incident had shook-up the entire SIU staff, and Mindy was especially taking it hard. "Mindy, everything's going to be okay. Spano is with Frederickson's wife and they'll call us when he's in a room." Mindy appreciated the calm approach that Harper had taken.

Detectives Allen and Adams paced in the Conference Room, not sure what to do. When Harper walked in the room she saw that Adams' fist was clenched. "Adams, you okay?"

"Yeah, just wish I could do something to help."

"Only natural, but we still have a job to do. Spano will call when he knows more." Detective Harper was taking control of the situation. She knew she had to be a pillar of strength for the staff and they saw determination and resolve in her approach. "Adams, we're not standing still on this. I want to know everything about that damn initial crash."

He looked back at her, "What do you mean?"

"From everything we're getting from the command post at the scene the garbage truck hit Detective Frederickson's car from behind. Was it intentional? Who owns that trucking company? We need to get to work on this and you can do some real investigative work for the team." She had fired so many questions at Adams that he appeared flustered. "Adams, I'm calling the rest of the team. We can use everyone possible on this." Harper knew that Detective Spano had called both Detectives Askew and Tindall, but wasn't sure what he had told them. She planned on contacting the two detectives to get the whole team working on the investigation.

\*\*\*

Nancy Frederickson stood near the bank of windows along the west wall of the waiting room on the second floor of the DMC when she spotted two officers and a nurse pushing a gurney down the hallway. "Joe, there he is!" Running to make sure it was her husband; she met the team pushing the detective toward his room. "Oh my God, honey," bending down and kissing him on the forehead with tears of joy and sobs pouring out, the two officers and nurse both smiled and were glad to witness the reunion. Detective Spano stood a few feet behind her. He had flashed his badge to the group as he and Nancy were approaching them. The last thing he wanted was the two officers stopping Nancy from greeting her husband. Spano was happy that Frederickson was wide awake and surprised that he actually gave his wife a little grin. The group proceeded down the hallway with Nancy gripping onto the right hand of her husband, looking like she'd never let go.

The two officers stood back with Spano as the nurse and Nancy entered the hospital room getting Don settled in the bed. The doctor that Spano and Nancy had met downstairs approached. He nodded to Spano and entered the room. While Detective Frederickson was getting settled into his hospital room, Spano asked, "Why the police detail?"

"Chief Mathews ordered it. We were ordered to keep a 24/7 guard on the detective's room until further notice."

Spano had a puzzled look, "24/7 guard?"

"Chief's orders."

Joe Spano moved away from the front of room 244 and decided to dial Detective Harper. She had to know more right now than he did. "Amy, this is Joe, I'm with Don's wife and they are getting him settled in his hospital room. Hey, the Chief has a 24/7 guard on his room. What's going on?"

"Not sure Joe. He hadn't communicated that news to us. One

thing I can tell you, this wasn't an accident. They're keeping Frederickson's name out of the news. The Chief doesn't want anyone to know where he is or even that he was involved."

"Makes sense, maybe we can flush them out if they don't hear any details about his condition."

"How do you know that?"

"Instinct, Joe. Just feel it in my gut."

Spano said, "Now you sound just like Frederickson."

"I'll take that as a compliment, Joe. "We've got some new details from the scene. Witnesses are saying that the garbage truck weaved through traffic and rammed Don's car sending him over the center median. This was intentional."

"Why would someone try to hurt or kill Frederickson now? We got Fotopoulos and his entire organization either behind bars or dead; who's left?"

"I'm not sure but the team's not sitting here and doing nothing. The Chief has us on the case and I've called Tindall and Askew to come in. I've put a call in to the Chief updating him. Joe, we're going to be at the forefront handling this investigation."

Spano was surprised at the stern resolve in Detective Harper's voice. "Okay, I'm with you. I'll be right in once I get to talk to Don. Maybe he will remember something from the collision that will help us."

"Great idea, once the Chief calls me back, I'll let you know what he approves us to do. Joe, make sure you tell Don that the team is thinking about him."

"I promise." Spano hung up and watched the doctor leaving the room. He moved closer to the entrance and wanted to give Nancy a few minutes alone with her husband. Turning to one of the officers at the door, "What is the guarding rotation plan?"

"Rotation of personnel taking four hour stints. We're all from Woodward North Precinct and this is in our coverage area."

"Good, has anyone given you possible suspects to be on the lookout for?"

"Not really; we just can't let anyone in except those with proper credentials or known family members."

Spano was hoping to get more details but the guards didn't have anything more than he did. He peeked into the room and saw Nancy waving to him. He gladly walked into the room and was surprised to see Frederickson lifting his right arm and waving to him. Joe moved closer, "Wow, some people will do anything to get a day off." That brought a chuckle from both Nancy and Don. "Boss, we're all so glad that you're okay."

"Joe, do you think this looks okay?" That brought a few more laughs. "I'm hooked up to these damn tubes and they tell me that dancing is totally out of the question." Nancy smiled at her husband while holding tightly on his hand. He looked up at the detective, "Joe, get these guys."

Spano was sure that his boss didn't know the outcome of what had taken place after his car was hit from behind. Not sure what he should tell him, Spano eased into the conversation. "Don, what do you remember from the crash?" He watched as Nancy gripped her husband's hand a little tighter.

"I'm not sure that I'm going to be a good witness. Everything is kind of blurry."

The nurse leaned in and whispered, "He's still in shock, detective, give him a little time."

Joe smiled back at her and turned toward his friend. "Don, I know this is a little uncomfortable for you to be in this position. Anything you can remember will be helpful."

"I know that Joe. I left headquarters after the press conference and had to grab a car from the motor pool. My vehicle was still at the warehouse along the river after our drug bust."

Nancy leaned in, "Joe, do you think this can wait?"

Frederickson immediately stopped his wife, "Honey, this is critical to solving the case."

She understood, "You're right. Just remember, the doctor said you need your rest."

Spano turned to her, "You're right Nancy. Don, just a couple questions then I'm heading back to the office."

Frederickson looked at his detective, "Shoot Joe; ask anything that you need to."

"Don, do you think you were hit on purpose?"

Don took a deep breath, "I saw a garbage truck driving erratically behind me. Once I merged on to 94 from the Lodge Freeway it was weaving through the lanes and I wondered what in the hell he was doing. Joe, I only thought that the truck wanted to get off at an upcoming exit and didn't think it was planning anything else."

"So you don't think it was aiming at you?"

"Not at first, not until I moved to the center lane and saw the truck gaining on my bumper. Joe, I tried to move back to the left lane, that's when all hell broke loose. Joe, I'm sure now that he aimed at me. It's hard to remember anything else, I think I went airborne and tried to grab onto the steering wheel."

Spano felt he had what he needed for now. "Don, Nancy's right, you need to get some rest. Detective Harper and the team is on it right now. I'll be back tomorrow." Spano tapped Frederickson's hand and gave him a smile. "We're all so glad that you're okay and will be on the mend." The two men had become very close during the short time that the SIU team had been in operation. It was a true friendship of people that both liked and respected each other. Once Joe was heading to his car he called Detective Harper. "Harper, first thing is, he's going to be fine. Same old Don, joking but has a pretty good recollection of the events before he was hit."

"Good, Joe, I talked to the Chief. He's still at the crash site and he's on board with us handling the investigation into the crash, at least the events that started the whole thing. Joe, I hope you don't feel that I jumped into this without checking with you or Don."

"Harper, you did exactly what any of us should have, I'm glad you're taking the lead."

"Thanks, Joe. I just wanted to do what you and Don would have done."

Spano filled her in on what Frederickson had told him from his recollection of initially spotting the garbage truck coming up from behind him, as he was trying to avoid the truck when he was sure it took aim at his rear bumper. They both knew this wasn't over. Someone was still trying to kill Detective Frederickson, but who?

# CHAPTER EIGHT

**Vinnie La Russo had his key men together in the office at the** Eastern Market. "How did the damn news people put the garbage truck crashing into the police car as the cause of this?"

Dominic Parma sat across the desk from La Russo hoping Mario had something for the boss. Mario shifted in his chair before answering, "Boss, I promise, we ain't got nothing to worry about; that truck isn't registered to any of our companies. Nobody will put it together with the Fotopoulos case, Castellanos or you."

Vinnie quickly answered, "Mario, that's all good but wasn't the damn driver you hired one of Castellanos' guys? If they get him talking we've got a big problem. How come your guys haven't located him or that detective? We haven't heard anything from the news about the condition of the detective."

Mario didn't know what to say. Dominic quickly jumped in, "Boss, I got my guys looking for our driver right now. We're searching both downtown hospitals and we'll find him. Our guy that was following the garbage truck planned to pick up the driver but he got caught up in the crash. He reported that he saw the guy who seemed to climb out of the garbage truck but then looked like he fell to the pavement. He must have been injured because emergency technicians on the scene were working on him and carried him to an ambulance. I thought they would take him to the DMC downtown. Our guy also saw a man pulled from the wrecked police car, he's sure that it was Frederickson."

Vinnie leaned forward, "What condition was he in?"

"He said the guy looked bad. My man tried to get closer and said that the techs were working on him next to the two vehicles. His head was covered in blood and unresponsive to the emergency workers."

Vinnie was happy to hear this news, "You got someone at the hospital?"

"I'm on top of that now. Two of my guys are combing the hospital for both our driver and Frederickson. There are so many people that have been taken there that it's impossible to get any information from the hospital staff. I've told them to stay there and check every room if they need to."

Mario had listened to this, "We'll make sure that we'll find out where he was taken?"

Dominic added, "Yeah, all the people hurt in the first crash were taken to the DMC. Once the explosion happened, I'm sure people were also taken to Harper and Receiving Hospitals. I sent guys to both places in case they was taken to one of them."

Mario and Dominic waited for Vinnie's reaction. Both men were a little uneasy as they sat across from him. La Russo was contemplating the information that they had given him. "First, we got to get your man; if he's identified as the driver of the garbage truck we'll have more problems. With the hospitals slammed with people, your men should be able to move around pretty easily. Dominic, I want this taken care of, and right away, you know what I mean?"

"Yeah, I'll take care of it." With that Dominic got up and tapped Mario on the shoulder. "Let's go." The two men made their way out of the upstairs office past the secretary. Once they were at the bottom of the steps Dominic turned toward Mario. "This ain't gonna cause us a problem. I want two guys at every downtown hospital searching for him. When someone finds him, I think he's going to have complications."

Mario nodded, knowing that Dominic would kill the driver and anyone else who got in their way.

*** 

Lieutenant Jackson stood up when the Chief walked back into

his office. Looking at her watch, she was sure he'd be at the scene the rest of the evening. "Chief, I didn't expect you back here."

"Me either, Lieutenant, but we have so many people dead and or injured. Until I have a better handle on this thing I'm staying put right here. Call upstairs and ask Detective Harper to come on down." Jackson sat down once her boss walked into his office and called upstairs to the SIU team. Detective Adams answered. Jackson stated, "Detective, the Chief wants Detective Harper to come on downstairs."

Adams quickly answered, "Harper is filling the team in on the investigation. I'll tell her that the Chief wants her in his office."

"Thanks, detective."

Adams and Tindall walked over to the group that was in the Conference Room. Spano had just arrived from the hospital as Harper was giving the team assignments. "Detective Harper, the Chief wants you to come on downstairs," Adams said.

She looked over at Spano, "Maybe you should come on down there with me."

"No, you've got control of this. I'll continue to finish what you've started up here. Go fill the Chief in on what we have so far."

"Okay Joe." Amy Harper grabbed her folder and headed downstairs to Chief Mathews' office.

This wasn't her first time in the Chief's office, but it was the first time she would be in there alone.

The Special Investigative Unit continued plotting the details that Harper and Adams had been working on. Spano, Askew and Johnson had the city map pinned on the crime board with the freeway highlighted and pins at all the hospitals where accident victims had been taken. Joe turned to the detectives, "Harper is right; we've got to find that driver from the garbage truck. Until we do, we're not going to know who may behind all of this. One thing for sure, someone is trying to kill Detective Frederickson."

They all knew Spano was right, but who could it be? Everyone involved in the Fotopoulos case was in custody. Adams looked at the board that the men studied, and asked, "Whatever happened to the owner of the trucking company."

Spano looked over at him. "Castellanos? We never found him. Harper and Agent Williams from the FBI cased out the place. Once we connected Castellanos with Fotopoulos, the Bureau shut the place down."

Adams listened; then said, "So Castellanos is still missing, and his place is locked up by the FBI. Seems like a good case for wanting to get revenge at the guy who was responsible for that."

"You're right, Adams. You take Johnson and head to the trucking company. We never found any signs of garbage trucks in their fleet; all their records showed that they were a supplier to local fruit markets. It would make a lot of sense that it could be a great spot to hide a garbage truck." Adams grabbed his jacket as he and Johnson headed out of the office. Spano knew that they at least had a plan to look for the missing garbage truck driver. Thinking that he needed to put an APB out and search every hospital and medical facility to see if the driver may have been brought in with injuries. As he headed to the desk phone he suddenly stopped. *"Shit! We don't even know what the damn guy looks like."* He was right, how could they search for someone that nobody had any idea what the guy looked like. There had to be dozens of men brought in the hospitals from the accident site that would look fit the description of a truck driver. Suddenly, he realized, it could be a woman that drove the truck. Spano slumped in a chair, *what now, he thought, what now.* Spano felt his best lead might be to get the head of the EMS units on the scene. Maybe they remember what the driver of the garbage truck looked like. It was just a chance, but he had to start somewhere.

# CHAPTER NINE

**Dominic Parma made his way down the long corridor of the** Detroit Medical Center. He spotted a young nurse holding a clip board. Ducking into a restroom, he splashed water on his face. He wanted the nurse to think he had been crying. Making sure his gun was tucked in and his shoulder holster was well hidden; he walked back out and saw that she was talking to an older woman. Dominic strolled over, almost mumbling and holding a tissue, "Miss, could you please help me?"

The nurse looked at the big man who had red cheeks and it appeared that tears were running down his face, "Sir, are you okay?"

He stuttered. "My brother, I can't find my brother." Dominic did his best acting job to convince the young lady that he needed help.

Putting her hand on his shoulder, she tried to calm him, "I'll try to help if I can." This was maybe the twentieth person she had talked to with the same request.

Dominic continued with his act, "My brother, Ben, he was on the freeway in that terrible accident. I can't get anyone to help me."

"What's your brother's full name?"

"Ben, Ben Walker."

She looked down at the clip board and ran her finger down a list of names. Dominic peeked over her shoulder as she checked the listing. Taking a breath, she turned and looked at Dominic. "Can you give me a little more information, how about a physical description of your brother or his birth date?"

Her questions made him think that the garbage truck driver was there. Waving his arms and shaking his head, Dominic said, "Sorry but I'm kinda confused. My mom was sure he was taken to Harper Hospital, I've been there searching, he's not there; they said he must have been brought here."

"I understand, but we have some people here that didn't have any identification on them and our only way to classify them is by possible age."

"I hope you don't think I'm a terrible brother but I can't remember Ben's birth date. He's thirty-four or thirty-five. Ben has brown hair and is six foot tall."

She again looked at the clip board, "The last name again?"

Dominic repeated, "Walker!"

"I don't see anyone listed here with that name, although we do have three people that are in the same age range but they don't have an ID. I'm not sure if any of them are your brother."

Dominic wanted to grab the clip board from her but knew that wasn't a good idea. "Where can I find those people to see if one of them is Ben?"

"The hospital is updating the list as soon as people are admitted. I get a new list every fifteen minutes. You can check downstairs at the main desk near the Information Office. They may have a more updated list."

Dominic tried to smile a little, "Can I walk down there with you to see if a new list is available?"

"I'm sorry, but they'll bring it to me when it's updated. I'm stationed here to help people who are in the same situation as you are."

"Thanks for your help." He walked away and dialed Mario. "Did you find anything out?"

"No, I'm downstairs at Admitting. They don't have either our driver or Frederickson on their list."

"Okay, did you call the guys that headed to Harper Hospital?"

"Not yet, I wanted to make sure they weren't here first."

"Call them and meet me at the front door. They do have three guys without identification being admitted. We should send some guys to head over to Receiving Hospital, maybe Frederickson is there." Dominic headed downstairs to the entrance of the hospital. When he got to the door his cell phone rang, it was Vinnie. Dominic wanted to have something to tell the boss, he hated to tell him they hadn't found Ben or Frederickson. "Yeah, boss, we're searching the DMC and Mario is also talking to his guys at Harper Hospital right now." He listened as Vinnie was barking out orders. "Vinnie, I got it, we'll handle this." Once he was off the phone he spotted Mario coming down the hallway. "Tell me you got something!"

"I just got off the phone with the guys at Harper, no sign of Ben or Detective Frederickson there either. I told them to stay put. Dominic, maybe our driver was using an alias. Do we have any knowledge of other names he has used?"

Dominic hadn't thought about that. They only had been asking about patients by Ben's name and description. If Ben used a different name he might be in a room, recovering. "I'm going back to check with that cute nurse upstairs. Maybe you're right; he could have been here the whole time." Dominic headed back upstairs with Mario trailing behind him. "Mario, I'm not asking that nurse, let's start searching rooms."

"How are we going to get away with that?"

Dominic stopped and turned, "I'm not sure but we've got to find him. Vinnie isn't going to accept that we can't find him. If necessary I'll kill everyone brought in from that crash."

Mario looked back at Dominic shaking his head, "We need to talk about this."

"I'm done talking, time for action."

*** 

Detective Harper sat across the desk from Chief Mathews as they went over the situation. She told him about the plan the SIU team was putting into place. "Sir, once we found out that it appeared that the garbage truck hit Frederickson's car on purpose we decided to search records and any possible tie in to Castellanos Trucking. I'm thinking this was a crime of retribution."

The Chief studied his young detective. "You sound pretty sure, Detective."

"Chief, we never found the driver of that first incident from last year when the garbage truck killed Detective Forsyth in St. Clair Shores. My gut feeling is that someone out there is looking to get even."

"Detective, this is your case. Just make sure we follow procedures. What do you need from my office?"

Harper looked back at her Chief, "Just your approval to proceed with the investigation."

"Detective, you've got my full support. If anyone gives you or anyone in the SIU team a problem tell them to call me." With that the Chief stood and extended his hand. "Detective Harper, I'm putting you in charge of SIU, report any changes or details to me or Lieutenant Jackson. I'll tell her that you'll be following up for me."

She stood and shook his hand. "Thank you for your support, sir. We won't let you down." Amy Harper walked out of the Chief's office feeling ten feet tall. Her only concern was what would the other guys think about her being in charge? Heading back upstairs, she decided not to mention that to the team. Harper had another issue, the one about her friend, Andy Jones. How could she get more involved without blowing the information that Tom Baker gave her. She made her way back into the SIU office.

Detective Spano had sent the team's secretary, Mindy, home. She wanted to stay and help but he insisted, "We're going to need everyone fresh, go home and get some rest." He was at Mindy's desk looking through her computer when Harper walked in. "What did the Chief say?"

"He gave us a green light. This is our case. Why are you at Mindy's computer?"

"I knew she filed the information from Detective Forsyth's crash. I was hoping to print the details so we don't have to repeat what we've already done."

"Good, let's put everything together. Because Forsyth was killed in a collision with a garbage truck it only makes sense that it's related to our case. Bring whatever you find to the Conference Room. I'll update Adams, Askew and Johnson." She waved to the two detectives that were working at their desks. "Guys, I know it's late but let's put everything together in the Conference Room." Walking to the large room in the corner of the office she hoped that they were following her. Once she reached the door she heard Detective Adams telling Johnson, "Harper's good people, she'll be the best one to lead this investigation." That comment made her feel much better.

*** 

Dominic Parma took Mario's suggestion but didn't have any luck with the nurse getting information on the possibility of Ben Walker, or anyone his age being brought in, dead or alive. The hospital didn't have any bodies from the crash that matched Ben's or Frederickson's description. Dominic and Mario needed to have something to tell Vinnie, and soon.

Vinnie La Russo paced in his office and was getting very impatient. *How could Ben Walker have disappeared?* Vinnie also knew there had to be more information on the condition of their target. His two key men haven't come up with anything and Vinnie wanted to get some news. He called his secretary, Gloria. "Call next door and get me something for dinner."

"Okay, corned beef sandwich?"

"Yeah, get something for yourself unless you plan to go home."

"No, Mr. La Russo, I'll stay as late as you need me." Hanging up she called downstairs and placed the order. Gloria had been with La Russo for seven years. Her father had worked for Vinnie, back in the day, and La Russo had known her since she was a little kid. He liked Gloria; she was very efficient and kept his affairs in order. Of course Gloria knew what Vinnie's business entailed. She not only was his secretary but also kept the office professional for anyone that inquired. More than once she had to fend off news reporters wanting to get an interview with her boss. Gloria was a real looker, and that sometimes had people take her as just another pretty face. Gloria graduated from Detroit Mercy College, with a Master's Degree. Vinnie paid for her college costs after her dad was killed working on a job for him. She appreciated everything he had done for her and was loyal to her boss. Gloria did everything possible in her job to make Vinnie appear as a normal businessman. Along with Mario and Dominic, she was a key individual in his organization.

Dominic walked along the second floor of the DMC when he spotted a police officer stationed in front of a patient's room. He stood back, watched for a minute and called Mario. "I think I found one of our guys!"

"What, where?"

"Meet me on the second floor across from the nurse's station. They got a cop in front of a patient's door." As he waited, Dominic grinned, why else would a cop be guarding a room if one of their own or the guy that caused it all wasn't in there. When Mario saw Dominic, he walked past him and stopped in front of the drinking fountain. Dominic followed his partner and quietly stated, "Look down the hallway, there's a cop in front of a room and I've seen two other guys enter. I believe they're cops too."

Mario peeked up and saw what Dom referred to. It had to be the detective's room. "Okay, what now?"

"We need to finish the job." The two men decided to create a plan but stayed on the second floor, out of sight of the officer guarding the doorway.

# CHAPTER TEN

**It had been a long night for everyone working the freeway** tragedy. The Detroit Fire Department had the freeway blaze finally under control and area hospitals were getting back to normal after the influx of so many injured or killed in the crash and explosion. The Department of Transportation informed the Mayor that the westbound side of I-94 from Woodward to Mt. Elliott would be closed for close to a week while they tried to clean the mess. The Director explained, "Some pavement will have to be replaced along the two mile stretch." The body count from the explosion numbered seven dead and over one-hundred injured. Many people suffered burns and lacerations from the explosion. Among the dead was Dirk Stanfield, the chopper pilot, and Aaron, the reporter on board. The news team at Channel 4 was still in shock and many in the control room had treated for stress. Calls of condolence came in from every station in the city and national news correspondents decided not to air the incident out of respect for the families of the two station employees killed in the crash. Investigators from the NTSB and FBI were called in to make sure this wasn't a terrorist action. They closed off the Interstate from Mt. Elliot to I-96. There were signs diverting drivers around the closed area.

Lester Holt, with NBC news, was at the site with a live broadcast along the closed section of the Interstate. Television viewers watched as he walked along the burnt pavement with the Mayor, who explained, "Lester, our Police and Fire Chiefs have done a great job clearing the majority of the wreckage. We hope that the FBI will allow us to remove the remains of the chopper and tanker later today once they've had time to inspect them."

Lester asked, "Mayor, have they told you what they are looking for?"

"No, the FBI is just making sure nothing else may have been involved causing this terrible incident."

"Any clues as to what they suspect?"

"No, right now the FBI is working closely with our Police Chief and the National Traffic Safety Board. The only fact we have is from initial reports. Witnesses stated that a garbage truck driving erratically caused the chain reaction vehicle crash."

"Do you know who was driving the garbage truck?"

"Yes, the driver has been transported to a local hospital and is being protected by our police department until he regains consciousness. He's there along with many of the people involved in the initial crash."

Lester Holt asked, "So your people haven't been able to talk to him yet. Was this a deliberate act?"

"No, we haven't talked to him. He's listed in critical condition and has been unresponsive. The FBI, along with our police force, haven't been able to interview him. It appears that he suffered a blow to the head and has been unconscious. We have officers stationed outside his room hoping to get answers once he comes to. The medical staff working on him hopes we might be able to talk to him soon."

Watching the interview with great interest at his office at the Eastern Market, Vinnie La Russo moved to the edge of his seat. It was early as the television broadcast beamed in the corner of his office. This new information was what he feared. He called out to his secretary, "Gloria, call Dominic, now!"

***

The morning brought new assignments for the detectives in the Special Investigative Unit. They were working the investigation into the freeway crash headed by Detective Harper. She had dispatched Detectives Adams and Johnson to Castellanos Trucking checking for more details on the possibility of the ownership of the garbage truck from last year's crash. Could it be the same ownership of trucks from the St. Clair Shores Trucking Company? Detective Spano was running down the information on the Forsyth crash with a garbage truck from last year. When he checked details on Mindy's computer yesterday, he discovered that they never found a tie in to the garbage truck and Castellanos Trucking. So many missing pieces made him wonder how they were all related to this new crash on the Interstate. Once the team started on their task, Amy Harper dialed the phone number Tom Baker had given her.

Tom looked down at the screen on his I-phone but didn't recognize the number. He decided to let it go to his message box. Tom and his partner were downtown at the Medical Examiner's office waiting for the identification on the two bodies that were transported from the scene on Jefferson Avenue earlier. Tom's partner was talking to the M.E. when Tom moved in closer. She was telling them, "We've got a problem with one of the bodies because there aren't any fingerprints or DNA on record to reference; however, we've got the ID on the other body."

*Tom Baker knew what she was going to tell them.*

The M.E. turned toward the two detectives; she had a solemn look on her face. "Detectives, one of your bodies is not only in our data base, it's that of a police officer."

Baker's partner was stunned, he asked, "Shit, who is it?"

"Records show his name is Andy Jones."

Tom knew he had to let them know that he knew Andy Jones. "Are you sure?"

"Positive, you're both aware our data base has more identification points for police officers than the general public."

Tom moved closer to the group, "I was in the academy with an Andy Jones." Tom didn't want to give away that he was sure that he knew who it was all along.

The M.E. looked back at them, "Not sure how many Andy Jones have been in the force, but our office has called this in to the

Chief's Information Director." Once they were done both detectives thanked the M.E. and headed out. Tom's partner looked at him, "Baker, what did your Andy Jones look like?"

Baker looked back at his partner. "It was a lot of years ago, but he was a tall white guy, my age, nothing else jumps out at me." Baker knew his partner wondered why Tom hadn't asked more questions from the M.E. He continued walking toward their car when his phone rang again. He stopped, "Hey, I've got to catch this call." Tom turned back toward the building on Beaubien Street and answered his phone. His partner watched for a second but figured it must be personal.

"Tom, it's Harper, do you have any more details for me?"

"Amy, I'm just leaving the Medical Examiner's office. They've confirmed Andy's identification. Kinda funny though, the M.E. said she didn't see any visual track marks. They said that they'll contact the Chief's office once they confirm the cause of death and have the toxicology report. It won't be long before it's on the news. Amy, she said he is a police officer, no mention of being an ex-cop."

That was confusing to both of them. They had been under the impression that Andy had been kicked off the force. "Tom, that doesn't make any sense. Keep me filled in, please. I'll need to find time to contact Andy's mom. Do you have any idea when they will release the details?"

"No, that's above my pay grade. Amy, would you like me to join you when you contact Andy's mom?"

Amy was surprised and happy when he asked. "That would be great, Tom. I'll call her and let you know when we can go over there." After she hung up she opened her desk drawer. Taking out a small photo album she turned a few pages and stopped at one that had her standing along the river at Hart Plaza. Amy stared at a photo of her standing with two other people.

Mindy approached Amy's desk, "Who's in that photo?"

Amy was surprised at the question. She hadn't seen Mindy

coming toward her. "Just a few friends from the police academy;" she didn't want to hide what she was looking at knowing it would only cause more questions.

"Is one of them the guy who called you earlier?"

"No, he's not in this picture." She showed the photo to Mindy. "This was the last week of the academy training and we all went downtown to celebrate." Mindy smiled as she leafed through the ten page album. Amy stood, "Mindy, I'm going to head out and see if I can find out more details from the scene on the freeway."

"Okay, if anything comes in I'll call you right away. I just wanted to thank you and Detective Spano for helping me when we got the news about Detective Frederickson."

Harper smiled at Mindy, "We're all concerned and glad that he's doing okay." Amy moved closer and hugged her. The team was pretty close, that was part of the key to their success. Once Mindy walked back to her desk Harper slid the photos in her purse. "Mindy, I'll call to see if you have anything from Detective Spano or the hospital."

"Are you going to stop by to see Detective Frederickson?"

"I should. If I do I'll let you know."

"Let me give you some money for flowers."

"That's not necessary. I know the Chief sent something from the department. Maybe once he's home we'll go over and take dinner to him and Nancy."

"I like that idea."

\*\*\*

Mary Ann Jones lived in Grosse Pointe just past Seven Mile Road. Amy Harper had been there with Andy a few times for dinner when they were in the academy. Mary Ann liked Amy and she was glad that her son once dated her. When she was pulling up in front of the Jones' house, it brought back a rush of memories, ones that she hadn't thought about in a long time. Amy dated Andy for a few months after they graduated from the academy. She liked Andy, and his mom was always great to her. Soon they were both assigned to different precincts and then she lost contact with him. Nothing bad happened, they just became involved in their new careers. She heard he was assigned to a task force that monitored drug traffic along East Jefferson near Mexicantown. Amy remembered hearing disturbing news about Andy that he was using drugs. She called and talked to his mom to help but Andy refused to talk about it. Harper looked at Baker, "Tom, Andy soon stopped talking to either his mom or me and we both feared he was hooked. Reports were that Andy had been dismissed from the police force and hadn't been seen in over a year by his mom."

She lowered her head, "What is it?" Baker asked.

"Tom, I should have done more to help find him, It's probably my fault that he's dead now." Now she stood in the street in front of his house and had to tell Andy's mom the news, news no parent was ever ready to hear. Turning to Baker, "Tom, I really appreciate you doing this with me."

Baker knew how hard this was, "Amy, none of this is your fault. We both know that many people fall into drugs, alcohol and other vices. I'm happy to be here, for both you and Andy's mom. I know this is tough and it's better that she hears it from friends instead of on television." Tom was surprised when Amy leaned closer and gave him a hug. The two of them walked to the door and waited for Ms. Jones to answer. Mary Ann Jones was glad to hear from Amy when she called. Little did she know what Detective Harper was about to tell her.

# CHAPTER ELEVEN

**Nancy Frederickson spent the night at the Detroit Medical** Center with her husband, refusing to leave his side. None of the personnel involved guarding the detective could blame her. The officers stationed outside Frederickson's room called in a concern when they spotted two men that passed their position late last night. It had to be close to midnight when first one, a big gruff looking guy walked by twice. Calling it in to his captain, he was assured that they would send a second group of officers to help secure the second floor. The officer relayed the description of the men he'd seen to his captain and was sure he had seen one of them earlier when he came on duty in the lobby talking to a young nurse. The Captain dispatched two squad cars to the DMC and advised Chief Mathews' office about the report.

Detective Frederickson spent a restless night; Nancy watched him toss and turn and tried to comfort her husband who mumbled in his sleep. She leaned closer, hoping to hear what troubled him. Although he was almost inaudible, she could tell he kept saying, '*Smoke, I smell smoke.*' It was the only thing she could make out for sure. Nancy held his hand and with tears in her eyes she tried to calm him down, "Honey, you're safe, we're in the hospital." The officer at the door peeked in but realized that this was more of a private moment. He wanted to ask if she needed help but guessed that she'd call if she did.

The staff nurse assigned to Frederickson's room made her round and the officer at the door checked her credentials then let her pass. "Mrs. Frederickson, is everything okay?"

Nancy looked up, "He keeps having nightmares or something like that."

The nurse understood, "That's not unusual, especially after the trauma of the crash. The doctors gave him some potent medicine and that may be causing the restlessness."

She had tears running down her cheeks and looked back at the young nurse, "It's just not like him to be like this."

"Let me check his vitals." Grabbing her stethoscope and checking his pulse the young blond watched the monitor above the detective's head. "Mrs. Frederickson, his heart rate and pulse are good." Nancy watched the monitor, not really knowing what she was looking for, except that it helped calm her nerves.

Just then the detective's eyes opened, startled, he mumbled, "What's going on?"

Both Nancy and the young nurse jumped, "Don, you're okay, I'm here!"

Moving his head from side to side, blinking his eyes, Frederickson took a deep breath. "Where am I?"

Nancy leaned down wiping tears from her eyes, looking into her husband's face, "Honey, you're at the Detroit Medical Center, don't you remember, you were in a car crash."

It was still fuzzy to him, although he didn't answer her right away; he looked over at the nurse standing on the other side of the bed. He cleared his throat, "Yeah, I remember, what day is it?"

Nancy looked back at the nurse with concern. The nurse grabbed the cup next to the bed and held the straw, "Detective, take a sip." Once he did she took Frederickson hand, "Detective, can you answer a few questions for me?"

Frederickson still had a glazed look on his face but looked back at her, steely eyed, "Sure."

"What's your full name?"

Although he took a few seconds to answer; "Detective Don Frederickson."

"Who is the lady standing next to you?"

He looked over at Nancy who looked pale and shaky, "Honey, are you okay?"

Nancy nodded, and smiled for the first time in a while, "You goof, just answer her."

"Of course, she's my wife, Nancy."

"Good, we just have to make sure you're long term memory is clear. Do you remember what happened to you?" She watched thinking that this seemed to puzzle Frederickson, and the nurse patiently waited for him to answer.

"Yeah, I was in a car crash, I think it was on the freeway." Nancy smiled, happy that he got it right.

"Good."

"If you're done, now I've got questions for you!"

Both women laughed, and the nurse looked back at him. "Okay, but I might not be able to answer them."

"When can I get out of here?"

"Oh, you'll have to ask your doctor that one. You've had a pretty hard hit to your head, and a few broken bones. They set your broken leg and the doctors are still concerned about the broken ribs and chest bone injury. It's going to take a while to recover."

Nancy kept hold of his hand, "Don, the nurses and doctors have been careful making sure that you'll be okay. Your recovery will be steady, but because you suffered broken ribs and your breast bone was cracked, it's going to take a while." He looked up at his wife, and she smiled down at him; "Honey, I'll be right here all the time with you."

The nurse standing along the bedside continued checking his vitals and adjusting the flow of medicine through his intravenous bottle. She looked back down at him, "Mr. Frederickson, I'm right down the hallway, if you or Mrs. Frederickson need anything just press your call button." She lifted the cord with the button and made sure he knew where it was.

He looked back at her, "Thanks, thanks for everything."

\*\*\*

Chief Mathews saw the information that his Captain had sent in and contacted Detective Harper to update her about the situation from the hospital. "Detective, we had a call last night from the DMC that they thought that someone may have been watching Frederickson's room."

"Sir, I'll head over there right now."

"Wait, detective, Captain Oliver dispatched an extra security team to the hospital. We have two men stationed in front of Detective Frederickson's room. I've also arranged officers to be stationed outside the room of the suspected garbage truck driver."

"Chief, has the driver come to yet?"

"No, the doctors said that the EMT team thought he was okay at first but he collapsed at the scene and hasn't regained consciousness since. Did your team find any more information on the garbage truck?"

Harper had sketchy information from both Detectives Spano and Johnson from their investigation at Castellanos Trucking. "Chief, we ran the license plates and vehicle identification number. The plates were titled to what appears to be a shell corporation. Spano is contacting the DMV and running a trace through the corporate data base to see if we can tie it to any company. I've sent Detective Johnson to the trucking lot. We might need to put a squad out there."

"Thanks, detective, I'll call Captain Glass from St. Clair Shores to see if they'll help with that. Regarding the details at the hospital, Captain Oliver has dispatched two more squad cars to the DMC making sure that his team has Frederickson and the garbage truck driver protected. Our only hope is that the guy comes to and we can get some details out of him."

Harper knew the Chief was as frustrated as they were. "We're going to find out who's behind all of this, Chief."

"I understand, detective, but we need something and need it soon."

\*\*\*

Vinnie La Russo waited to hear from Dominic and Mario. *How could they have let the driver of the garbage truck become protected by the police? Dominic Parma was better than this*, he thought. Gloria knocked on the door to his office. "Mr. La Russo, Dominic called."

"Put him through."

"He left a message." She knew her boss was upset and waiting to hear from his two men. Standing in the doorway, after opening the door, "Sir, Dominic said, he and Mario are making another trip to the DMC before heading back here."

"Why didn't he talk to me, Gloria?"

"I don't know except that he said they were in a rush and will call back."

The man was concerned, if his two men didn't succeed, what was their back-up plan. Vinnie stood and moved toward the large glass window overlooking the action at the Eastern Market. Gloria was still standing in the doorway as Vinnie seemed to be watching something outside. Vinnie couldn't help but think that he needed to do something, but what? He turned surprised to see her still in the office. He thought she had a strange look on her face, "Gloria, is there something else?"

"Oscar is outside; he wants to talk to you."

"What in the hell does he want?" Vinnie was on edge, but knew Gloria was just trying to help. "Send him in!" She backed out of the doorway and Oscar White soon appeared. Vinnie was now standing with a scowl on his face behind his desk, "What do you want?"

Oscar shifted from one foot to the other. "Dominic called, he wanted me to get some men together and head back to the warehouse. We've got to get rid of the three trucks."

"When did he call you?"

"About an hour ago," Oscar hated coming to Vinnie's office, let alone coming there by himself.

"So, get some men and do what he told you to!"

Oscar cleared his throat, "I need the warehouse keys; Dom said you have them."

La Russo leaned down and opened one of the desk drawers, fumbling through; he grabbed a set of keys. "Here, these are the keys that you'll need." Tossing the set to Oscar, Vinnie sneered, "I want to know when this is done."

"Yes sir, I'll get it done right away." Oscar turned and hurried out of the office.

Vinnie slammed his fist on the large mahogany desk, startling Gloria, who sat just outside the office. "Gloria," Vinnie yelled, "Call Dominic, now!"

# CHAPTER TWELVE

**Detective Harper had her team working every angle of the** case. Chief Mathews had great confidence in Harper and his SIU officers. She listened to the message with an update from the teams that covered both Detective Frederickson's hospital room and the room of the suspected garbage truck driver. The officer relayed, "Frederickson's talking to his wife and starting to remember what had happened on the Interstate." That was cheered by the SIU team. Members had made a visit to his bedside but their number one task was to solve the case. Once she had her update, Harper made her second trip to the freeway accident scene. Studying the tanker and garbage truck along with Captains Williams and Oliver who were assigned to the scene along with the Michigan State Troopers, she was sure this was intentional. Along with details from witnesses, it all became clearer that Detective Frederickson was the target. Williams pointed to the garbage truck that still teetered over the top of the police vehicle, "Detective, everything we know now is the garbage truck was weaving through traffic and rammed Detective Frederickson's car, sending it over the center railing." Pointing across the lanes, "The Detective's car was hit head on by on-coming westbound traffic after it went over the rails, causing the action of the other side of the freeway." Harper nodded as he continued. He pointed to the burned out hull of a truck, "That tanker was hit by two speeding vehicles causing the first explosion." Both of them looked further down the freeway where the burnt shell of the chopper still draped across the pavement.

Harper turned toward Captain Williams, "My team has run down every angle on the ownership of the garbage truck but they've come up empty."

"I understand; the Chief told us that your team was taking the lead in that part of the investigation. The State Police are handling things on the freeway. How can I help?"

Amy was pleased that the Captain expressed his continued support for her team. "Captain, I'll keep you informed on anything we find."

Nodding, he said, "I appreciate that." The Captain continued going over the details for Harper making sure that he covered everything. He knew Chief Mathews wanted his SIU team to pilot the case, but he appreciated them keeping him at the forefront of the action.

*** 

The investigation into the two dead bodies found off of Jefferson had taken a surprising turn for the detectives in the Eastern District. Once the Medical Examiner confirmed that one of the bodies found off the wooded area was a police officer, it became more personal to those on the force. Although only Tom Baker personally knew Andy Jones, many of them understood the pressures of the job. Maybe Jones did become involved in drugs; however his death, especially the way his body was found, was extremely upsetting. Many officers had been known to develop some problems, but there was a support system for those that tried to get help. It was a well-known fact that many police officers abused alcohol. Tom Baker answered questions from fellow officers about Andy Jones. How he wished he wasn't the only one in the District that knew him. It was awkward and Tom felt he was being judged by some of the others because he was in the Academy with Andy.

Making the situation worse, The Detroit Free Press ran an expose' in the evening paper about personnel problems in the police department. The reporter had cited past cases of officers who had legal troubles. One of those cases they centered their article on was the case of Lenny Johnson, who last year had taken his family hostage in their own home. Chief Mathews was mad as hell about the story and had his Public Relations' officer complain to the editor. The Chief wanted to know why they chose Johnson's case to highlight. His team never released what had happened to Johnson after the standoff at his home last year. Mathews didn't want a reporter digging any deeper into the case. His team relocated Johnson and his family with assistance from the FBI into witness protection. Johnson, after all, helped uncover the corruption in the force last year, and pinpointed the involvement of the Mexican Cartel in the drug trade. After the success of that investigation, it was critical to relocate them. Chief Mathews didn't need the newspaper again linking another officer with problems, especially one with drug issues.

Lieutenant Jackson, along with the department Public Relations' officer, was in conversation with the paper's editor. "Sir, we have valuable information that we can supply to the press, however this comes with a great amount of restraint." The editor knew there was a catch, but he listened to the offer. Jackson stated, "The case of Officer Lenny Johnson should not be linked to your investigator's story. If you're willing to meet here at headquarters, the Chief will give you full disclosure."

The offer was too good to be true, but he was curious. "I can't promise anything but I'm willing to listen to what the Chief has to say."

"Good, let's say tomorrow around noon?"

It was silent for a few seconds, "I'd like to bring my field reporter with me."

"Only if it's understood that everything is off the record."

"Deal, we'll be there." Once he hung up from the call from Lieutenant Jackson and the department's Public Relations' head, the editor hurried upstairs to his managing editor. Heading up the cascading staircase to the large office on the top floor he headed into the office. Out of breath and talking a mile a minute, "Have I got a scoop! That article on police corruption really got a rise out of the Police Chief. They agreed to meet with me and Blake tomorrow. They promised more details on the Lenny Johnson case. We touched a nerve here." The Free Press had run many stories in the past on both political and police corruption but never did the Mayor's office or Police Chief ever offer to enlighten them on details. This was different. Neither man knew what would come of the meeting but both were excited at the prospects.

*** 

Dominic Parma looked over at Mario after hanging up with the Vinnie, "He's really pissed." Shaking his head, he started walking back down the hospital corridor. Mario followed him, knowing that his uncle's temper often was out of control, especially if things didn't go his way.

"Dominic, let's take one more pass down the second floor and then head back to the Market. We can send a couple guys to keep watching the two hospital rooms."

"Okay, we've got Oscar taking care of the trucks. I'll get a couple more guys down here." The two men separated, Dominic taking the stairs to the second floor and Mario took the elevator. Once Dominic reached the top, he opened the stairway door. He watched two police officers in the middle of the hall, they had stopped Mario. Dominic turned in the opposite direction, keeping an eye on what was transpiring. Mario was waving his arms in the air while the officers stood in front of him. Dominic slid his hand to the gun holstered on his left side. He took a few steps toward the action down the hallway. Mario was still moving both hands up and down but neither officer seemed to be making an aggressive move toward him. He wondered, *what's going on, they hadn't stopped either of them last night or earlier today, what changed. Could the garbage truck driver have come to? Did he finger them?*

Dominic ran all the scenarios that he could think of in his mind. As he moved further down the hallway, he watched as Mario turned back toward him, walking slowly to the end of the hall. Once Dominic knew Mario saw him, he headed to the exit at the other end of the hallway. Both men got in the west elevator and took it to the first floor. "What the hell was that all about?"

Mario looked back at Dominic as they headed to the car in the parking lot. "They wanted to know why I was on the east wing of the second floor."

"What did you say?"

"I did my best imitation, speaking Italian and arm waving." Demonstrating his imitating act, "I'ma gonna see my brother. When they pulled out a chart scanning a list, my English got worse; thank goodness the big black guy and mick are typical dumb cops."

"Shit, you looked like a plane trying to find a place to land." Mario smiled but Dominic wasn't in any mood to laugh. "Guess they got the whole damn corridor locked down now."

Mario nodded, "Looks like they planned to increase protection on both the detective and our guy."

The two men reached the exit on the first floor. "This calls for a change, we need to get a nurse or doctor in there, instead of a gun, a needle in either of them will do the job." Dominic made his way to their vehicle without saying anything else.

Mario knew that his frustration was high, "How about some of our boys to take turns watching things for us until we get it handled."

Walking without turning back, he mumbled, "Sure, call Lefty, but they need to keep a low profile." Neither man wanted to give Vinnie anything else to worry about, they agreed to keep the situation to themselves for the time being. Dominic kept walking to the car then turned, looking back at the DMC, "If necessary, I'll blow the whole damn place up!" Mario just stood there, stunned. He looked back at him, what the hell was he thinking.

# CHAPTER THIRTEEN

**The investigation continued into the bodies found along** Jefferson and it was getting a lot of unwanted attention; Tom Baker's Captain got a call from downtown. "Have your two detectives handling the case in the Chief's office," was all that he was told. *What's going on*, Captain Oliver wondered. Just another drug related murder. Once Oliver learned that Baker knew the police officer, who was one of the two bodies discovered, he thought that Tom might have more on the case. Tom didn't reveal that he visited Andy Jones' mother to deliver the bad news, he also didn't tell his Captain that Detective Harper went with him. Detroit was still considered by many as the murder capital of the country, this didn't help deter that impression. The national news teams were still covering the explosion on the Interstate and many of the reporters picked up the story on the two dead bodies. To add to their problems, unfortunately, last night there was another shooting at a gas station on Grand River and Six Mile that added to the city's murder reputation.

Baker and his partner stood in the Chief's lobby at Police Headquarters, "Tom, what in the hell is this all about?"

"Shit, I don't know; the Captain said the Chief wanted us in his office, and wanted us now." The two men stood, shifting from one foot then the other, waiting, not sure why they were there.

Baker watched as an attractive woman moved into the lobby, "Detectives Baker and Samson?"

Tom jumped to his feet, "Yes, I'm Detective Baker, can you tell us why we're here?"

Without answering his question, she said, "Follow me," she turned walking quickly toward the large double doors. Baker and

Samson looked at each other, and followed. She opened the right hand door and stood waiting for the two men to enter the room. Baker entered first then Samson moved into the room and there behind the large desk sat Chief Mathews with two men in dark suits sitting across from him.

"Detectives Baker and Samson, thanks for coming in. I need you both to take a seat," pointing to the leather couch against the wall, Chief Mathews stood waiting for the detectives to be seated. "Gentlemen, it looks like we have a problem here. Your unit discovered the two bodies in the field, apparent drug related murders?"

Baker cleared his throat and watched the men seated across from the Chief; turn in their chairs, and one of them leaned to the edge of the seat. Baker answered, "Yes Chief, our unit got the call around midnight. Samson and I met two uniform officers at the scene. They found the bodies after a tip from the owner of the liquor store down the street; he said some kids said they saw the bodies when they cut through the lot." Samson clasped both hands in front of him, not sure what this could be about.

Chief Mathews nodded and looked back at his other two guests, "Detective Baker, your Captain said you personally knew one of the dead men."

Samson looked over at his partner; did they think Baker had something to do with this? "Yes sir, but not until the Medical Examiner confirmed the identification."

"Detective Baker, are you sure about that?"

Baker squirmed as the leather seat made a creaking sound. "Sir, I wasn't sure at first."

This wasn't going good, and Tom Baker knew it.

Chief Mathews took a step closer to the men on the couch, he raised his voice and both of them straightened up, "Detective, I haven't got time for this shit; I need the whole story and now!"

Baker looked at the Chief, "Sir, when Samson and I got to the scene the uniformed men said both bodies were mutilated beyond identification. I pulled the tarp back and saw the tattoos on one of the bodies. I was sure right away that I had seen that tattoo. When I was in the Academy, one of the cadets, Andy Jones told me that the names tattooed on his arm were the guys in his unit that were killed in Iraq. I thought it had to be him, but honestly Chief, I thought that might be something many soldiers did."

"Okay, who else had you told about the body?"

"I'm not sure what you mean?"

"Detective, I'm asking how many people know that you're aware of the identification of Andy Jones as one of the bodies in the field. Who have you told?"

"My Captain knows that I was in the Academy with Andy Jones." Baker took a deep breath, "I also told another officer who was in the Academy with us."

"Detective, this isn't a game show, I need everything you know; you don't know how important this is."

"I called one of the Detectives in your SIU squad, Amy Harper. She and I were in the Academy with Jones. I thought she should know."

For the first time one of the men seated across the desk asked, "How did she take the news?"

Baker looked confused, "I'm not sure what you mean?"

"Was she surprised, upset, what did she do?"

"She was definitely shocked; she even stumbled when I told her."

"So you told her in person?"

"Ah, yes, I thought it was the best way to handle that."

"When did you tell her?"

"The next morning after we found the bodies, we met and I gave her the news."

The Chief asked, "Detective Baker, anything else we need to know?"

He thought for a second, "Detective Harper and I broke the news to Andy Jones' mother."

Turning to Detective Samson, "What do you know about all of this?"

Samson was confused, "Only what I've just heard here."

"Thanks Detective Samson, you can go back to your precinct, however, you're not to repeat anything you've heard here, understand."

Standing, Baker's partner stuttered, "Yes sir."

"Detective Baker, you'll need to stay here while we complete our investigation."

Samson still standing, looked back at his partner, "Guess I'll see you back at the Precinct?"

"We'll get him back there eventually, Detective Samson." Tom Baker watched his partner walk toward the double doors and wondered what was going on and how much trouble was he in. Once Samson was out of the room, the Chief looked over at the two men still seated. "Where do we go from here?" Baker was terrified, what was going on?

One of the men that was seated stood, he was tall and slender, maybe six-foot-three. He had a hard look on his face, and peered down at Baker. Tom thought he might be Hispanic or Indian, "Detective, tell me about Andy Jones' mother's reaction."

Tom thought that was a weird question. "She was stunned, cried. Detective Harper held her for a long time. She kept saying that Andy wasn't on drugs, he promised her he was clean."

"Anything else, it's important."

Tom shook his head, "No, like I said, Amy told her the news; she asked me if she could do that, during the Academy they were close."

"So you decided to tell Detective Harper because they may have been a couple?"

"Yeah, I don't know, Harper and I hadn't talked since the Academy. I heard she was promoted downtown, so I called her, seemed the right thing to do."

"Okay, detective, you're going to be here a little while. We'll call your Captain and let him know." Turning back to the Chief, "We're going to need to talk to Detective Harper." Lieutenant Jackson came in and escorted Baker back into the outer lobby; he was sure that he was in deep trouble. He felt his palms and they were wet, he felt moisture running down the back of his neck from sweat and wondered who the two guys in the Chief's office were, maybe Internal Affairs. He was breathing hard and Lieutenant Jackson asked if he'd like a bottle of water. He nodded; *Harper's going to kill me.*

In a few minutes the door opened to the lobby and Detective Harper walked in, she looked at Tom, "What are you doing here?"

Before he could answer, Lieutenant Jackson approached, "Detective Harper, the Chief is expecting you." Harper saw the worried look on Baker's face. *What was going on, why was Baker in the Chief's office.*

Lieutenant Jackson was standing in front of her, "Detective, the Chief is waiting for you." Amy Harper opened the large door to the Chief's office and saw two men standing with the Chief. *This wasn't good*, she thought, not knowing what she was walking into.

Chief Mathews greeted Detective Harper, "Detective, thanks for coming down here so quickly. I need to introduce you to Inspector Hershel of the RCMP and Special Agent Downey from the DEA." Harper's eyes grew wider, *Drug Enforcement Agency, Royal Canadian Mounties, Oh shit, what's going on?* "Gentlemen, this is Detective Amy Harper, she's running our Special Investigative Unit and heading our investigation into the crash on the Interstate." Both men extended their hands and Harper forced a smile, not sure why she was in here and what Tom Baker had to do with all of this. "Let's all sit at the conference table."

Once the group was seated, she asked, "How can I be of assistance?"

Chief Mathews started the conversation. "Detective, how much do you know about Andy Jones?"

This was a curve ball she didn't expect, "Andy?"

"We understand you were close to him in the Academy and recently visited his mother to inform her about his death."

"Yes, that's right. Andy and I were real good friends in the Academy and kept in touch for a few years after we both graduated. I found out that he was having a possible drug issue and tried to help but he didn't want anything to do with me helping him, in fact he was the one that broke off all communications."

"When exactly was this?"

Shaking her head, "I'm not sure, a couple years ago. I tried to keep in contact with Andy's mother but as time went by I lost touch."

"Did Andy ever tell you what he was doing or about his drug involvement?"

"No, in fact he was pretty secretive about it all. I offered to get him in a rehab group or to a special doctor but he refused. That's kind of when we stopped talking. Can I ask, what's this all about, Chief?"

Mathews looked over at Special Agent Downey. "Agent, I think it would be in our best interest to bring Detective Harper into the loop."

"Okay Chief; it's your call." Downey was a tall guy, olive skin and was wearing what looked like an expensive suit. Harper sized him up when she walked into the room, he didn't fit, not dressed like a cop. "Detective, four years ago we were sure that a drug ring was operating out of the precinct that Officer Jones was assigned to. My team did extensive research on the members of the Third Precinct. We were sure that Officer Jones wasn't involved. He was recruited and went undercover for the DEA." Harper had a surprised look on her face, but it almost seemed to be a smile to Downey. "You okay, detective?"

"Yes, just thrilled that Andy was working for you on this."

"Not only working with us, but he was influential in getting to the main source and the members that were involved. We had to keep his identification under wraps so we spread the story that he was implicated and resigned from the force. Officer Jones joined the DEA task force with permission from your Police Chief. He was currently working undercover in the Eastern Market area on a tip. The last communication we had with him was that he had been picked up by someone with a trucking company."

"Okay, have your guys checked that out?"

"I've got two men on it."

She asked, "What does Tom Baker have to do with all of this?"

"Baker, we're not sure. We'll need your help on that."

"Do you think Tom had anything to do with Andy's death?"

Agent Downey looked back at Chief Mathews, "Chief, do you want to take it from here?" The Chief nodded. "Detective, when we found out that Tom told his Captain that he recognized one of the bodies that was discovered in the vacant lot we became concerned. How did he know Andy Jones? The M.E. said he acted a little strange when she ran the identification and gave Tom and his partner, Detective Samson, the news. This all was a red flag to our joint investigation. The DEA thought that Andy's cover was blown and maybe it was someone from his past that exposed him."

Harper quickly said, "I can assure you that Tom was as shook up as I was when he learned that Andy was one of the men found in the field. He called me to meet him. Tom told me in person about Andy. I don't think he'd get me involved if he was in on the hit."

"We agree with you now after hearing his story. Detective, Inspector Hershel and his team have been working the case with us. We're sure that someone in the Eastern Market is distributing drugs. We also think they may be using scab laborers to move the stuff. Andy was posing as day laborer in the Market area for the past few weeks trying to get a line on the investigation."

"How can my team help?"

Chief Mathews held a hand up, "Right now your main task is finding who is responsible for putting a hit on Detective Frederickson. We needed you to confirm Baker's story, but this information we've given you has to stay right here. You cannot tell anyone, not Baker or even Andy's mother. We'll make sure he's cleared once we solve the case so his mom will know what a great asset he was to the department."

"Sir, he deserves a proper funeral."

"You're right, but it will have to wait. I promise that once we can, we'll make sure Andy's mother has all the benefits that she deserves from a fallen officer and he will be recognized for his outstanding service."

Agent Downey stood and extended his hand to Harper. "I know you'll keep all of this to yourself for the time being. I'll keep in touch, if it's okay with you, Chief?"

"Certainly."

Harper asked, "What do I tell Detective Baker sitting outside?"

Mathews was quick to answer, "I'll handle Baker, he'll get the riot act for involving you in his case and we're taking him and Samson off the investigation. I'm sure he'll lay low for a while but if he calls you, I'll expect you to tell me."

Detective Harper stood, "Yes sir, anything you or the DEA or RCMP need." They all shook hands and Mathews walked her to the door.

"I need to give you a little help with Baker, so follow my lead." When he opened it he gave her a stern look. "Detective, I hope you understand this isn't over, you'll be called back if needed."

She answered with her head down, "Yes sir, I promise not to involve myself in anyone's case but my own." Amy walked past Baker, never looking up at him.

"Detective Baker," the Chief loudly stated, "Come back in here!"

The Third Precinct was buzzing when Tom Baker arrived. Detective Samson walked over to his partner, "So what happened after I left?"

Tom kept his head down leafing through paperwork on his desk, "Best if you don't ask, I still got a job but half my ass was eaten off." He tried to keep focusing on the papers when his Captain called out, "Baker, my office now!"

# CHAPTER FOURTEEN

**Tom Baker knew he was about to get another chewing out, this** time from his Captain. He was barely in the Captain's office when the man barked out, "Baker, what in the hell's going on; I just got off the phone with Chief Mathews, and he's not exactly happy with you or our team. You and Samson are to go back downtown to the M.E. office and see if they have an identification of the second body found in that field." Baker stood quietly while the Captain paced in the office. The man kept talking, "The last thing I need is having the Chief running our investigation. Now get your ass out of my sight and report back to me, not anyone else, is that clear?"

"Yes sir, got it." Detective Baker headed out of the Captain's office and everyone was looking at him. He walked to his partner's desk, "Samson, the Captain wants us to follow up with the Medical Examiner." His partner followed him out of the precinct not sure what was going on but didn't want to ask. They were hoping the M.E. might have the identification of the second body found in the lot with Andy Jones. Under orders from his Captain they were to report everything back to him and him alone. Upon arrival they were pleased that the Medical Examiner had the details lined out for them. She went over the details, "Both men were shot at close range with a twenty-two automatic weapon. This was the cause of death," pointing to the bullet holes in the man's head. "Detectives, the bodies were mutilated close to an hour after they were killed. We haven't identified the second man yet. We don't have any prints or dental records to go on and nothing in the data base to help."

Baker looked back to Samson; then answered the M.E., "Thanks for your help, please call if you get that identification."

Turning to his partner, "Let's head back to the scene off of Jefferson, maybe we'll find something else to help with the case."

The ride back to Jefferson and Lenox took about thirty minutes. Samson couldn't wait any longer, "Okay, are you going to tell me what in the hell all of this is about?" Baker turned toward him, shook his head and kept driving. "Tom, this is bullshit, I'm your partner, and I've got to know what's going on."

"Sorry, but honestly I'm not really sure what's going on. The only thing I can tell you is that I did call another Detective about the bodies we found. Guess the Chief and whoever those two suits in his office were weren't happy with that."

"That doesn't make sense. Who in the hell were those two dudes?"

"I'm guessing Internal Affairs. I probably haven't heard the end of this." Just the sound of Internal Affairs scared the shit out of Samson. He decided to drop it for now.

\*\*\*

Vinnie La Russo was pacing when Dominic and Mario finally made their way up to his office. "Where in the hell have you two been?"

Mario looked back at his uncle, "We just left the hospital, and were trying to find Ben and the Detective."

Vinnie told them, "We got another problem, two guys were up here asking questions and Gloria was able to fend them off. They wanted information on the guys we picked up to drive the trucks."

"What!" Dominic yelled. "How in the hell did they connect us to picking up those guys."

Mario looked back at him, "Either one of those guys was a plant or someone double-crossed us."

"That damn Oscar, I don't trust him." Dominic was grabbing for someone to blame. "I'm going to drag his ass up here."

"No," Vinnie pounded on the desk. "You guys screwed this up.

Oscar only did what we told him to." Dominic and Mario just stood watching their boss who had lost his temper waiting for them to handle this. "You lost the garbage truck driver and now the cops got him. Detective Frederickson is most likely alive and now we got some guys, probably cops, snooping around the office."

"Uncle, we'll take care of this." Before Mario could finish Vinnie stopped him.

"I promise you this isn't going to be pretty for either of you."

"Boss, take it easy, we'll get it done tonight." Mario pointed to the door and they both headed out of the office. He stopped at the secretary's desk, "Gloria, Vinnie said two dudes came by asking about those guys we had in here the other day."

Gloria shifted in her chair and looked up at Mario, who now had his hands resting on her desk. "Yeah, they came in maybe a little after noon, they seemed to be hinting around that they knew we hired illegals and day laborers. I told them that we only employ members of the Teamsters. One of them said his friends told them that he was hired to drive a truck for us."

"What did you tell him?"

"Like I said, we only hire Teamsters. I asked if they had their Union card, we would take an application. They just smiled and left."

Mario breathed a sigh, "Thanks, honey, if they come back call us right away."

The two men walked down the stairs and Dom turned back toward the top, "What do you think this was about?"

"Not sure but it isn't good. If one of those three guys was a plant we're going to have problems. Best not to say anything to Vinnie right now, no sense adding to this situation." Dom agreed and they headed back to the DMC. Lefty and his two men that they sent hadn't reported any changes. Mario suggested, "Call Lefty, see what's going on with the guys guarding our two targets."

Dominic agreed, "Lefty, what's going on down there?"

"Dom, I got one guy sitting in the waiting room on the second floor near where two uniform officers are standing. People have been coming and going for the past two hours."

"What kind of people, other cops?"

"No, I'd say legal types, lots of suits with briefcases."

"Which room is all this action happening at?"

"Hard to see the room number but I'd say between 206 and 210."

"Keep your guy there, we're on the way. Meet us downstairs in the main lobby."

When Dominic hung up, Mario asked, "What's that all about?"

"Lefty said there's a lot of suits going in and out of one of the rooms, from what he said it has to be the one that Ben is in. Only thing to surmise is he's awake and talking."

"We should have killed that son of a bitch as soon as he climbed out of the garbage truck."

"That was the plan but our guy following got caught up in the crash and by the time he saw Ben on the pavement the EMS was already working on him."

Mario started driving faster and pounded on the steering wheel. "We've got to get into that room."

Dominic looked back at him, "I'm telling you, I think we need to blow the whole place up!" This time it didn't seem like a wild threat, Mario was afraid that he was serious. Mario didn't know what they should do next but the prospect of blowing up the hospital wasn't something he wanted to think about.

# CHAPTER FIFTEEN

**Tom Baker walked through the tall grass kicking at the tires** and trash that littered the open fields. Detective Samson was on the other side of the lot poking through the cluttered bags and cans with a long stick. "Baker, I think we need to talk to those kids that reported the bodies to the guy in the liquor store."

Tom stopped, looking back at Samson, who kept searching the field, "Did you ever talk to them?"

"No, once the uniformed officers called it in, they said that they interviewed both the kids and liquor store owner."

"That's right, we've got to find those kids, they may have picked up something and we don't know how it could help our case." Baker grabbed his phone and dialed the local precinct looking for the officers that manned the crime scene before they arrived. He told his partner, "Samson, the officers are on patrol and will head our way; I told their Captain that we needed a copy of their log." Both men walked back to the corner waiting for the officers to arrive.

A squad car pulled up to the corner of Jefferson and Drexel across from the Riverbend Shopping Plaza and two officers stepped out. When Baker approached, one of them, a young, tall, blonde officer immediately asked, "What's this shit about us reporting to you about our investigation?"

Baker wasn't in any mood to explain the request to this younger officer, "Hey, this comes directly from Chief Mathews' office; we need to review your log and the details of the conversation with the witnesses you talked to the other day."

It was obvious that the young officer had a real attitude, "If the Chief needs our log, let him call for it."

Baker was close to going berserk, "You stupid son of a bitch, we're not asking; I'm demanding your information and want it now." Both men were getting close to punches when Samson jumped between Baker and the young officer.

"Hey, buddy you're way out of line, we've all got a job to do and regrettably, we're all in the middle of it. I suggest you back up." Samson had his back to Tom Baker and hoped that he didn't jump around him at the young officer. "Now, do you want to work with us or should I call the Chief?" Samson had a stern look on his face and grabbed his cell phone and started dialing.

"Wait," the kid's partner yelled, "what do you need?" The tall officer turned back toward his partner, "Listen Jimmy, you're not taking me down this road with you again, go back to the car. Sorry Detective, what can we do for you?"

Tom Baker was still livid and after having both the Chief, then his Captain bite him in the ass today, he wanted a piece of someone, anyone would do and this young officer was his target. Baker yelled to the young guy, "You better go back to your squad car and let the men handle this." The young man started yelling back and now a small crowd had gathered watching the action. Samson saw what was happening and put his arm around Baker, "Okay partner, look over at that group standing on the corner."

The second officer also turned and saw what was happening, "Jimmy, go back to the car now before we're all on the news." They saw one of the people on the corner aiming their cell phone and it was pointed at them, probably filming the action. "We've got to make this go away now."

Jimmy looked at Baker, "We'll meet again, and you're not going to like it." He moved to the squad car watching the small group that had gathered, "Nothing going on here, let's move on!" He stood next to the car and waited until the group started to disperse.

Detective Samson extended his hand to the second officer, once they shook, he said, "Thanks for your help, you gotta get that kid in line or we'll all have a problem."

"I know, this isn't the first time. What can I do for you?"

Samson continued handling the request knowing that Baker was still steaming from his interaction with the young officer. "Our Captain and the Chief have become involved in this case and we've got no idea why but just following orders. We wanted to talk to the kids that originally told the liquor store clerk about the bodies."

"Understand," looking at his memo pad, he said, "I talked to the kids, Jimmy talked to the clerk in the liquor store. We put it all in our report. I can get you a copy. As far as I can remember the kids, two of them, said they were cutting through the lot behind the old hotel when they saw the bodies."

"We're concerned that they may have picked up something that's critical to our case."

The officer nodded, "Let me call in to the precinct and get a copy of the report for you. I know I got the kids' names and addresses. Just hope they gave me the straight shit. At the time it just looked like another body dump."

The two men again shook hands and Detective Samson handed him his card. "Call me when you've got the report, I'll meet you wherever you need." The second officer made his way back to the squad car. Samson could see that the young officer was arguing with his partner but got into the squad car. "Baker, just think you could have that shit for a partner." Samson let out a big laugh, and Baker smiled back at him. "I suggest we cross the street and talk to the guy in the liquor store." Walking into the store the two detectives flashed their badges, "We're here following up on the call about the bodies from the lot across the street."

The store clerk looked back at the two detectives, "I didn't make the call to the police."

"A couple days ago someone from here called in about two bodies in the lot across the street."

"Yeah, that was my nephew, he opens up. I'm the owner of the store. He's not here now."

"We need to talk to him, it's important."

The clerk started looking through some papers taped up above the counter, "I got his number up here somewhere, here it is." He handed the sticky note to the detective, "Do you want me to call him, he lives down the street or do you want to do that?"

"I appreciate your help", taking the note from the clerk, "I'll call him," he wrote down the name and number and handed the sticky note back to the clerk. "What did you hear about this?"

He said, "The kids told him what they saw, he called the police then he called me. The only thing I know for sure is Samuel said it was two bodies in the field across the street. Sorry to say but this isn't the first time we've had bodies in that field."

Detective Samson understood, how ironic he thought, just a

mile and half down the road it changes from Detroit to Grosse Pointe. You immediately saw the difference in the houses, stores and neighborhood. Didn't seem right, but it was reality. "I'm going to call your nephew, hope he can come down here soon." Samson dialed the number and a woman answered, she spoke broken English but he understood that she'd get her son for him. Once the man came to the phone the detective introduced himself, "Samuel, I'm Detective Samson with the police and your uncle gave me your phone number. We need to ask you a few questions about the events from the other day when you called in the report on the bodies in the field. Can you come back to the store or should we come to your house?"

"No, I come down to the store. You don't need to come here. It will take ten minutes, is that okay?"

"Yes, perfect." Samson told Baker that the clerk is on the way. He walked to the back of the store and slid open the cooler and grabbed a cold Coke. "Tom, you want a drink?"

"No, I'm good." Baker paced around the front of the store still upset at the run in with the young officer.

Samson made his way back to the front and put a five dollar bill on the counter. "Oh no, Detective, it's on the house."

"Thanks, but I can't accept that, please let me pay for it." The man took the five and gave Samson his change. He walked over to where Baker was looking out the front door. "You okay buddy?"

Baker looked back at him, "Thanks, that whole thing could have really got me fired. What in the hell was wrong with that jackass? Did he truly threaten me when he left?"

"Bet his partner will take care of that for us. Wasn't the first time the kid reacted before putting his brain in gear. It's going to be okay, Tom."

The doors opened and a short young man walked in and saw the two detectives who were standing up front. "I'm Samuel, are you the detective?"

"That's me," Samson handed him his card. "We need to go over the events from the other day when those kids told you about what they saw across the street." The young man opened his hands with fingers pointed out like telling the detectives that he didn't know anything. "Samuel, just tell us exactly what happened and what the kids told you."

Samuel's English was a little sketchy but he started relaying the details. "I opened up early and two boys, I see them in store before, they come in. They say; dead bodies across the street, what I said. They say two dead bodies, smashed in faces, in field. I called 911 and tell the lady what they said and where we are."

"That's good Samuel; did the kids have anything they might have taken from the bodies?"

"What do you mean?"

"Did they buy anything in the store?"

"Yes, they buy pop and chips."

"How did they pay for it, did they use a twenty dollar bill or bigger?"

"Yes, one-hundred dollar bill," turning to his uncle, "I check like you told me with that special pen."

This was a break maybe just what the detectives needed to know. The kids must have searched the bodies and found the money or who knows what else before crossing the street and telling the clerk. "Thanks Samuel, that helps. Do you know where these kids live?"

"No, just close by, they're here a lot."

"Have you seen them since?"

"Yes, they bought more pop and chips yesterday."

"Okay, this is important, if you see them again don't tell them we were here asking about this." The young man seemed to understand. Samson and Baker walked out of the store and back across the street. "You thinking what I'm thinking," Samson asked.

"Yeah, they'll be back soon to spend more of that money. We should camp out here for a while. If we found drugs on the bodies, so did those kids and who knows how much money they may have found?" This might be the first break in the case for the two detectives. Baker felt he needed something good to get out of the dog house with both the Chief and his Captain. "We've got to get our car out of sight." Pulling around the corner, Samson looked back at his partner, "You okay?"

Baker turned, "Thanks for jumping in, did you get that asshole's name?"

"Actually, I think it was Jimmy or Jim. His partner said he will take care of that for us; however, we should report it to the Captain. I'm concerned that group on the corner was probably filming with their cell phones. I don't think they could hear what was being said." The two detectives sat waiting, hoping the kids came back to the store. Samson's cell phone rang; he didn't recognize the number, "Hello?"

"Detective, this if Officer Thompson, I have the information you needed from our interview with the two kids that spotted the bodies."

"Thanks for getting back to me so soon, where can we meet?"

"Actually I made a copy of the report and can drop it off if you're still in the area."

"That would be great; we're parked on the corner of Drexel and Jefferson, hoping to find the kids that your partner talked to. I hope Jimmy isn't coming with you."

"You don't have to worry about that. I told my Captain about the incident; I've been assured that Jimmy will be on desk duty and probably under investigation soon."

"Good, we appreciate your help."

# CHAPTER SIXTEEN

**The black and white squad car pulled off of Jefferson behind** the detectives' vehicle. Officer Thompson stepped out and Detective Samson got out and greeted him. Thompson had a folder in his right hand, and handed Samson the packet. "It's the three page document from our investigation including everything the two boys told us."

While leafing through it, Baker stepped over to the officer. "Thompson, thanks for bringing this, we thought that those kids will show up again and maybe we'd get another crack at talking to them. The clerk said they gave him a hundred dollar bill for the snacks they bought." Baker looked over at Samson, "We wanted to let you know that this is your case too, and we'll keep you in the loop."

"I appreciate that, my Captain wanted to know how we could be included, so this helps me let him know that you're working with us."

Samson reiterated, "We're on the same team."

As the two men were talking Thompson looked up and pointed to the corner, "There they are, the same two kids crossing the street."

All three men waited until the kids entered the liquor store. "We better get to them now before the clerk lets them know something is up." They headed to the front of the store. They were in front of the mini-mart when both kids came bursting out of the liquor store. The chase ensued, "Stop, Police!" yelled Baker. The kids split up, one took off running across Jefferson and the second one turned the corner on Lenox and headed off, running into the alley. Baker pointed to the kid that crossed Jefferson, "I got that one." Detective Samson and Officer Thompson chased the second kid that headed down the alley. Tom Baker was about ten yards behind the kid he was chasing, as the kid zig-zagged through the open field behind the old Lenox Hotel. Baker called out, "Stop or I'll shoot!" The kid picked up speed when he made it to the pavement and turned to see where the man chasing him was; he didn't see the box that was in the middle of the alley, and went crashing to the ground. Baker was right there, gun drawn, "Don't get up; don't move!" With his knee in the kid's back and cuffing him, Baker pulled the kid to his feet.

"I didn't do nothin, man, what do you want?"

"We just wanted to talk to you, why did you run?"

"The store clerk told us that cops were here looking for us."

"He's right, but now you're in real trouble." Leading the kid back across the street he saw his partner and Officer Thompson standing with their suspect. With both kids in custody, now they might get the rest of the story. Baker shook his head as he joined his partner, "Samuel warned them."

Thompson asked, "Do you want me to go in and get him."

"No, we got what we needed; I never know why people can't just follow what we tell them."

Thompson nodded, "Everyone wants us to solve crimes but no one ever wants to cooperate with us."

They all understood, they shared the same frustration. Baker suggested, "Let's take both of them back to your precinct."

Thompson was pleased, "Great, I'll take one of them and you can bring the other guy in. My Captain will appreciate this."

"Like we said, it's your case too." Baker and his partner hoped that they may have gotten the first break in this case, one that may lead to who killed Officer Andy Jones.

\*\*\*

Things hadn't improved at the DMC and Mario was becoming more concerned about Dominic and his erratic statements about blowing up the hospital. He knew that they needed to solve this and solve it soon, but blowing up the hospital wouldn't be the answer. "Dom, let's see what Lefty and his guys have for us."

Dominic wasn't saying much on the ride back to the DMC, once they pulled into the lot he climbed out of the vehicle, "I'm not waiting too long, either we get this handled or I'm taking action. Back in the day we'd just walk in, guns drawn and mow the whole group of them down." He walked faster and Mario followed, not sure how to answer that. "Lefty better be there or else." Dominic said. Mario knew he had to get control of the situation. Lefty was sitting in the outer lobby talking to a young girl. Dominic motioned to him, and watched as Lefty stood and smiled back at the cutie. As he approached the two men, Dom grabbed Lefty, pushing him into the wall, "What the hell you doing, picking up some piece of ass?"

"Get your hands off of me!" Pulling away, Lefty yelled back, "You're crazy!"

Mario jumped in between them, "Hey, we're getting too much attention. Let's go back outside."

Lefty quickly said, "I'm not going anywhere with him unless he apologizes." This wasn't good and Mario knew it was about to get worse.

"Lefty, come with me." Mario was looking back at Dom, "I'll handle this." Lefty followed but kept an eye on Dominic; once they got outside Mario tried to calm the situation down; "Lefty, we've run into so many problems that both Vinnie and Dom are losing it."

"I've been here doing exactly what you both told me to do, yes I was hitting on that sweet thing, wouldn't you?"

"Sure, don't worry about that." Trying to change the subject, he questioned Lefty, "What's been going on, you said your guy is near one of the rooms watching the action going in and out of the rooms on the second floor."

"Yeah, suits, lots of suits been in there for a while, two of them with briefcases, I suspect lawyers or something like that."

"Oh shit, which room number?

"The one that is further down the hall, you suspected that it's the one Ben's being kept in."

Mario thought out loud, 'If he's awake and talking we've got big problems.' "Lefty, I'm going to tell Dom and you get back in touch with your guy upstairs. We need to know if those suits are still in there and how many cops are outside. Keep me informed on what's going on."

Lefty nodded but said, "Okay, I'll do this for you, just keep that big asshole Dominic away from me."

Mario walked back into the hospital lobby, and saw Dominic talking to a nurse. He watched for a few seconds. The big man was arm waving to him behind his back and the nurse appeared to be searching the computer in front of her. Finally he saw the nurse hand Dominic a piece of paper. Turning toward the hallway, Mario made sure that Dom saw him and would follow. He stopped at the bank of elevators and waited. Dominic followed down the hallway and stood next to him. Once they got in, Dom said, "I think I've got a lead. The nurse said that one man fitting Ben's description was brought in from the crash, but he hasn't been identified and still unconscious. That doesn't make sense, why are there men in suits coming in and out if he isn't awake. Her report has him listed in critical condition on the third floor. Maybe we're wrong, maybe it's not Ben that's being protected on the second floor."

"How did you convince her to give you the room number?"

"I told her all about Ben, how he's my kid brother and our family's been searching every hospital for him. She just wanted to help. If it's him, we'll settle this right now."

"I hope you're right, what's the room number?"

"Three-ten." They got into the elevator and Mario pushed three as Dominic looked at him, "What did you tell that son of a bitch Lefty?"

"I told him that he needed to be all business, girls could wait." Dom smiled, Mario figured that he would just forget about Lefty. *Dom didn't need to know what Lefty said, better leaving this alone for now.*

The elevator doors opened and Dominic pointed to the wall that showed directions to rooms 301 to 320. "I'm going to head down there, and then you follow in a couple minutes. Make sure the coast is clear; I don't want anyone coming in and stopping me from completing the job. If he's in there I'll take care of it." Mario hoped that Dom was right. Maybe they could finally have something good to tell Vinnie.

Mario watched as Dominic disappeared into the room on the right. He continued checking out the hallway watching that no one was heading in their direction. Mario spotted a nurse and doctor pushing a cart and coming in his direction. Walking toward them, planning to give Dom extra time, Mario moved toward them and stood in front of the cart, "Excuse me, I'm looking for our brother that I thought was on this floor."

"What's his name?" The nurse asked.

"Ben, Ben Walker, he was brought in late yesterday and the

lady downstairs said he was on this floor. I checked everywhere and he's not in here."

The nurse turned and motioned to the desk in the center of the hallway, "If you stop at the desk they can help you, maybe he's been moved or he could be downstairs for a test." The doctor wished him good luck and continued heading down the hall as the nurse finished talking to Mario. He saw Dom who was now walking back toward him. Either he had taken care of the situation or it wasn't Ben in the room. "Thanks for your help." Mario headed to the bank of elevators as Dominic followed. He pressed the button and saw Dom getting in. Both men got in without talking when another couple followed them into the elevator. Mario pushed the button for the first floor and looked over at Dom, who shook his head; he knew Ben wasn't in the room. They were now back to square one. Mario needed to inform Dom about what Lefty told him regarding the suits coming in and out of the room on the second floor.

Dominic was moving at close to a trot as Mario hurried behind. Dom turned, "Mario, where did Lefty go to?"

"I sent him back to the second floor, and told him to keep a watch on the original rooms we gave him to watch. I'm sure that Ben is in one of those rooms. That's where the suits are."

"Has to be, but we're out of options."

"Dom, Lefty said that suits have been in that room, it's the one we suspected to be where they're holding Ben. I think we need to get someone in there."

Dominic stopped and looked back at him, "We tried that, too many people checking ID's, my girl was turned away yesterday."

"I understand, however, we might be able to get a cop in."

This was a great idea, why didn't he think of that. "A cop, who are you thinking about?"

"We've got to have someone on the force in the precinct handling the protection on the second floor. I'll call Vinnie and see if he has a name for us."

"Okay, but if this doesn't work, I'm handling this anyway I need to." That's what Mario was afraid of.

# CHAPTER SEVENTEEN

**Chief Mathews knew that the DEA planned to take the lead** handling the murder of undercover officer, Andy Jones. Although there was always competition between law enforcement officials, this was the second time the DEA shared information with his office in the past year. Mathews wanted to keep his detectives in the SIU involved in the case, especially knowing that Detective Harper had a previous personal involvement with Jones. The Chief was pleased that Agent Downey agreed to have Detective Harper involved when needed. The DEA expressed concerns that the death of Andy Jones may have been more than a random murder; could the people who perpetrated this have gotten names of other undercover agents? Agent Downey covered more details with the Chief than anyone had before. Mathews also had to keep Detective Baker in the dark about the implications that Jones was not only undercover but that the DEA was involved. Too many people involved could be a problem, most of all; he couldn't have any of this leaked to the press. The Chief gave Amy Harper directions to fill Detective Spano in on the details of the investigation, but limit it to just Spano for now. He trusted his SIU team to keep everything on the down low.

Detectives Harper and Spano were going over the events when Lieutenant Jackson called. "Detective, the Chief wanted me to give you an update from the Third Precinct. Detective Baker and his partner have the two kids in custody that discovered the body of Andy Jones." Just the sound of Andy Jones' murder made Harper shudder again. "Harper, looks like the kids took items off the bodies before it was called in. Detective Baker, along with the officers from the Third, are questioning them right now and we hope that they have more for us soon."

"Thanks Lieutenant, I'll follow the Chief's orders and wait for any further updates from your office." Once she hung up, Detective Harper filled Spano in on all the details. Spano felt that she had been hiding something, not knowing what it was before, this revelation now made it all clear. The Special Investigative Unit was a good team and Harper and Spano complimented Detective Frederickson's leadership.

\*\*\*

Detectives Baker and Samson arrived at the Third Precinct with their suspect and parked behind Officer Thompson who had his young man with him. The men escorted the two young men into the building to a round of applause from the officers on duty. Baker looked surprised, *hadn't got a reception like that before.* The Captain from the Third walked over, hand extended, "We appreciate your cooperating with our team on this investigation." Pointing to the Interrogation Room, they led the two suspects in. "I'm going to have Officer Thompson stay in here with both of you if it's okay."

"Absolutely," Tom Baker said. "I told him this investigation belongs to both of our units." Once they separated the two youths, Baker and Thompson questioned the one that headed across the street behind the old Lenox Hotel. Samson had the other young man in another room and waited to question him until his partner finished with the first suspect. Detective Baker cuffed his suspect to the table without saying anything.

"Why am I here, I told you I didn't do nothing."

"Yeah, that's why you took off running from the store, just because you didn't do anything. I need your name, address and age."

"I want a lawyer!"

"Sure, that's your right, you also have the right to remain silent, anything you say or do can be used against you in a court of law, you have the right to an attorney, although it might take a while before someone from the Public Defenders Office can get here. I'll just leave you here and we'll make the call. See you in a couple hours."

Baker and Thompson got up and started to walk out of the room. "Hey, wait, you can't leave me here like this."

"You asked for a lawyer, we can't talk to you now."

"Stop, I don't want a lawyer, I just want out of here."

"Okay, so you're telling me that you'll write it down that we offered you an attorney and you refused."

"Yeah, just get me out of these cuffs." Officer Thompson un-cuffed the young man and slid a paper and pencil over to him. "Write it down now!" He took the paper and started to write, "What do you want me to write down?"

"Let's start with your name, address and age. Then write down that we offered you a lawyer but you rejected that." Baker and Thompson remained standing watching the young man write it out. When he was done Baker took the sheet of paper, "Okay, Denard, you're eighteen and live on Lenox, is that right?"

"Yeah, glad you cops can read."

"Don't be a smart ass or I'll just have Officer Thompson put you in the bullpen with those other dudes."

"No, don't do that. I got a driver's license; can I reach in my pocket and get it? I'll prove that's the right information that I gave you." Baker nodded. Denard pulled a money clip out of his front pocket, and separated a driver's license from the bills.

"Leave it all on the table, Denard. What's your buddy's name?"

"LaVonn, he lives down the street from me. I didn't do nothing, why'd you pull me in here?"

"Denard, you stole money from one of the dead bodies, probably drugs too. If you call that nothing then I'd hate to see what you'd call something. Maybe we'll let you go, but first what else besides the money did you take from the two dead bodies in the field?"

Denard looked up at Baker, "We didn't take no money."

"Oh yeah, then where do you work because not too many teens have a hundred dollar bill on them."

"My mom gave me the money."

"Guess she will say that when I call her."

Denard immediately shouted, "Call her, go ahead."

"Okay, but she'll really be pissed when she has to come down here to bail you out. Guess that's on you." Baker grabbed his cell and punched in Denard's name and address. Got it, your phone number is 313-555-1423, I'll dial and see if your mom wants to come down here and pay your bail once the District Attorney sets it."

"Man, why you gotta be like that, hang up, I'll tell you what you want to know."

"Denard, I haven't got the time to play around with you, maybe LaVonn will be more cooperative. Officer Thompson, see if he's got anything else of value to say. I'm going to talk to LaVonn." Detective Baker walked out of the room, hoping that Denard would be more willing to talk to Thompson. Meanwhile he joined Samson who had the second young man in another interview room. "Hello LaVonn, Denard had a lot to say about you."

"He been lying, I ain't done nothing."

"Not what he said. He told us that it was your idea to take the money and drugs from the two bodies before you told the clerk at the liquor store."

"I did nothing like that. It was Denard that took the three hundred dollars. He even kept two of them and only gave me one."

"Okay, who kept the drugs?"

"I ain't got no drugs. Didn't see any drugs."

"Don't lie to me, what else did you two take, LaVonn?"

"Me and Denard saw the two bodies. He said that one dude had an envelope in his pocket. The only thing I saw was three one-hundred dollar bills."

"Who kept the envelope?"

"Denard, he put it in his pocket. I just got one of the bills. He took the rest."

"Okay, write it all down for Detective Samson. Include your name, address and if you have any identification give it to the detective." Baker walked back out and returned to the first Integration Room. "Officer, what has Denard given you?"

"He's said that he and his buddy each found a one-hundred dollar bill. That's all he said that they took."

"Funny, that's not what LaVonn had to tell us. He said you took an envelope from one of the bodies with three one-hundred dollar bills and a packet of something else. Guess we'll have to let LaVonn go, it's all on you, Denard."

"That's bullshit; he took some of the money too."

"Last chance Denard, where's the envelope and drugs?"

Denard put his head down, "I tossed the envelope, it had three one-hundred's in it and two packets. Looked like some blow of some sort."

Baker pounded on the table, "Where is it?"

Denard almost jumped out of his chair, he didn't see Officer Thompson come close to laughing out loud. "Got it at home, hope you're satisfied."

"Looks like we got to call your momma anyway, Denard."

Once Thompson and Baker left the room they met with Officer Thompson's Captain. Baker filled him in on what they got from the two suspects. "How do you want to proceed Detective?"

"Your guys handled the original case so I think they need to contact Denard's mom and get the packets he said they found. Maybe we'll get lucky and it will have fingerprints that will lead us to the killers. I'll call this in to our Captain and let him know what we're doing."

"Thanks, Detective, do you want me to call in for a search warrant?"

"Yeah, it should be your search."

"Detective Baker, our team really appreciates how you and your partner have handled this. Thompson told me about your run in with Jimmy, and you can rest assured that I'll be taking care of Officer Jimmy Smart. He won't be around much longer."

Baker and Samson were pleased that they had answers for their Captain, maybe Baker might be off the hook, at least from his Captain. The Captain at the Third said he'd call once the search netted the envelope and, hopefully, packet of drugs.

***

Captain Mathews contacted Agent Downey with the details that Detective Baker and Samson uncovered at the Third Precinct. Once the officers from the Third recover the items from Denard's house it would all be ready for the DEA to pick up. Everyone understood that every precaution would be taken to insure the integrity of the packets, hopefully for analysis by the DEA. Mathews was pleased that Baker had success while re-investigating the case that they got the original call on. Mathews never informed Baker that Andy Jones was undercover with the DEA, but now planned to bring him into the loop.

Detective Baker got back to his precinct and his Captain immediately waved him into his office. Baker wondered, *what now, I don't have any ass left.* He looked back at Samson who held his hands up in the air. Walking with his head down, Baker went into the Captain's office.

"Shut the door, detective." Baker was about to explode, he closed the door and saw Samson watching through the fish bowl office glass. The Captain sat behind the desk and smiled, "Congratulations Detective, great job. I just got off the phone with the Chief and he wanted to thank you and your partner for the investigative work."

Baker felt like an anvil had been lifted off his chest, he was sure this was another ass chewing; he didn't quite know what to say. "Thanks Captain, just doing my job."

"Well I'm going to dial the Chief and let him talk to you. Tom, I'm happy this has gone well for both of us." The Captain dialed and Lieutenant Jackson answered, "I'll get the Chief for you."

Once the Chief came to the phone he talked to the Captain for a minute then the Captain handed Baker the phone. "He wants to talk to you alone, Tom." His Captain walked out of his office and Baker took the phone.

"Chief Mathews, this is Detective Baker."

"Detective Baker, great job today. You and your partner made some excellent decisions and keeping the Third Precinct in the loop was a good call. Because of your findings I need to update you on a couple of things." Baker listened as the Chief gave him the details, "Baker, Andy Jones was on an undercover assignment with the DEA. Detective, my SIU team is aware of all of this and although you and Harper are old friends it is still in both of your best interests for now to keep your cases separate. If something changes I'll let you know. Once we have our forensic team check out your findings. I'll make sure you get the results."

"No problem sir, Detective Harper and I will not communicate until you approve it."

"Thanks detective, if anything else develops in this case my office will advise you."

Tom Baker left the office and his Captain extended his hand in front of the rest of the unit. "Congratulations Tom, nice job. I told Detective Samson what was happening and that the Chief wanted to talk to you alone."

Baker, said, "Thanks." Once the Captain walked off he turned to his partner, "Samson, the Chief wanted to thank you too but something came up and he had to handle it." Baker moved to his desk and shuffled papers. Everyone else wondered exactly what happened but he wasn't talking.

\*\*\*

Things were finally starting to get cleaned up on I-94 with the removal of all the damaged and charred vehicles on this the third day after the inferno. The Fire Department, along with Michigan Department of Transportation, had their work still cut out for them. Close to a half-mile of pavement will have to be removed and replaced and the remaining part of the Woodward overpass also had to be removed. The M.I. Light Rail Project had taken half of the bridge down and the blaze finished the job. The projection was that the Interstate would be opened by the end of the week, with only one lane operational for downtown traffic. It would be at least ten more days before the entire project was completed.

Chief Mathews studied the final death toll from the incident. It remained at eleven; almost a miracle, he figured, given how many vehicles and people were on the Interstate at the time. He read further that close to forty people were treated by the DMC, Harper and Children's Hospitals; with sixteen still in critical condition. *He thought that among them were Detective Frederickson and the suspected driver of the garbage truck who witnesses claimed started the whole chain of events.*

Channel 4, as well as the morning Free Press, announced the plans for the funeral for Dirk Stanfield, the chopper pilot, and Aaron, the reporter, that were killed in the crash. The Channel ran a special report recognizing Dirk's heroic military career and his family was appreciative of the attention they gave him. They included details about Aaron and his highlights as a television reporter.

There were still questions remaining about the events but the Chief and DEA hadn't planned to release any of the details, at least not yet. The Mayor and Police Chief both planned to attend the funerals along with local and National NBC News teams. Detroit was still in the news with questions regarding how all of this happened and who was responsible. Chief Mathews' office kept as many details out of the press as possible, however, with reporters from CNN and all the local affiliates clamoring for the story, it was hard not giving them something. Never was there any mention of the action or the DEA's involvement.

# CHAPTER EIGHTEEN

**Dominic and Mario waited for their contact that Vinnie called** from the North District Precinct. The officer, Charles Ventimigilio, had been on Vinnie's payroll for years. Dominic was pacing and not happy waiting for Charles, "Once he gets here I want him to go upstairs and check out who's in the room with all those suits coming in and out." Mario hoped Charles could resolve the questions about who was being guarded on the second floor besides Detective Frederickson. They at least knew now that Ben failed to kill Frederickson, and was probably in custody. "I should have thought about this earlier, Mario, why didn't you think of it?"

"Guess I was like you, running in three directions at the same time. Good thinking, Dom."

Charles made his way into the lobby and saw Mario and Dom; he thought that they seemed to be arguing. "Hey guys, I got the message you needed me."

"Yeah, follow me outside." Dominic walked out the lobby doors and both Charles and Mario followed him. Once they were outside, Dominic spun around, "Here's the deal. Your department has one of our guys being held upstairs. We've got to get to him."

"Guess you're talking about the driver of the garbage truck? Vinnie filled me in."

"Yeah Einstein, if he's in there we gotta get him out or make him go away."

"Dominic, the whole force is guarding that guy and someone else upstairs. There's no way I'll get anywhere near him."

"This ain't a request, Vinnie's counting on you."

Charles knew that he had to try something, Vinnie wasn't one to let down. "You gotta give me something to go on; I can't just walk in there."

The three of them stood outside mulling their options over. Mario snapped his fingers, "I got it. Charles goes in and says he's visiting a friend downstairs, he thinks he sees someone in the lobby that looks a little suspicious, maybe causing a bit of trouble."

Dominic turned, "You dip shit; we're the ones in the lobby."

"Wait a minute," Charles interrupted. "That might work. I know one of the officers on this shift and it wouldn't hurt to give that a try. I could tell them I'd help upstairs while one of them checks it out."

"Okay, but who stays here in the lobby?'

Mario looked back at Dom, "We don't stay down here, one of us goes upstairs and follows Charles and I will have Lefty hang out down here in the lobby. I'll fill him in on the plan. He looks fishy doing nothing." They all laughed at that.

Charles headed to the elevators and Dominic followed him. "Dom, don't get out on two, send the elevator to three then come back down and get off at two. I should have worked the story by then. If it doesn't work you'll be able to tell because I'll be back at the elevators." The two of them got in and Charles pressed two and three. He got out on two and Dom stayed in, going to three.

Mario instructed Lefty who was standing in the lobby and gave him the plan. "You pace the room, if a cop comes down here, turn away, kinda like your guilty or hiding something. Try to keep him busy down here for a few minutes."

"Sure I got it, I'm for anything that doesn't have to do with Dominic. What if they decide to take me in?"

"You're not really going to be doing anything wrong, I need you to just look guilty. If necessary and they take you in, we'll get you out of this." Lefty nodded and Mario went back outside and kept an eye on his cell phone in case Charles or Dom called.

Charles got out of the elevator and walked down the hallway on the second floor. He was close to room 210 when one of the men guarding a room ahead stopped him, "Sir, you can't be up here. Oh, Charles, what the hell you doing up here."

"I was visiting someone on the first floor when I thought there was a guy in the lobby that looked suspicious, maybe familiar from mug shots. I knew you guys were on special duty up here so I thought I'd let you know."

"You got a description?"

Charles described Lefty to the officer on guard. "You want me to help you up here while you go check it out?"

"No we got it, I'll call it in to the Captain, his orders were don't leave the post unless there's an earthquake." They both laughed.

"You know the Captain; this guy is maybe the key to something big."

While they were talking, Charles noticed Dominic getting out of the elevator. He tried to motion to him not to come down the hallway without the officer seeing. Charles started re-telling a funny story about the Captain and both men were laughing. "Hey, this guy you're guarding, he finally come to?"

"Yeah, they've had every suit from the D.A.'s office in here but I hear he ain't giving them anything. Heard one of them say he can't remember anything from the crash. Charles, let me call this guy in the lobby in to the Captain. Would you pass the description to him on it?"

"Sure, anything to help." Charles knew the plan didn't work but at least he had something for Dominic and Mario.

While the officer dialed the Captain he turned and asked, "Who you here to see, Charles?"

Before he had to come up with an answer the Captain was on the line, "Captain, Ventimigilio is here visiting someone and he says there's a suspicious guy hanging around in the lobby. Yeah, he's right here." He handed Charles the phone.

The Captain wondered why one of his men was at the DMC, "Ventimigilio, what the hell you doing up there?"

"Visiting my neighbor, he's downstairs, had an operation..."

"I don't need your life story, Ventimigilio. What does this suspicious guy look like?" He described Lefty to the Captain and he could see Dominic still hanging around down the hallway. Charles thought, *Wish he'd go back downstairs.*

The Captain came back on, "Good work officer, didn't expect that you'd be help to us, I've got two guys in the lobby right now and we'll take care of it."

Charles handed the cell phone back to his buddy, "Says he's got men handling it now. Man, that asshole hates me, How about you, can I help; maybe you need a break?"

"Wish I could take you up on that but I'd be busted to traffic duty or worse if I left my post."

"I understand, been there, the Captain is pretty tough. So this guy you're guarding, have you talked to him?"

"No, they got him bottled up; especially once he came to, they have had suits in there all day long. If he ain't giving them anything, I wonder why they are still interested in him?"

"Do you know the guy?"

"Never saw him, why are you interested?"

"Just curious, a lot of manpower for a guy who was in the crash."

"Sorry Charles, I gotta go. See you at the station."

"Later," Ventimigilio walked back down the hallway, glad that he didn't see Dom still down there hanging around. Getting back in the elevator he pressed one and waited.

When the doors opened he saw everyone in the lobby watching the action in the corner of the room. Two officers were questioning a man that they had cuffed and pressed against the wall. Another officer had people pushed back from the group in the corner. One officer had Lefty's wallet in his hand and was going through his identification. Charles and Dominic made their way toward the lobby and stopped, Charles asked a lady who was watching the action, "What's going on?"

"I'm not sure; they got a guy in there and looks like he's causing trouble."

Charles motioned to Dom, he needed to go back and now. He stood watching and waited like everyone else. The officers that were questioning Lefty escorted him out of the lobby and everyone was buzzing about what was going on. No one knew for sure but it did give people something to talk about. Charles walked outside and didn't see Lefty or the two officers. He looked around and saw Mario standing near cars parked along the entrance. Walking over he asked, "So where's Lefty?"

"They took him away. I told him to act a little squirrely but he must have overdone it. Hope he didn't have any open warrants because they looked pretty serious when they put him in the squad car. What did you find out upstairs?"

"The officer on the second floor confirmed that it's your garbage truck driver that they have secluded and under special security. Good news is, he's not talking. Seems that he said he can't remember anything about the crash. My buddy said they've had attorneys in there but he's holding tight to his story."

"Thanks Charles, now we've got to figure out how to get in there. Do you think your Captain would put you on the security team guarding him?"

"I'm not one of his "go to" guys, there are times I think he hates me, and other times I know he does. I could try but don't count on it."

Mario had to tell Dominic the news; he didn't know how he'd react.

# CHAPTER NINETEEN

**Amy Harper listened to the message, Lieutenant Jackson** said it was urgent. "Detective, the Chief advised me to contact you right away. We have a development on the murder of Andy Jones. Detective Baker and his partner were able to recover an envelope and packet of drugs that were taken off of either Jones or the other body discovered in the field. Forensics has identified fingerprints from the packet and he wants you to meet him at the DEA's office as soon as possible."

Harper wondered why Chief Mathews wanted her to head to the DEA's office. "Lieutenant, I'll head right over although I was told not to contact Detective Baker or involve myself in his case."

"I'm not sure Detective, he did say it may have to do with your case too."

Detective Harper moved over to Mindy's desk, "I have to meet Chief Mathews at the office of the DEA and will call after the meeting. Let Detective Spano know where I am and that I'll fill him in later." Harper thought the case was puzzling enough and now more pieces were being added that didn't fit, at least not the case she was working on. *What did this have to do with the crash and attempt on Frederickson's life.* The drive to the DEA's Office was quick from Police Headquarters, Harper turned onto Michigan Avenue toward Howard Street. Pulling into the lot she flashed her badge, "I'm here to meet with Police Chief Mathews and DEA Agent Downey." She was escorted through to the visitor's lot and up to Downey's office. The agent that walked with Harper never said a word, just kept his head down and led Harper to the fourth floor office.

She extended her hand, "Detective Harper," Agent Downey smiled. The Chief wasn't in the room and Harper wondered what was going on. "Detective, your Chief will be back in a minute, we have some new developments in our case. Two detectives found an envelope and drugs that has helped us identify a possible suspect in Andy Jones' murder. The forensic team has identified the fingerprints and Chief Mathews wanted you involved."

"How did you get DNA results so fast?"

"It normally takes twenty-four hours even with a rush order. We got lucky on this one. The lab had two sets from the evidence lab brought in, both were run on separate equipment and we got a hit in less than eight hours on the first set. The second sample also hit about an hour later, both pointed to the same suspect who handled the packets."

Detective Harper sat listening, not sure how this all had happened but intrigued her. Within a few minutes Chief Mathews entered the room along with two other men. "Detective Harper, this is Agent Hollis with the DEA and Commander Duke from our North District." Harper thought, *more puzzle pieces.* "I'm sure Agent Downey has filled you in about the break in the Jones' murder case. Their forensic team was able to get a seven point fingerprint match from a packet of drugs that was taken off one of the bodies. It matches that of a onetime felon, Oscar White. Our investigation has him currently working at the Eastern Market for a trucking and stowage company. There's no record of him being involved in any criminal activity for close to fifteen years. We don't want to pick him up right away because more people are probably involved. We need to get close to this White fellow."

Harper appreciated being involved, "That's a big break, Chief; how can the SIU Team help?"

"That's why you're here; we need to put a couple of people undercover in the Eastern Market. I want to use one of your detectives, maybe Askew; he's new to the team and not well known to people that could be involved. The DEA already has another agent undercover there but with this revelation we need to concentrate on this Oscar White fellow."

"Askew is a good choice, sir."

Agent Downey invited everyone to head to the conference table in the adjoining room. "If I may Chief, our team of agents had been working on the drug trade with possible suspects in the Market area. This is a known source of problems for contraband as well as drugs. With trucks traveling across the border to Canada on the Ambassador Bridge daily, it would be easy to move almost anything. This White fellow has never shown up on our radar, neither he, nor the trucking company he works for, have been suspects in our investigation."

"What trucking company does he work for?"

"La Russo Trucking, primarily a vegetable and produce company. They've been in operation for years, however, we've never been able to link them to illegal activity."

The name of the trucking company sparked Detective Harper's memory, she asked, "Agent Downey, last year during our investigation into the murder of Lieutenant Forsythe, we looked at a link to a company in St. Clair Shores, Castellanos Trucking. Could it also be part of La Russo's operation?"

"Chief Mathews has already been working on that and currently we haven't found any connection. That doesn't mean there isn't one, and I agree with you, Detective, it does bring up a red flag so we'll both keep working on it."

Turning to Chief Mathews, Harper asked, "What do you want me to tell Detective Askew?"

"Agent Downey has two men that have been undercover at the Eastern Market in the loading and unload areas. One of the guys is working in Shed Five, the same one that Oscar White handles. Downey had Jones working on the day laborer aspect. The question was the possibility of them using these guys for running the drug trade. We think they are using day laborers that they pick up on Gratiot for some of these illegal jobs. The men don't know anything about the operations and most are illegals so they naturally hide from authorities. My two guys are working in loading and unloading trucks but I need someone to get close to this White fellow."

Chief Mathews added, "We don't have enough yet to charge White, probably he's just a pawn in this. We want to get whoever is at the top of the food chain. With our team and the DEA working together, we have a much better chance to uncover who was behind the murder and maybe crack the case of drugs and contraband moving in and out of the area. The Canadian authorities are working their side of the border on the same case."

The group planned the combined operation with the DEA running point and the Detroit Police Department handling the backup support. Detective Harper hoped this didn't interfere with her team's handling of the Frederickson case but pleased that the Chief had her involved.

***

Lefty was being booked downtown for disorderly conduct and the two officers handling the arrest reported back to their Captain, "Ventimigilio, may have been on to something. This guy acted irrational when we walked up to him and immediately began arguing. Not sure what he was up to but, Captain, he's still yelling in the holding cell."

The Captain thought, *maybe he underestimated Charles.* He'd check into him a little more, maybe he'd use him in other cases to see how he handles himself. The Captain told his officers, "Bring this guy to the Interrogation Room, I want to question him."

Lefty sat in the cell, proud that he did exactly what Mario told him. He didn't want to be held over too long so he thought, *I need to cool it for now.* The officer unlocked the cell door, "Come with me," Once Lefty stood he cuffed him and escorted him down the hall to an Interrogation Room.

"Hey, where you taking me?"

"Be quiet, you're here for causing a disturbance and resisting arrest. You want us to add more charges?"

Lefty put his head down, "I didn't do nothing."

"Well you can tell that to my Captain." The officer cuffed Lefty to a table and the Captain walked in.

He held a printout and studied his prisoner without saying anything for over a minute. Lefty was uneasy in the hard chair and finally said, "I didn't do anything, I want a lawyer."

"Sure, but if you want a lawyer it would probably be later today or tomorrow before a public defender would get here." The Captain stood and headed to the door.

"Wait, I didn't do nothing, your cops grabbed me in the waiting room for no reason."

"Sorry, you asked for a lawyer, I can't talk to you unless you retract your request."

"Okay, I don't want a lawyer, but why am I here?"

Sliding a pen and pad over to Lefty, and taking the cuffs off, the Captain said, "Write it all down, we offered you a lawyer but you don't want one. Understand, anything you say can and will be used against you in a court of law."

"Sure, but I'm innocent."

"Yeah, that's what everyone in here says." The Captain watched as Lefty scribbled on the pad and slid it back across the table; reading Lefty's statement the Captain still standing asked, "Why were you at the DMC?"

"I was there looking for friend."

"What's your friend's name?" Lefty seemed to act like he didn't understand the question. "Hey jackass, what's your friend's name that you were looking for?"

"He called, said he needed a ride home, I couldn't find him."

"You must be an idiot, what's his name?"

"His name?"

"Oh my God, yeah dumbass, what's the name of your friend that needed a ride?"

"Santorio, he called said he was in the lobby but wasn't there."

The Captain was frustrated, Lefty was talking in circles and making him ask multiple questions for the same answer. "Santorio what?"

"His name, you asked for his name, it's Santorio."

"Is Santorio his first name or last name?"

"First name."

He was about to grab Lefty and pull him across the table, "Jesus, what's Santorio's last name?"

This had gone just the way Lefty hoped, maybe he'd get the Captain to give up. "Santorio, I don't know his last name, it's just Santorio."

The Captain slammed open the Interrogation Room door, "Officer, take this asshole back to his cell."

The officer looked at his Captain who was shaking his head, "Got it Cap't." Cuffing Lefty he escorted him back to a holding cell. Lefty smiled as he was taken back. The officer wondered what, if anything, the Captain had learned.

\*\*\*

Amy Harper returned to the SIU office and Detective Spano

immediately walked over to see what had transpired at the DEA Office. "Why did they want you to come to their office?"

She motioned for him to follow her and continued walking to her desk while she filled him in, "The Chief and the DEA have a lead in the Jones' murder case. They want to use Detective Askew in an undercover operation and needed to fill us in."

"Murder case, what does this have to do with our investigation?"

Harper slumped in her chair and asked Spano, "You better sit down." She decided to tell Spano everything, including her initial meeting with Tom Baker at Palmer Park.

"Amy, why didn't you tell me about this?"

"I know I should have but I thought that I could handle it without it interfering with our investigation. Joe, I was wrong. Sorry, but I'll never do that again."

Spano stood and put his arm on her shoulder, "You can't try to handle something like this on your own, and we're family and want to help. What can I do?"

"Just knowing that you're here for me right now is enough. Until the Chief gives me more details, I plan to work with you on our case."

Neither Detective knew how, or if, the murder case of Andy Jones related to their investigation but would follow the Chief's orders.

# CHAPTER TWENTY

**Detective Frederickson was being wheeled down to the X-Ray** department for more tests to confirm how his injuries were coming along. Two officers, along with a nurse, escorted him downstairs. "You know this isn't necessary." He felt the protection was excessive. "You guys must have other things to do other than walk around the hospital with me."

"Detective, we're just following orders from the Chief."

Nancy Frederickson sat in his room waiting for him to return; she was pleased with all the protection her husband was given. She told the officer upstairs, "We still didn't know if Don was the target but I'm afraid that someone is trying to kill him." They couldn't confirm or deny her opinion. His room was filled with flowers and well wishes from the Chief, friends and the SIU team.

Before he went down for his test he told his wife that his room looked like a funeral parlor, "You need to donate those flowers to people that can appreciate them."

While Frederickson was downstairs, there was action outside that directly related to his security as well as the suspected driver of the garbage truck. Mario and Dom needed a plan, Mario called and talked to Gloria, hoping he didn't have to talk to Vinnie.

Gloria hesitated to offer a suggestion but knew they needed something, "Mario, my friend is a nurse, do you want me to call and see if she can help." He was very interested, "Jean is a traveling nurse and I think she covers three or four hospitals downtown. Mario, she's divorced and probably could use some extra money."

Once he hung up he headed straight to Dom, "We've come up with a great plan to get into Ben Walker's room. I talked to Gloria, and her friend is a nurse. I bet she can get into the room."

Dominic was frustrated, "Shit, what do we know about her?"

"She might be our last hope, and Gloria said she could use the extra money." Mario detailed the rest of the conversation with Gloria to Dominic. "I've already called her, she's on the way."

Dominic pounded his fist into his right hand, "Why in the hell didn't we think of this before?" Mario saw him smile for the first time in a while. They both were relieved and Mario said he'd wait outside for her.

It was maybe an hour later when a lady wearing a nurse's outfit strolled out of the emergency entrance and approached them, "Excuse me, are you Mr. La Russo?"

He looked at her, "Yeah, I hope you're Jean?"

"Yes, Gloria called and said that you might have a job for me."

Mario nodded, "Exactly what do you know?"

Jean quickly answered, "You've got a guy in the hospital that you want to disappear."

"Disappear yes, but the key thing is we need to silence him. It could be very financially rewarding." He reached in his pocket and handed her a small roll of bills. "This is just a sample of what I'm talking about. Get the job done and we'll have a six figure amount deposited into your bank account." Jean was pleased when she saw the hundred on top and Mario said, "They're all hundreds." The roll had to be two inches around.

"This is great. I'm on the hospital staff here as well as two other hospitals. I called my contact at DMC and got a special staff assignment for the weekend. They're always shorthanded and with everything that's happened this week they needed everyone available."

Mario went over everything again, one more time, "You know we got a guy upstairs on the second floor, we don't want him to disappear; we need him dead. The cops have two men guarding him and checking everyone in and out."

"Give me his name and do you know the room number?"

"Ben Walker and everything we've found is that he's in room 210," Mario asked her, "I hope you've got something to get the job done."

"Oh yes, I've got the easiest way to do this and leave no trace, just like you want. I'm going to give him something to cause a heart attack, most importantly it will break down naturally in his body." Taking out a vial, "This is Potassium Chloride; once I put it in his I.V. it will slowly mix with the other solution and do the job in about a half an hour or less."

"How are you going to get in there?" She showed Mario her

name tag. "Shit, this looks real!"

"Oh, it is. I'm a traveling nurse. I rotate between here and three other hospitals. It's all legit."

He thought, *sure glad Gloria gave me her name.* Mario watched as she made her way across the parking lot. He was glad he talked to her and not have Dominic do it. Dom had almost gone ballistic with Lefty and Charles, he didn't need him to scare off this lady.

***

The guards on the second floor had just changed shifts and the first group filled them in about the events from earlier. One of them said, "You wouldn't believe it, but Ventimigilio comes upstairs telling us that a strange guy was hanging around the lobby. He says we need to check it out."

One of them was shocked, "Ventimigilio, you gotta be kidding. The Captain thinks he's lazy at best and I'm surprised he's still on the force."

"Yeah, we're kinda surprised too, but seems like they got the guy at the station and he's a real nut. We heard he about drove the Captain crazy when they tried to question him."

While the four officers were talking, a nurse approached, showing her badge she said, "I'm supposed to be checking on his I.V., do one of you need to come in with me?"

"Wait, you're not the normal nurse on duty?" He checked her name tag and looked at the roster that the hospital gave him. "Your name is not on my list."

"I'm not a duty nurse, I'm the surgical anesthetist. We always follow up on our patients." Jean casually stood there, "Call the desk, they'll tell you who I am."

"Let me call down and just check, but keep the door opened." When she entered the room, she saw that Ben was asleep. The officer moved into the doorway and watched as Jean picked up the chart and studied it. She appeared to check his arm bracelet and was looking at the I.V. bottle. The patient opened his eyes and the officer moved closer.

The officer peeked in, "The girl at the desk said you're a

traveling nurse on staff, so I guess everything is okay." While he continued talking to her, Jean continued to take Walker's vitals and wrote something down on the chart.

She turned to the officer, "His heart rate is a little elevated; Mr. Walker, are you having any chest pains?"

"No, but I can't sleep." The officer watched and the nurse continued doing some test. He moved back to the doorway and motioned something to his partner.

While he did this, Jean continued working on Walker, it was a stroke of luck that Walker already had a rapid heartbeat. She continued talking to Ben, "The record shows you were unconscious for a few days and having trouble remembering. I have something to help you relax." Walker appreciated her efforts.

The officer at the door was still talking to the other officer guarding the doorway, He told his partner; "The nurse said he's having a problem, do we need to call this in?"

"No, I'm sure the nurse will report it, just make sure she's not doing something she shouldn't?"

"Hell, I'm not a doctor, what do I know?"

"You'll know if she kills the dumb shit."

He laughed, "Okay, I got it." When he turned back toward the nurse it appeared that she completed her review of the patient and Ben Walker was sitting up in the bed talking to her. The officer watched her make more notes on his chart and then she headed his way. He asked, "Is he okay?"

"Yeah, probably nothing but I'll fill the desk and doctor in, his blood pressure and heart beat are a little high but not in a dangerous range. They might prescribe something for him."

The officer watched Jean finish and asked his partner, "Hey, did those other guys leave already."

"Yeah, they said this duty is so damn boring that eight hours on their feet took its toll."

Jean walked out of the room, "I'm going to inform the desk about his issues. They're not unusual but they'll send someone to check on him in a little." Jean headed down the hallway and stopped at the desk. The officers watched her and were sure everything was okay. The two men kept their position checking people that came down the hall. It was a little over a half an hour later when a Doctor approached; showing his identification, they let him in Walker's room. He was in the room for a few seconds when he called out, "Code Red." One of the officers at the door ran into the room and two people rushed down the hall with a crash cart, "Move out of the way," a nurse called out. Red lights flashed at the nurse's station and the officer watched as hospital personnel rushed into the room. The nurse who accompanied the crash cart put a substance on the paddles and the Doctor who had pulled the front of Ben's hospital gown open, pressed them to the man's chest. "Clear!" He repeated the process twice. "Clear!" One more time, the doctor yelled "Clear." He watched the monitor that still showed a flat line pulse and heartbeat. Two doctors and the nurse continued trying to revive the patient for a couple more minutes but it was hopeless. Both officers were standing in the corner of the room, panic on their face, not sure what to do, but certain that this wasn't good.

\*\*\*

The officers downstairs in the X-Ray lab got a panicked call from their Captain. "Where's Frederickson?"

"Sir, we're with him, he's having a test right now downstairs in the lab."

The Captain was almost yelling, "Go in there right now; make sure he's okay!"

Pushing the door opened, holding the cell phone he entered as two technicians tried stopping him, "Hey, you can't go in there."

"I gotta see that the Detective is okay."

Frederickson heard the commotion, "I'm good, what the hell's going on?"

"Hold on Detective, my Captain wanted to make sure you're okay. Captain, he's fine."

"Don't let anyone else near him; see if you can get him back into his room."

"What's happening Captain?"

"Not sure, stay with the Detective. I'm on my way right now. Our suspect upstairs is dead," with that he hung up.

The officer looked at the face of his cell phone thinking; *did he say dead, did someone kill him?* Immediately calling out to Frederickson, "Detective, we need to get you back upstairs."

The nurse looked at them, "But we're almost done, just need one more X-ray of his chest."

"It's going to have to wait, we gotta go now." The officer told his partner, "Watch the door, I'm getting the Detective out of here." The technician wasn't happy but turned off her equipment. Along with the nurse, the officer helped Frederickson back in the wheelchair.

Detective Frederickson held his hand up, "I'm not going anywhere until you tell me what's going on?"

"I'm not sure but my Captain wants us to get you back upstairs now."

"What aren't you telling me?"

"Nothing, just we gotta go."

"Listen son, I'm not going anywhere until you tell me everything you know, got it!"

The officer didn't know what to do, finally he decided to tell Frederickson. "The Captain said that the suspect on your floor is dead, I don't know any more than that."

"Okay, but before we move you need to get someone upstairs to protect my wife, right now!"

The second officer called in to his Captain but didn't get an answer. He dialed the squad that was assigned to the lobby. "I need someone to head upstairs to Detective Frederickson's room, make sure his wife is okay."

The guys downstairs asked, "What's going on, the Captain called, said he's on his way. Do you know what happened?"

"No, just get someone upstairs and call me once you get there." The officer turned to Frederickson, "Okay Detective, I've got someone headed upstairs, we gotta go now."

The nurse pushed the wheelchair and the two officers walked with her, one in front and another behind with weapons drawn. Everyone that approached stepped out of the way, not sure if the guy in the chair was a prisoner or being protected. They got on the elevator and the officer told people waiting, "Sorry, you'll have to catch the next one." Getting in they stood in front of the wheelchair blocking Frederickson from view. Once they arrived on the second floor, one officer got out and checked the hallway first then motioned for the nurse and his partner to proceed. They got to the Detective's room and the nurse got him settled back into bed.

Nancy was standing, "What's going on, an officer came in asking if I was okay, when I asked what was going on, he just said he was supposed to check on me."

The arriving officer said, "We're not sure, just the Captain wanted him back up here where we can protect both of you."

Her hands were shaking, "Don, what do you know?"

"Not much hon, they said that the guy down the hall had a heart attack. Nancy, we don't know anything else."

It was just a matter of minutes when the Captain entered Frederickson's room. "Detective, glad you're okay. We need to take extra precautions until we know what happened down the hallway."

"What aren't you telling us?"

"Nothing yet, we have the lab checking the toxicology report, hoping that they can tell us their findings soon."

"Sounds like you suspect foul play?"

"A Doctor making his rounds found the man unresponsive. He did all that he could. Our officers outside the room said a nurse came in earlier maybe a half an hour or more before and checked on the guy. She said he seemed to be having an issue and she informed the desk."

"Did you check on that?"

"Detective, we got this, I promise. My officer confirmed that she stopped at the desk and they have her report. We've located her and she's giving us a complete report. Her notes showed that he was having an elevated heart rate and his blood pressure was up slightly."

Nancy was listening and didn't like what she was hearing. "Captain, I think you need to double the police guard."

Frederickson patted his wife's hand, "They got it handled honey; we'll be okay."

"Mrs. Frederickson, I've already put a second team on the floor and I promise were doing everything to keep you both safe. Chief Mathews is aware of everything and is headed here."

"Thanks Captain, I wasn't trying to tell you how to do your job."

"It's understandable, you're worried; we are too. Until we

know what happened down the hall we'll take extra precautions." The Captain turned and gave his two officers their orders. One of them pulled a chair into the room and sat in the corner and the other man sat in the doorway. Two more men came upstairs and took their position outside the room on both sides of the hallway. Once he did that, he told the original two officers to come with him. "Okay guys, let's go over this one more time."

They filled him in on the events, everything checked out, especially since the nurse in question was still in the hospital. She wouldn't do something and hang around, would she?

# CHAPTER TWENTY-ONE

**The commotion on the second floor of the DMC had** become obvious to everyone on the hospital staff and patients. The second floor corridor was in a virtual lockdown and officers were stationed along the hallway on both ends. Chief Mathews arrived and was in Frederickson's room. "Don, our people are indicating that the suspect suffered a fatal heart attack. We haven't received the toxicology report yet but all signs appear to be that of a health related death."

The Detective wasn't convinced, "Chief, it seems odd to me that he came out of the coma and appeared to be okay and now, suddenly has a massive heart attack."

"I know where you're going, however it doesn't do any of us any good to start guessing without facts." Turning to Nancy, the Chief smiled, "I'm sorry, I know all of this seems to be suspicious and we've got the best people on the case, but until we know more we'll just be diligent in protecting you and your husband."

"Thanks Chief," she felt that she may have overreacted but after all she was sure someone out there was trying to kill her husband and she was just being very protective.

The Captain from the North Precinct walked in and the Chief moved over to talk to him. "Chief, the lab has run routine Cardiac Enzyme tests that have all come up normal for a patient who suffered a heart attack. I'm not a doctor but they tell me that in a heart attack the enzymes and proteins leak out of damaged cells, thus the levels rise to extremely high levels. That's what they have found in our suspect."

Mathews listened to what the Captain was telling him, "Can we get the doctor who did the testing to come up here to talk to us?"

"I'll make that request."

The Chief turned back to Frederickson and his wife. "I've asked the doctor who ran test on our suspect to come upstairs and fill us all in." That brought a nod from both Nancy and Don. "I promise we'll make sure everything is checked thoroughly." As they talked, close to twenty minutes later, a doctor in her lab coat entered Detective Frederickson's room flanked by a police officer.

"I'm Doctor Nagappala, head of Pathology; I understand you wanted a more complex answer to our testing of the patient that suffered a heart attack." She held a printout, "We ran all the normal tests and they came back normal for someone who died of a massive cardiac event. I plan to perform an autopsy and we'll run further tests but it will take more than eight hours to get accurate results."

The Chief answered, "Yes, thank you doctor, the individual was a key suspect in our case and we need to make sure nothing could have been done to cause this heart attack. Do you test his blood?"

"Yes, that's one of the things that the lab does in any case like this; however, we did not find any foreign substances in either his blood stream or enzymes that would point to foul play. We, in the medical profession, know that there are things that can be hidden in the body's blood stream that could cause a rapid heartbeat, maybe even bring on an attack but they usually show up in the testing we've run so far."

"Thanks for coming up here and giving us this information."

"My team downstairs will perform more tests when we do the autopsy and if we find anything that looks suspicious I'll immediately let you know." Both Frederickson and his wife thanked the doctor and Chief Mathews walked with her out of the room.

"Doctor, I know you're aware of our situation, I just can't have anyone that's not on your normal staff taking care of my Detective, especially with this new event."

"Sir, our team of nurses and doctors will provide the very best care for your Detective. I'll make sure that everyone who isn't aware of the situation is filled in at once."

\*\*\*

Mario and Dominic were driving back to the Eastern Market to go over everything with Vinnie. Gloria had been instrumental in their success and the two of them were grateful for her help. Mario made the call that would get both of them off the hook with the boss, "Vinnie, Ben Walker is dead."

"You're sure? Did you see his body?"

"No, but Gloria was instrumental in getting us a name to get the job done."

"Gloria, what did she do?"

Mario had to admit that Gloria gave them the help they needed. "Her friend, Jean, is a nurse, once she arrived, the plan went just as planned. She injected Ben with something and he had a massive heart attack. Vinnie, we saw the staff at the hospital in a panic, I know it's done."

Vinnie appreciated Gloria more than ever, when he got off the phone he went to the outer office, "Thanks Gloria, I knew I'd be able to count on you." He gave her a peck on the cheek.

Although she didn't want to take credit for the success, she said, "My friend made sure it all looked like a normal heart attack."

"Why don't you go out and buy yourself a new outfit," peeling off a few bills from a stack of hundreds, Vinnie handed them to her. "It's late, take the rest of the night off."

"Thanks Mr. La Russo but this isn't necessary, I'm willing to stay as late as you need me here."

Vinnie smiled at her, "No, Mario and Dom should be coming back soon. We'll be okay, see you tomorrow." Vinnie knew his two men would come back to the office to finally gloat about their success. Why not, they got rid of the only witness that could tie them to the crash. La Russo and his company were in the clear, he was sure no one would suspect anyone from the Eastern Market in any of this now.

***

To help with the work load Chief Mathews contacted Detective Baker to come downtown to meet with him. *What did I do now*, Baker wondered as he parked in the visitor lot. He made his way into the Detroit Public Safety Headquarters on Third Avenue remembering his last visit, that didn't turn out so good. The Chief's large outer office was intimidating as Lieutenant Jackson manned the desk. She had Baker sitting in one of the huge chairs, nervously in the corner. He was there only a few minutes when Detective Amy Harper walked in. Baker's heart beat rose, *this can't be good.*

Harper stood next to where Baker was sitting, "Tom, the Chief said he called you in too; looks like we might be working together on this."

Baker had no idea what she was talking about, but that comment made him feel much better already. The last time he was here he remembered what the Chief said, "Don't call Detective Harper and just do the job he was assigned." He looked up at her, "I'm not sure what's even going on."

"I'm not positive either but the Chief wanted us to both be here and he'd fill us in. Tom, he said you did a great job finding critical evidence in Andy's murder, evidence that might break the case wide open."

As they stood there talking, Jackson walked over, "Detectives, the Chief will see you both now." Harper walked in first followed by Baker. Lieutenant Jackson walked in behind both of them and shut the door.

Chief Mathews motioned to the conference table at the far end of the room, "Let's sit over there." All four of them sat at one end of the large oak table. The leather chairs had wrapped arms and the seat backs were ornate, almost like each one had been hand carved. Baker was still nervous and his eyes shifted from the Chief's desk back to the large conference table. Mathews stated, "Detective Baker, I want to congratulate you in person on your investigation at the murder scene. It has led us to a suspect that is of interest to both our office and that of the DEA." Baker just sat quietly, not sure where this was going but happy that he wasn't on the receiving end of another ass chewing. Mathews continued, "Detective Harper and her team have become involved in an undercover assignment in this case. Because it was you and your partner that opened the investigation when you found the bodies in the field and now found critical evidence, we felt you should be part of the next step."

Baker didn't know where any of this was going, "I appreciate that Chief and will do anything you need to help solve this."

"I know that, Tom; Detective Harper has said some good

things about you and I trust her instincts." Baker looked over at Amy and a slight smile crept into the corner of his mouth. "I'm prepared to bring you in on everything we know so far." The Chief went over the details from the forensic lab pointing to Oscar White as a suspect. He also told Baker about an investigation now taking place at the Eastern Market with questions not only about White but whomever might be involved. "Baker, this Oscar White guy isn't a rocket scientist; he handles loading and unloading of trucks. He's the tip of this thing and who knows how high it goes. I've talked to your Captain and for the time being, you're being assigned to the SIU team upstairs. Detective Harper will be your commanding officer; do you have any problem answering to her?"

"No sir, I'd be happy to help the team anyway possible."

"Good, I'm going to let her take you upstairs and fill you in on your role in this investigation. I had Lieutenant Jackson make the necessary personnel changes and your assignment for now is temporary." Once that was agreed to, the two detectives stood. The Chief shook Baker's hand and he followed Detective Harper and Jackson out of the office.

When they got to the bank of elevators at the end of the hallway, Tom Baker cleared his throat. "Harper, thanks for everything you said to the Chief, I appreciate this opportunity."

"I only told him what I believe to be true, Tom. Andy Jones was a good friend and I was happy that you told me right away about his murder. Neither one of us knew where this would lead to but apparently Andy was undercover with the DEA and on special assignment. Now it's up to us to help catch his killers and solve the case he was working on." The elevator doors opened and both of them stepped in.

*** 

The next day brought the start of the new undercover assignment headed by the DEA to the Eastern Market. Detective Askew had been filled in on the case by Detective Harper and the representative of DEA. Askew was the newest member of the SIU team, he told Harper, "I'm pleased that you chose me for this assignment."

"Detective, you're an important member of the team, glad

you're on the case."

It was almost five in the morning and Askew met his contact on the corner of Gratiot and Beaubien. The introduction would be simple, just work as hard as possible and you'd fit in. He would be in this undercover assignment working in Shed Four unloading vegetable trucks with the DEA operative who had infiltrated the working staff. Both men would be under the auspicious detail assigned to Oscar White, the suspect in the murder of Officer Andy Jones. The Detroit Police would be handling some of the background investigation along with the Drug Enforcement Agency. Both entities would keep the Canadian authorities in the loop on their investigation. The Border Patrol had been brought into the case and increased their inspection of trucks crossing at both the Ambassador Bridge downtown and Blue Water Bridge in Port Huron. If drugs were being moved over the border it made sense that they were coming in and out via these two routes. The investigation would be entering the next stage, the most important one that could solve the murder and possibly the route the drugs were using to enter the country.

# CHAPTER TWENTY-TWO

**Oscar White continued pressing his men to get the two** trailers of produce unloaded and stacked into the open stalls in Shed Four. The men, mostly day laborers, pushed crates of lettuce, tomatoes and cabbage into the assigned areas for vendors to set up their stands. Although it was only six in the morning, people always arrived at dawn hoping to get the freshest and best selections. White was ordering the men, "You men have to move faster, we'll have people tramping all over the place soon and we have to set up." It was a normal Saturday morning with hundreds of people strolling with their carts and wagons through the massive display of fruits, vegetables and plants in the historical market place. Oscar walked over to the next Shed to see how they were doing. He watched the new guy that one of the vendors and his supervisor had suggested that he hire. The guy was working hard and out pacing the other seven men unloading the trucks. Oscar was happy to have a new man who worked hard on the job.

While Oscar was overseeing the work being done, Dominic Parma walked into the Shed. "Hey Oscar, come here, I gotta talk to you."

Oscar really hated Dominic and always preferred doing business with Mario. He wished Vinnie sent his nephew instead of the brutal enforcer. The man was crude and treated everyone like shit. "Make it fast; I have to get all these trucks unloaded."

"You don't tell me what to do; I'm here because Vinnie wants you to do something for us."

Oscar wondered, *when will it ever end*, "Okay what?"

"Those trucks that we moved from Castellanos' lot a couple days ago, we gotta get the stuff out of them tonight."

"Okay, let me get these trucks unloaded and I'll come up to Vinnie's office."

"We ain't got time for that; you need to get a few of your guys to go with us."

"When do we need to do this?"

"Soon as possible."

Oscar resisted telling Dominic that it was Saturday and his men were too busy, "Hope it ain't going to be like the last group we took to move the trucks?"

Dom stood; arms crossed just starring at Oscar, "Bring two or three of your most trusted guys to the office at four, we need ones who can get it done quickly. I'll have Mario go with you to get this all done."

Oscar watched Dominic walking away and wished Vinnie didn't send him to the Sheds while they were working. Dom always caused a stir, after all how many people do you see with that God awful scar on his face; all the guys always wondered who he was. When Oscar looked back to the group they were watching the conversation instead of moving the crates, he hollered, "This ain't a picnic, let's get these crates off the trucks." He noticed that one of the new guys was double stacking crates and working harder than everyone else. Oscar walked over, "Nice job kid, keep it up. What's your name?"

"Askew, Jimmy Askew, thank you sir."

"No sir's here, all of us are just doing our job." He continued watching the new guy stacking and moving crates, *Glad I got this extra guy, he seems pretty good, wonder where did he come from.* Oscar waved to his foreman, "Where did this Askew guy come from, what do you know about him?"

"He came well recommended by the guys working the trucks unloading at the meat market. One of the vendors said they've known him for years, said he's a hard worker."

Oscar nodded, "I can see that, he's out performed everyone on the dock. When we're done bring him to my office, I'd like to talk to him."

Saturday was always one of the busiest days at the Market, and this wasn't any different. Trucks from local farmers arrived with loads of fruits and vegetables. Blueberries and strawberries were still in season and patrons knew they could get a great buy on these items.

Jimmy Askew pushed the carts with loads of vegetables, sweat rolling down his face. He knew his role, get close to Oscar White, impress him with his work efforts and gain his confidence, if it meant working like a dog, he'd do it. Askew had a benefit, as a kid he grew up on a farm and understood the process of handling produce. The DEA informer, who worked his way all the way up to the foreman at the Market, had set up Askew's background so that he'd fit in right away. They wanted him to use his real name, much easier on a short assignment to not get crossed up when someone called you. After all there were hundreds of Askew's in the Detroit phone book.

Oscar walked back to his office along the outside wall of Shed Five mulling over what Dominic wanted. He had helped move the trucks a few days ago, just like Vinnie wanted and then they even ended up killing the two guys they used doing the job, *what more did they want from him.*

The Market was bustling with trucks lined up along the streets and cars were vying for parking spots. It would be a long day with the work starting at sunrise and clean up lasting into the early evening. Oscar had two crews, one to unload the trucks and another crew of less experienced men to sweep and clean up the stalls. He would only use his morning crew to do extra work, work like what Vinnie proposed. He'd get with his foreman to pick the crew for the special job.

***

Detective Harper was meeting with Tom Baker and Joe Spano at the crack of dawn, again covering key aspects of the case. "The Chief has agreed that the DEA should head this up", she told them. "They have infiltrated the Eastern Market with two undercover agents and Detective Askew joined them today." She went over the details that they had on Oscar White who was the target of their investigation. Although he was known as a low level person, it was his fingerprints that brought the investigation to the Eastern Market. Questions revolved around who White worked for? What did Andy Jones find out and how did that get him killed? That was what the teams were working on.

While Askew was working undercover, Harper planned on circulating the Market as a shopper, hoping to keep an eye on her Detective. "Tom, your Captain has been apprised that you'll be assigned to our staff. Once we get to the Market, Detective Spano might have a problem being recognized because he had been in an undercover assignment there before. That's where you come in. With Askew there, we need to make sure he's okay." Both of them understood that Harper wanted to protect Askew; they couldn't have another member of the team injured or worse.

Detectives Baker and Spano listened to Harper with her plan to keep an eye on Askew. Tom Baker was impressed with Amy Harper's leadership, her understanding of the assignment and how she was handling her leadership role. He asked, "Detective, what do you want me to do?"

Harper looked back at both of them, "Tom, I'm thinking that you and I will walk through the Market, acting as shoppers." Smiling at Tom, "I think we'd look like a normal couple. Spano, you've been down there before so we need to keep you out of sight."

Spano nodded, "Great idea, I like it, I could handle monitoring information from the car. If you both circulated the Stalls, hopefully, you'll spot Askew and this White fellow. I'll track any unusual movement by the suspect. We don't want to spook him."

Baker agreed, "I'm in."

Harper grabbed her phone, "I'm going to leave the Chief a message so he knows what we're planning." Once she did that the three of them headed downstairs to the garage. Spano walked ahead of them. Detective Baker walked next to Amy Harper, wanting to say something but not sure how to approach the subject. Once they got to the cars Amy turned to him, "Tom, I appreciate your willingness to help our team. I know taking direction from me might be kind of weird."

"No, not at all, in fact I'm proud to be part of your SIU team, even if it's only temporary."

She stopped and turned toward him, gently touching his hand she smiled, "Maybe we can make it more than temporary when this is all done." The two continued to linger in the moment when Detective Spano pulled around the corner in an unmarked SUV.

Spano pulled up in front of them, "I got this vehicle from the motor pool; I thought the two of you could use it. We don't want someone to spot you arriving in a squad car."

"Thanks Joe, good idea, Tom and I will head down Michigan Avenue and you can follow us. I'll try to find a spot along Russell

Street." The detectives knew that the Market would be very busy on a Saturday and Harper wanted to get there as early as possible.

\*\*\*

Oscar White made sure his men had completed the last assignment when he asked his foreman to bring three crew members to his office. It was close to eight and the Market was bustling with people everywhere. Shoppers had wagons, carts and armloads of fruits and vegetables. The coffee stands had lines of shoppers and Amy Harper and Tom Baker stood in a line at the busy beverage shop along Shed Four. Harper held a small hand basket with vegetables sticking out of the top as Tom placed their order. "Honey, would you like a donut?"

Amy looked a little surprised, "No, just the coffee, sweetie." She smiled back at him as he placed their order.

Tom returned with two cups of the special roast and handed her a cup, "Let me carry the basket." She handed it to him and they strolled down the right side of the pavement looking at the displays of fruits stacked high along the path. "How about sweet corn to go with that roast you're making?"

Harper almost laughed out loud, she hadn't cooked a thing in months, let alone a roast. "Maybe, if you're planning on making it." They walked toward the next Shed that had displays of flowers and shrubs along with vegetables. Harper elbowed Tom when she spotted Askew wheeling two crates of lettuce to a stall. She hoped to signal that they'd have him covered.

Tom Baker quietly asked, "How did Askew get placed in here so quick."

"The DEA had two men working here, they've been undercover on another case and we could use them to help us." It was all making sense now to Baker; the Eastern Market was under surveillance for possible drug running and with the information about Oscar White being involved in the murder of Andy Jones, this was the center of their investigation. Harper continued, "Tom, if we could break this thing open it would mean a lot to me. I know Andy's mom would appreciate the news that we found who killed Andy."

Baker nodded, "I'll do anything necessary to help solve this case."

They walked closer to where Askew unloaded crates. Baker asked the vendor standing next to the stall that Askew was working in, "Hey, can you tell me where I can find raspberries?" The vendor shrugged his shoulders.

Askew still stacking the crates pointed down the aisle and said, "Mister, I just unloaded some in the stalls along Shed Four, I can show you." Askew wheeled his cart toward where Baker and Harper stood. While still pointing down the walkway he quietly said, "Something's going down, not sure what but I was told to come to White's office when I'm done." The two thanked Askew for his help and walked back toward Shed four.

Harper and Baker walked all the way to the next Shed before saying anything. "Tom, I'm going to call this in to Agent Downey. Maybe one of his undercover guys knows a little more."

# CHAPTER TWENTY-THREE

**The call into the DEA office from Detective Harper** confirmed what Agent Downey had heard from his team at the Eastern Market. They were ready to put their undercover agents into action. The new information that the DEA discovered confirmed that there was a connection between a known mob figure, Dominic Parma, to Oscar White. That might have changed their whole approach. Agent Downey passed new details to Harper, "This Parma fellow has a checkered past including serving eight years of a fifteen year sentence at the U.S. Supermax prison in Lewisburg, Pennsylvania. While he was incarcerated his reputation as an evil, narcissistic Neanderthal grew. Rumors swirled but nothing was every confirmed. Harper, we've got to see how he fits into this investigation. The new question is; who is Parma, and who is he working for?"

The DEA had Agent Hollis tailing Oscar White after the meeting with Parma, maybe this would reveal the connection they were looking for. Downey suggested that Detective Harper continue keeping a low profile but stay in place at the Market. Harper relayed the details to Detectives Spano and Baker. "We need to watch White from a distance and keep an eye on Askew. Something is obviously up, but we're not sure where this will go."

Spano continued communicating via cell but wanted to be more involved. "Harper, how about I track this Parma fellow?"

"Joe, the DEA has an agent doing that, maybe you can move your position to building Five. If White is meeting with Parma we know it might be critical to our investigation."

"Okay, I'll park along the right side of the Shed and will let you know if he's heading somewhere."

Harper filled Tom Baker in on her conversation with Spano, "The DEA is running a complete background check on Parma along with Lieutenant Jackson checking from the Chief's office." She continued, "Detective Spano is moving his position so we need to keep an eye on Askew and Oscar White." Things were progressing faster than either detective figured. Maybe they would get the break they needed to solve Andy Jones' murder and connect Oscar White to the DEA's suspected drug case. The two detectives continued their undercover shopping expedition along Shed Five with Baker carrying the basket in his left hand filled with fruits and vegetables.

As they stood along the far end of the walkway, Detective Harper spotted two men who seemed to be watching them. She tapped Baker on the shoulder, "Check out the two guys over there."

He turned slowly and saw exactly what she meant, suddenly to her surprise Tom slipped his right arm around her back and pulled her closer, she was sure he was about to kiss her. She momentarily stiffened, but Tom nestled his cheek next to hers. He whispered, "Either we make sure we're seen as a couple or this will fail."

Harper lifted her hand to the side of his face, gently touching him then kissed him on the cheek. "Then this should help."

An older couple walking near smiled, the lady turned to her husband, "Why can't you be more like that?" Harper overheard her and chuckled. The lady's husband had a quick comeback. "If you looked like her, I'd kiss you out here too!"

The two detectives looked over at the older couple who were now about five feet from them. Harper blushed, "Sorry, we were recently married."

The lady responded, "Enjoy it while you can honey, it doesn't last long." All four of them were now laughing.

The older lady extended her hand; "I'm Maggie, what's your name?"

"Harper, um, I mean Amy."

"That's a sweet name, where was the honeymoon?"

Harper turned to Tom Baker for help, he quickly jumped in, "I know it seems cliché, but we went on a cruise. Floated down the Danube River and visited Vienna," he reached over and fingered Harper's necklace, "We bought this charming item in the Central Market Hall."

"That's so romantic," she turned back to her husband, "Why can't you be more like this?"

Tom Baker reached out to shake the man's hand, "Love is grand."

The man shook his head, "I don't remember!" That brought out more laughs. The four stood talking and Harper thought this was the best cover that could have happened. She looked over and saw the two men that she suspected of watching them, turn and walk away. The two detectives were in good position near Oscar White's office and right where they needed to be.

Once the older couple walked away, Harper looked at Tom Baker, "That was very sweet."

He smiled, touching her hand, "You're easy to be sweet to."

***

One of the DEA Agents stationed at the Market followed Dominic Parma as he left the impromptu meeting with Oscar White. He watched Dominic as he headed into the building off of Russell Street. The sign indicated that it housed two trucking companies, a restaurant on the first floor and a storage company. La Russo Trucking and Carmen's Produce had large signs showing that they were on the second floor. The storage company's directions pointed to the back of the building, hopefully this narrowed their target. The information was called in to Agent Downey, "Stay in place," were his orders. Downey contacted Chief Mathews and both men agreed to meet just off of Gratiot across from the famous meat market that bordered the Eastern Market.

Mathews told Lieutenant Jackson, "I want you to search our data base for any connection of either business to Castellanos Trucking. If we could find a relationship of either to the now closed trucking company in St. Clair Shores, it would help our investigation." Jackson searched every owner of both companies with no results of a connection to Castellanos. Carmen's had been originally a door-to-door supplier of produce on the lower east side before moving into the Eastern Market. The owner, Gino Carmen, was over eighty and his two sons now ran the operation. La Russo's also was originally a door-to-door produce supplier to neighborhoods. Now they're primarily a restaurant vegetable and produce supplier. They were the larger of the two companies with close to fifty trucks operating throughout the city. Both businesses appeared to be a dead-end with no connection to Castellanos. What was Dominic doing at either one?

Agent Downey met Chief Mathews and both planned to discuss their combined operation and how to best use their undercover personnel. Downey was confident that his two men had an inside track to Oscar White. "Chief, my guy is one of the foremen for White that has your guy working on unloading trucks. If Askew sees something coming in that appears illegal, he's to tell my guy."

"Sounds like a good plan. My SIU Detectives are keeping an eye on Detective Askew and they said he's sure something is going down today."

Downey didn't like the Chief using his SIU Detectives but understood. Downey took a deep breath, "Chief, I thought we'd agree to use one of your detectives, not the whole team." He put his right hand on his hip and shifted his weight, showing his displeasure.

Mathews knew how the Bureau operated, regardless if it was the DEA or FBI. He stood his ground and moved closer to Downey, "We agreed to run this as a cooperative investigation; that means both departments using whatever was best to achieve our joint goals."

"Okay, Chief, but your people can't get in the way. Our agents are in control of the situation."

Mathews looked away for a second hoping to gain composure, after taking a breath he said, "Remember, Andy Jones was one of my officers, and if it means catching the guys that killed him, we'll be right there."

Downey didn't like that the Chief had his detectives involved but nodded. "Okay, Chief, but let's make sure everyone keeps us apprised of their movements."

"I agree; my detectives will keep us informed on their position." Both men appeared happy with their stand and Mathews added. "On another point, I'd like to know what details your team has discovered on the companies that Dominic Parma was seen going into?"

Downey was surprised that Mathews knew about Parma and his visit to Oscar White. How did he have that information? "I'm not sure what you mean?"

"You know exactly what I mean; we couldn't find any connection to the owners of either La Russo Trucking or Carmen

Produce to any underworld activity. There also isn't a connection to Castellanos Trucking in St. Clair Shores from the storage company in that building. Castellanos is the trucking company we closed last year with the Feds." Maybe it was just an illusion but Mathews seemed to be standing taller than before.

"Listen Chief, our investigation hasn't found anything yet, as long as I can, I'll share what we find with you." Downey was using his Federal Department card, something that both the DEA and FBI always seemed to push. Mathews didn't like this but it was clearly a standoff.

Mathews' cell phone rang; he answered and was nodding as he listened to the details. Mathews broke out in a smile, "Thanks Detective, make sure you keep an eye on him."

Downey listened in anticipation, once the Chief hung up, he asked, "So what's that about?"

"Sorry, I'll share what I can but right now it's too soon to tell." With that the Chief walked toward his car parked in front of the meat market on Gratiot. Agent Downey stood there with a puzzled look on his face.

# CHAPTER TWENTY-FOUR

**Detective Harper was pleased that she had some progress** to report to the Chief. She kept her team in place while things appeared to be changing. Detective Spano moved his position to be in front of the building that Dominic Parma went into hoping that he'd re-appear. The team back at headquarters was running background searches for Parma, La Russo Trucking and Carmen Produce, as well as, the storage company. Parma was the key to the search, nothing pointed to him being part of either business; however, great details were coming to light. Mindy relayed the information the team had so far, "Detective, here's what we found on Parma, he was born August 6, 1979 in Detroit; dropped out of school when he turned sixteen. He had been sent to juvenile detention twice, once at eleven for breaking and entering at a gas station and again for destruction of property two years later."

Harper listened but wished there was more, "Mindy, anything later?"

"Oh yeah, his checkered past became more illuminated when he was a murder suspect at seventeen. The charges were dropped when another individual confessed to the crime. The case against Parma wasn't very strong and the District Attorney took the easy path with the confession from the second suspect. He was sentenced to fifteen years for murder two years later at a Supermax prison but was out in eight years. He disappeared from records for a few years until 2006 when he was accused of a brutal beating of two men outside an adult nightclub. The charges were later dropped when the men recanted."

Harper recognized that it was obvious that Parma was a bad guy, but who did he work for.

Jimmy Askew was keeping his undercover assignment in place and completed emptying the last crates from the trucks in Shed Five. "Hey kid," Jimmy turned to see the dock foreman walking toward him. "Mr. White wants you to head to his office once you've stacked those crates." Askew hoped it was something that would help with their case. He nodded and pushed the cart to the open stall ahead. He needed to let Detective Harper know what was happening.

Detectives Harper and Baker continued their stroll through the Shed's while keeping an eye on where Askew was working. Detective Harper motioned to Baker, "I think Askew is headed toward the end of the stalls. Not sure where's he's going, we'd better move closer." He agreed. Both of them wanted to make sure they weren't singled out as looking suspicious so Tom Baker took Harper's hand and pulled her a little closer. She smiled at him, a look that he remembered from their time in the Academy. As they moved into the end of the area where Askew stacked crates, they could see him enter into an office door. "Baker, why don't you walk around the back of the building, I'll stay out here keeping an eye on the doorway." Tom Baker made his way through the stacks of vegetables and headed to the back of the building.

Oscar White sat behind the make-shift desk in the small office littered with handcarts and push brooms. "Mr. White, did you want to see me?"

White looked up at Askew, "Tell me your name again?"

"Jimmy, Jimmy Askew."

"Well, Jimmy, I like the way you work. I might have an extra job for you, interested?"

"Yes, sir, sure could use the money." Askew wanted to make sure he kept his cover intact.

"I'm going to need a couple guys to empty some of our trucks that are at another location." White knew that Dominic wanted him to bring two or three men with him but Oscar didn't trust that Dominic would actually send the guys back, especially after the events of their last venture together. If Dominic was going to kill these guys too, no sense losing some of his long time workers. "Okay kid, you're going to be gone for a while, any problem with that?"

"No, I ain't got anyone waiting for me, just got to keep my spot at the mission tonight."

Askew was just what White was looking for, another guy without any family. "Bring your gloves and we'll all head to my vehicle." Askew was concerned, did Harper or Spano see him go into the office? Where were they headed to? He couldn't ask questions, it would look suspicious, so he did as instructed. He followed the foreman who told him to come to Oscar's office and another man joined them outside. They all got into the older model Suburban that was parked along the side of the building. Jimmy Askew was seated on the right side of the back seat, looking out of the window, hoping he wasn't headed into danger.

\*\*\*

Downey took the call from his agent watching the building that Dominic Parma disappeared into, "Boss he's on the move!" Downey instructed his agent "Keep on his tail, looks like the guy is our new key suspect." His team still didn't have any more details on Dominic Parma than the local police did, but since Parma met with Oscar White, they figured that the two men were in this together.

Detective Spano was in position just across from the building where Parma was last seen, he watched Dominic getting in a vehicle. He immediately contacted Amy, "Harper, our guy is on the move."

"Thanks Joe, can you follow him? I've got a problem here, Askew got into a SUV with Oscar White and a couple of other guys. Baker and I are out of position."

"I'm on it, how about Askew?"

"Our car is too far away to get to it. I'm calling it in to the Chief." Harper and Baker were running to their vehicle that was parked across the Market. Once she hung up with Spano, she called Mathews. Out of breath, she said, "Chief, our guys are all on the move, Spano is following the other suspect, Dominic Parma, but we've lost Askew."

Mathews was concerned, he couldn't lose another detective in this operation, "How did that happen?"

"Askew headed into an office with Oscar White then they came out a back door and got into their vehicle. They've headed north on Russell."

"Okay Detective, I'll call Agent Downey, maybe they have a guy on it."

After the Chief hung up, Amy Harper feared that her team may have failed and Detective Askew was in danger. Tom Baker had made it to their vehicle as Harper rushed around to the driver's side of the car that was parked about a half mile away. Baker could see the look of panic on her face, "Harper, it's going to be okay, you know the DEA must have another team on this too." He was probably right but this was her assignment and she had to make sure Askew was safe.

She looked over at Baker as they pulled out of the parking spot, "We need to do something; I can't leave Askew like this."

Tom Baker wanted to help, "How about I make a call to the Third Precinct; the Captain there owes me one." Harper was willing to grab at any suggestions and she liked Baker's idea; she was extremely worried and couldn't come up with anything else.

"Okay, Tom, see what you can do."

Baker grabbed his phone, "Captain, it's Baker, I need a favor." Detective Harper leaned in closer hoping to hear something positive. "Captain, I lost a guy that we were tailing; he's driving a GMC Suburban." Tom gave the Captain the full details with plate numbers.

"How in the hell did you lose him?"

"Probably looking at a skirt." The Captain laughed, *same old Baker.*

"We got two cars in the area; I'll put an APB out for you. What number do you want me to call you on?"

"Here's my cell." Tom finished and Harper gave him a weird look.

"Looking at a skirt?"

He hung his head a little then glanced down at Harper's legs, "I didn't tell him what color the skirt was."

She smiled, "Thanks Tom."

"Harper, I promise, we'll find him."

Detective Harper was glad that the Captain assigned Baker to her team; *maybe she's been wrong about him.*

\*\*\*

The DEA Agent that was assigned to follow Dominic Parma

now stayed a few vehicles back while Parma drove in the left lane going east on Gratiot. He was driving a little over the speed limit in a new black Lincoln MKZ. Once he passed the junction of Gratiot and East Warren, a grey Suburban merged onto Gratiot and Dominic was seen motioning to the driver of the grey vehicle. The two vehicles fell into line and continued heading east. The Agent following called the information in to Agent Downey. Once the DEA had the news, Downey called Chief Mathews; "We spotted your grey Suburban. It's heading east on Gratiot, traveling behind our new suspect, Dominic Parma, whose driving a black Lincoln MKZ."

Detective Harper was thrilled when she got the call from the Chief. "Thanks boss, Baker and I will head that way." Once she was off the phone she turned to Baker. "The DEA spotted our guys. Guess you can call your Captain at the Third Precinct and thank him but we'll be back on it."

"Sure, I'll let them know."

She shifted in the driver's seat and looked over at Baker, "Make sure you thank him for me. You might want to tell him that the skirt is on the case too." She had a big smile on her face as they drove down Gratiot from the Eastern Market.

# CHAPTER TWENTY-FIVE

**The Detroit Medical Center was still buzzing with** personnel concerned that a killer was still on the loose in the hospital. Security was at heightened alert and the officers guarding Detective Frederickson stopped everyone that came anywhere near his room. Nancy Frederickson was concerned but didn't want to show that to her husband. The detective wasn't thrilled with all the security, "Hey guys, what's the possibility of you giving us some private time?"

Looking at each other, "Sorry, Detective, the Chief ordered us to stay in here."

Nancy tapped his shoulder, "Better to be safe honey, at least until they have the results from the Medical Examiner on the guy's death down the hall." He nodded but deep down wanted them out of his room.

The two officers decided to make a call to their Captain. Once they did one of them offered the Fredericksons an option, "The Captain said we can give you some privacy but you have to agree that you'll do whatever you need to but remember we'll be standing outside and might need to come back in. How about we give you five minutes."

Frederickson looked at his wife and they both started laughing, "It's not like that guys, we'd just like to talk without you hanging around." Now they were all chuckling. "Besides that, I'm not going to need five minutes, two or three would do." The laughter was contagious, all four were laughing; it was nice to see them relax after the events of the past day. The officers standing guard outside pushed the door opened, "Everything okay in here?" one of them asked.

"Yeah, everything's fine," the four of them were still smiling, causing the guards outside to wonder *what was this all about*. A doctor approached and the officer outside stopped him, checked his credential and the hospital roster making sure he belonged. He was the Chief of Surgery. The doctor entered the room and was surprised to see everyone seemingly laughing about something.

"I'm glad that you're all doing well."

"Thanks doc," Frederickson said. "Just trying to keep it light. Hope you have some information for us."

Doctor Guzzardo looked back at the officers; "Can we have some privacy?" the officers along with Nancy chuckled which the doctor seemed puzzled about.

"Okay doc, but we'd like to keep the outside door ajar." The officers moved out of the room with one of them monitoring the action inside. They didn't want to eavesdrop but couldn't totally remove themselves without keeping tabs on their protection duty.

Doctor Guzzardo had a stern look as he turned toward the couple. "Detective Frederickson, I've gone over your chart with our team and we're still concerned about the damage to your sternum."

Nancy leaned forward in her chair, "I thought they said it would heal in a few weeks."

"Oh it should heal normally but with what this shows we'll need to get more X-rays to make sure." He continued, "Checking the ones we took in the ER showed that the sternal fracture may be more severe than originally thought. I'd like to do another CT and maybe MRI to make sure that you don't have damage to your vital organs."

Nancy was concerned, "What exactly do you mean?"

"We have to check your heart, lungs and local blood vessels again. That's what we wanted to do when you were brought back upstairs yesterday. We need these examinations to rule out further treatment."

"If you find other issues, where do we go to next, Doctor?"

"Most likely we continue with bed rest, but if we find severe sternal fractures, you can have bone displacement that will require surgical intervention."

This was news that neither Nancy nor the Detective expected. Frederickson took a breath, "We'll do what you need, Doctor. I'd like to get back on track as soon as possible."

"I'll get our team to schedule the procedure. Guess we'll have to tell the officers outside so they can be prepared to adjust their schedule." Nancy wanted to express a deeper concern but decided that it might not be in her husband's best interest.

***

The DEA agent, Hollis, following Dominic Parma now had two vehicles to keep track of. Detectives Harper and Baker soon joined the parade, and radioed the details to the agent. The black Lincoln moved into the right lane and signaled that he was entering the east entrance of Interstate 94, the grey Suburban followed. Both the agent and Detective Harper's vehicles kept pace, a few vehicles behind the suspects. Detective Spano, who was following Dominic Parma from the Eastern Market, was also in on the chase. All five vehicles were heading east on I-94 with the destination unknown.

Harper contacted the Chief, "Sir, we're tailing the suspects and have an eye on the vehicle that Askew's riding in."

"Detective, I think we need to get a few more cars involved!"

Harper didn't pretend to tell the Chief how to run the case but suggested, "Chief, too many cars will tip the suspects off. We've already got the DEA, Spano and us following. They're possibly headed to the St. Clair Shores area. Maybe informing their department that we'll be passing through or involved in action there might be the best option."

"You're right, Detective. Keep me in the loop and I'll contact both the Shores and Grosse Pointe Chiefs."

Detective Baker looked over at Harper as she maneuvered their vehicle behind the grey Suburban. "Harper, where do you think they're going to?"

"Not sure but I'm calling Spano, he's in that unmarked vehicle right behind us." She filled Baker in about the Castellanos Trucking case. "Tom, last year we investigated a situation that involved a trucking company in the Shores. This might be the tie-in we've been looking for."

Baker was proud to be involved with the SIU team. This was the kind of action he joined the force for. "Harper, just tell me what part you need me to play."

She glanced over at him, "Tom, you're doing just great. Glad you're here." The chase continued along I-94 with the three cars in pursuit trying to stay out of the suspects' view. The Lincoln moved into the right lane just past Eight Mile Road. The grey Suburban followed and signaled that they were getting off at the Twelve Mile Road exit. Harper mumbled something to herself and Baker asked, "What's that you're saying?"

"The trucking company I told you about, it's just a little past here; Christ, Tom, could all this be connected to our case from last year?"

He looked over at her, "You've got a good chance that you're right."

Keeping an eye on the convoy of vehicles ahead of her, Detective Harper went over the events again. "Tom, one of our suspects was the owner of Castellanos Trucking. When the FBI and I went to check it out, he never showed up, in fact we've never found him."

"What did you think he was involved in?"

"Drugs, Castellanos was tied in with the group that ran drugs across the Detroit River from Canada."

"You got the head guys, didn't you?"

"Yeah, the owner of a Greektown restaurant and members of the Mexican Cartel were all caught but we never found Castellanos. Kind of funny, but one of his drivers was suspected of driving a garbage truck that killed Detective Forsythe."

Baker was putting it together, "And now we figure that a garbage truck is responsible for ramming Detective Frederickson." He looked back at Harper, "Could this Castellanos guy still be around?"

Harper hadn't thought that was possible, they always figured he was dead. "I'm not sure, Tom, but if they head off to Twelve Mile and Little Mack, that's the area that the trucking company I told you about is located."

The vehicles they were following turned right onto Twelve Mile. Traffic was fairly heavy so when the DEA Agent and Spano followed, it didn't look suspicious. Harper got caught by the light that turned red. She watched the cars that made the turn and knew Spano would keep her apprised of their location. Harper made the turn as traffic cleared and she contacted Detective Spano.

His voice was raspy, he rapidly spoke, "Harper, if they keep going in this direction, I think they're heading toward Castellanos' lot!"

"That's just what I was telling Baker. Doesn't the FBI have that place locked up? Joe, what's wrong with your voice?"

"Not sure, maybe I'm catching something. Anyway, when I asked the Chief yesterday about the trucking lot, he said it was under control of the FBI, so should be no worry there."

Harper wasn't sure but it was kind of eerie that they were heading in the same direction of Castellanos Trucking. Spano gave her his location and she quickly caught up. The black Lincoln was still in the lead as the grey Suburban followed. Detective Spano and the DEA agent kept switching places so that the suspects wouldn't see the same cars following. Harper and Baker stayed back a few car lengths, hoping this was soon coming to an end.

Agent Downey wanted to be in charge of the case and with this new development he really wished his team was the only one following the suspects. He paced his office and decided to contact his lead agent that was behind the two vehicles. "Hollis, what's the situation out there?"

"Boss, once the two vehicles met just east of downtown they appear to be on a mission. They've got a destination, just don't know where."

"Keep me in the loop."

"Will do, boss." Just then the Lincoln made a shape turn onto Little Mack and then to the right into what looked like an abandoned warehouse. The front of the building had three large bay doors and may have been used for shipping of some sort. "Boss wait, they're stopping." He watched both vehicles pull into the lot just off of Twelve Mile and Little Mack.

Downey yelled, "Hollis, where are you?"

"Greenlawn Street, just off of Twelve Mile Road. Both vehicles pulled into the warehouse lot."

Downey immediately instructed him, "Keep back, I don't want you or those cops that are following tipping your hand yet. I'm sending backup right now. Just keep an eye on the situation. This is just a stake-out for now."

Detectives Spano and Harper followed Agent Hollis' vehicle and all three drove past the warehouse. Harper pulled her vehicle around the corner and Spano followed her. "Joe, Detective Baker and I are walking back down to Greenlawn. You try to park near here and call it in to the Chief."

"Harper, don't do anything yet, let's wait for orders from the Chief."

"I'll wait, but I also want to keep an eye on Askew, I'm responsible for his safety."

Spano understood what she meant. "Okay, but be careful."

She started walking down the street and Agent Hollis jumped out of his vehicle, he was frantically waving at her, "Detective, stay in place."

She looked over at him; "I gotta get a better handle on this thing, Hollis." She stood with hands on her hips, aggravated but decided to wait. She yelled back, "I'll give it ten minutes Hollis, then I'm heading over there."

He didn't know what to do but hoped that things didn't get out of control.

# CHAPTER TWENTY-SIX

**Detective Harper wasn't pleased that the Chief ordered her** and Baker to retreat to their original position. She paced along Greenlawn and Baker tried to calm her down to no avail. "Come on, Harper, the Chief said he'd be here in a few minutes." She knew he was right but Askew was her responsibility. Joe Spano had pulled into the parking lot of the party store just down the street near the corner of Little Mack and Twelve Mile. He had a clear view of the warehouse from his position. The old building was large with three bay doors in front and a small passenger door to the far left side. Agent Hollis jotted down the information as he joined Spano at the party store. He pulled into the parking lot and decided to park next to Spano's vehicle. His boss was sending back-up, and Hollis shared that information along to Spano.

Detective Harper was impatient; she paced along the street, "What are they doing in there?" The team that followed the suspects had been in place for fifteen minutes. Because Oscar White had a couple other men with him made Harper feel a little better. Hopefully, one of them was the DEA undercover agent. Baker wanted to offer a suggestion but he didn't have anything to add. They kept their vigil, staking out the warehouse when a black Suburban pulled down the street and turned into the warehouse lot. Everyone watching the action was alerted that this could be another suspect in their case. Detective Harper could see the vehicle pulling in but didn't see who was in the vehicle. Calling Spano, "Joe, what's going on? Who's in that Suburban?"

"Harper, take it easy, I'm on it. Appears that one guy is getting out. Let me see if I can get a photo with my phone." The party store was at least one hundred yards from the warehouse and Spano's I phone six snapped off a dozen photos of the tall, dark complected man that climbed out of the vehicle. "Harper, I got a couple photos, not too good but maybe the lab can clean it up. I'm sending it to headquarters."

"Good job, Joe. I'm going to head to your location; waiting

down the street has me out of position in case we need to take action." Spano knew there was no stopping her, and she was right about being too far away. If something went down it would take her and Baker too long to join the fray. While he watched for Harper and Baker, another vehicle pulled down the street, two men piled out. The DEA agent smiled, "Guess Downey thought I needed help." The men walked back toward the party store, and nodded to Hollis. "Save the day, you're here to help." The sarcastic remark wasn't lost on the new arrivals. Agent Hollis from the DEA introduced Detective Spano to the arriving agents.

"Hollis, Downey's on the way. He's hoping this could be the big break we've been looking for in our case."

Spano was concerned that too many of them gathered across the street from the warehouse would tip off the men inside. "Guys, I think we're making a strategic mistake. If any of our suspects look across they're going to see us watching them."

Agent Hollis knew he was right, "Detective Spano is on to something guys. Let's spread out," Hollis looked across at the warehouse lot, pointing to a spot to the Agents that just arrived, "How about you two moving across to that building." It was next to the warehouse but closer to the street and would offer solid cover for them. They'd also be in better position if they needed to react to action inside.

While the DEA agents were moving into position, Detective Spano saw Harper make her way along with Tom Baker to the west side of the warehouse. They were now camped out into the brush that had grown out of control on the empty looking building. Spano wasn't sure if this was brilliant or a strategic bad move. Just then his cell vibrated in his right hand, it was Candice in the lab.

"Detective Spano, I got identification on your guy from the photos you sent."

He was shocked; he had sent them just minutes ago. "Candice, you sure?"

"Yeah, I'm sure, didn't even have to run it through facial recognition, the guy's on the front page of today's Free Press."

Spano was stunned when she said that, "On the front page, who in the hell is it?"

"Joe, its State Representative Matt Cusmano! He represents the district that encompasses St. Clair Shores."

Spano was holding the phone in his right hand and looked over at Agent Hollis. He questioned Candice one more time, "Why's he on the front page?"

"The article was an interview on the plans Cusmano hopes that the State Legislators will adopt for road improvements along Gratiot and the Eastern Market area."

Spano thought this was way too easy, "Thanks Candice." He looked back at the party store. "Hollis, I've got to grab something from inside." Agent Hollis wondered what could he be talking about. Spano disappeared into the store and quickly came out holding today's newspaper. Stuffing most of the paper in the trash can outside; he held the front section and was comparing something in the paper to his cell phone. "Son-of-a Bitch, it's him!"

Agent Hollis moved next to Spano, "What are you talking about?"

Spano showed him the front page, "This is our guy that just pulled up to the warehouse; he's the local State Representative." Both men stood, puzzled with this new development.

Detective Harper saw Spano holding a newspaper, *what was he doing?* She called him, "What's going on?"

"Harper, the guy that just joined our suspects, he's a State Representative, Matt Cusmano. Candice told me he's on today's front page."

Now she too was puzzled, "He's a State Rep, Spano you're sure?"

"Yeah, I better call this into the Chief."

*** 

The Chief of Thoracic Surgery, Doctor Guzzardo, walked down the hallway on the second floor of the DMC. He made his way toward Detective Frederickson's room. Like everyone, he was stopped and checked out by the security team. "Sorry, Doctor but we're just following orders."

"I understand." Once he was cleared he knocked on the door and one of the officers inside opened it. The security team wasn't taking any chances and everyone was checked. He was escorted in and saw Frederickson's wife sitting next to him, he made his way to the bedside. "Detective, I'm Doctor Guzzardo; I'm not sure if you remember me but I was the one who examined you in the Emergency Room a couple of days ago."

Frederickson nodded, "I think I remember; Doctor, this is my wife, Nancy. What do you have for us, doc?" It was becoming obviously painful to his wife that her husband was frustrated being relegated to lying in bed.

Doctor Guzzardo laid down a folder on the edge of the bed, "Detective, first thing is, you're sitting up too high." He took the controls and lowered the head position of the bed about four inches. "You're going to need to be totally flat for at least the next four weeks."

Frederickson looked back at Nancy, then asked, "They told me that I'd need to be on my back but no one said that I needed to be totally flat in bed. I already feel like a turtle lying here."

The doctor reached for the folder, "Detective and Mrs. Frederickson, I've brought these X-rays from the series we've run downstairs and I've taken a second look with our medical staff. I want to show you both our area of concern." He moved toward the wall on the opposite side of the room. "Nancy, you'll be able to see this pretty good; Detective, I don't know if you can see these so you'll have to listen as I show Nancy what we're talking about. I promise I'll bring you a photo to see once I show your wife the X-rays."

Nancy Frederickson moved closer to the lighted panel as the doctor placed the first X-ray on the screen. She turned back to Don, "I'll be your eyes, honey." He wasn't happy, but did as they said.

Doctor Guzzardo pointed to the center of the first X-ray. "Folks, we knew that his sternal fracture was most likely caused by the seatbelt or steering wheel. Even though his vehicle had an air bag, the blunt force of the crash was what caused you, Detective, to be thrust forward into the dash, not to mention the rollover when you went over the center guard rail."

None of this was new information and Nancy wondered why he re-iterated these details. "Doctor, is there something else you're not telling us?"

"It's not that we didn't tell you this, we didn't see it until we took another series of X-rays; that's what I wanted to show you. I brought the X-rays to point it out." He turned back to the detective, "Mr. Frederickson, please continue to lay flat, I'll bring a photo to show you what we're looking at." Both Nancy and her husband became more concerned. "Mrs. Frederickson, if you look closer you'll see a dark line, this goes across the corpus sternal bone." He pointed to the spot that Nancy was studying. "That's where the bone suffered the impact and the dark line is the crack. The good news is, it's not separated. The bad news is that a piece of the bone appears to be chipped. That's the problem; where's that piece of bone? We're concerned that the bone chip could lodge somewhere in his frame and cause additional problems."

Frederickson was still lying flat in the bed but called out, "Bottom line, what's the bad news, doc?"

"Detective, you could suffer a possible spinal column injury. This could be made worse with any movement." The Doctor brought a photo over to him, "You can see in this photo that I highlighted from the second round of pictures that it shows soft tissue swelling and bruising on your spine." Turning toward the couple, "Detective, I'm worried about two things, pulmonary contusion or possible cardiac injuries. We need to run more tests. I plan to talk to your security team and have a portable X-ray machine brought up here."

The officer listening was also concerned and he jumped in, "Sorry, Doc, but we'll have to call that in before you can bring anything in here."

"Okay, but you better do it now because we must get more information to insure Mr. Frederickson isn't in any other danger." The officer quickly grabbed his cell phone while the doctor stood with arms crossed, and waiting.

# CHAPTER TWENTY-SEVEN

**Chief Mathews was stunned when Detective Spano gave** him the news from the warehouse. He couldn't believe that State Representative Matt Cusmano was seen just joining their suspects. The Chief remembered that he had met Cusmano just a few months ago when they both attended an event that honored local students for their achievements. The Representative had made a positive impression on the Chief. This had to be a mistake, "Spano, you're sure that it's Cusmano?"

"Chief, I was able to take close to a dozen photos with my cell and sent them to the lab. Candice called me in minutes and confirmed that it's the Representative."

While Spano continued talking, Mathews looked down at his desk, there it was; Matt Cusmano right there on the front page of today's Free Press. "Detective, I'm holding the cover of today's paper, he's on the front page. Send me one of those photos you took."

"I'm sending the photo right now, sir. I know he's on the front page, in fact that's what Candice from the lab told me. I grabbed the paper from the party store where we're camped out and compared it to the photos in my phone. It's him, sir. I'm sure. I've sent you the best photo I have."

"Okay Detective, let me check it." Mathews hung up. He knew this new information will have everyone in the DEA and Detroit Police Department wondering where this investigation would now turn. Once Mathews reviewed the text with the photo he called Spano right back, "Detective, I'm heading out there right now." With that Mathews hung up again and yelled to Lieutenant Jackson, "Come on, we need to head to St. Clair Shores."

Jackson jumped up and called the Chief's security team. "Tim, tell them they need to be ready immediately; the Chief's on his way downstairs to the garage." Jackson trotted behind the Chief catching up, "Chief, what's going on?"

Mathews filled her in on the information that Detective Spano had given him as his driver made their way across I-94 to Twelve Mile Road. There was a series of warehouses along the Little Mack and Twelve Mile area, some of them had been abandoned since the recession of 2008. The Chief contacted Agent Downey to pass this new information along. "Thanks Chief, but Agent Hollis called me soon after he and your Detective had identified the State Rep. I'm not sure what this is all about but my team is running down more details on Matt Cusmano. Chief, I'm close to the warehouse, where are you?"

"I'm with Lieutenant Jackson and we just got off of I-94 and Twelve Mile Road. We'll be there in minutes."

"Okay, meet you there." Downey contacted Agent Hollis to see if there was any change in the situation.

"Sir, no one has left the building and I have our two agents stationed along the right side of the warehouse. There's only one vehicle parked in front, near the largest bay door. Detectives Harper and Baker are also along the other side of the building. Spano and I are still positioned down the street. If the State Representative comes out, do you want us to stop him?"

Downey hadn't thought about that, "Hollis, that's a good point, if he comes out alone I want you to hold him. Make sure you don't alert those others inside. I'd like to have us and the local cops raid the warehouse together."

"Got it, sir."

Chief Mathews contacted the St. Clair Shores Police Chief, "Chief, we've got a possible problem in your area and I'd like you to be involved." He detailed everything to him, "Chief Glass, this could have connections to a murder of an undercover police officer." Mathews didn't want this to get out of control but also wanted to make sure they didn't have a situation in the area that belonged to St. Clair Shores Police.

\*\*\*

Detective Harper turned to Tom Baker, "I've got to get the rest of our team checking into the possible connection of the State Representative to either Castellanos or La Russo Trucking downtown. This might be the missing piece of the puzzle."

Baker knew she was right, "Seems to make sense, they hadn't found any links in the past but maybe Cusmano is the key. It might all be linked back to him. If this guy's involved who knows where it might lead. Harper, you gotta be careful here, if we've got a corrupt State Rep., it could involve more people in the Legislature."

She knew he was right. Not too long ago there was a romantic involvement between two people in the State House that caused quite an investigation. "One thing I know for sure Tom, we've got the Chief and DEA behind our investigation." Detective Harper had the rest of her team working on tracing the State Representative and any possible connection to any of the others involved in their case. Questions now arose about him and why would he be at the warehouse in St. Clair Shores?

The stakeout at the abandoned warehouse was in the third hour and Cusmano had been in there for close to an hour and half. This all made Amy Harper wonder, *what is he doing here? Why did he get personally involved?* She asked Baker, "Tom, if you were involved in some kind of underworld activity, and a public figure, why expose yourself by showing up in broad daylight to the scene of a possible crime?"

"Good point, you wouldn't." They were both puzzled as they waited for further directions from the Chief or Agent Downey. While Tom finished his statement, two black Chevrolet Tahoes pulled down Little Mack after turning off Twelve Mile. "Looks like the guys in charge of this thing have arrived." Two vehicles pulled past the small strip center and party store across from the warehouse where Hollis and Spano were positioned.

Harper wanted to cross the street but Baker suggested, "Spano has a handle on this, let him update them."

She knew that was a good idea, "Yeah, you're right; besides we need to stay where we're located." Harper had another new appreciation for Tom Baker, not only did he handle the situation in the Eastern Market when she thought men were checking them out, but now he offered solid detective insight. Her cell vibrated,

"Harper here."

"Detective, Spano filled us in on the situation and we see your location as well as that of the two DEA agents on the other side of the building. Agent Downey and I feel we need to make a strategic decision soon. Either we wait for one or more of the suspects to leave the building or we all descend on them in full force. Detective, for now, keep your position."

She hung up and turned to Baker, "The Chief and Downey are deciding how to approach." Baker not only understood but was glad to be involved in a high level operation.

# CHAPTER TWENTY-EIGHT

**Dominic Parma had been pacing in the warehouse as the** three men stacked the final boxes in the back of the ice cream trucks. Oscar White thought using the ice cream trucks was a good cover to move the product. He walked over to where Parma stood; the man had his right arm on his hip and pointing toward White. "This is taking too long, get those guys moving faster."

"We're almost done; I don't need you to tell me how to load trucks." Oscar White had about enough of Parma busting his balls, he quickly turned away talking to himself. The guys loading the trucks watched them, wondering what was going on. Oscar coaxed his team along, "Come on, men, just one more pallet and were done." White planned on telling Vinnie when he got back that he was done doing anything with Dominic involved in the future, there was no pleasing him.

Matt Cusmano was standing in the small office at the end of the warehouse on the phone. He was talking to Vinnie, "Yes Uncle, they've got everything in the three ice cream trucks just like you suggested. I agree that's a great cover to move the product out of here." Matt didn't want to be here but had to do what his uncle wanted. Once he got off the phone he looked out to see the men closing the back of the last truck. He left the office and moved to where White was standing with his men. "Oscar, what's the plan?"

"We're going to move the product out of here to a different location just outside of Port Huron. Guess your Uncle is concerned about a couple of guys that came up to his office yesterday and were asking questions. Gloria sent them on their way but he's none the less worried."

Matt peeked back at Dominic who had been staring out of the small bank of windows on the north side of the warehouse. "That guy worries me."

"Tell me about it. He's a pain in the ass; the guy has a short trigger. He's going to get someone killed."

Matt nodded, "I guess Mario either wouldn't or couldn't make it so Vinnie asked me to oversee this. He, too, must be concerned about Dominic. What's this I heard about his recent threats at the DMC?"

Oscar turned to see where Dominic was before he answered, "Matt, I heard he told Mario that he'd blow the hospital up if needed when they were looking for Ben."

Matt was shaking his head, "You gotta be kidding me."

Oscar rolled his eyes, "Told you, he's nuts."

Matt looked back over at Dominic who was still looking out the windows, "So you think he's totally losing control."

"I'm not sure but this is the last time I'm doing anything with him. I've got to get these trucks moving and then we're out of here."

"Are your guys also moving the trucks?"

"Yeah, they're a couple of my most trusted men. We're taking the trucks from here, one at a time. It will be getting dark soon and that offers great cover for this."

Matt watched the guys who were completing the job and locking the doors, "What's the deal with that one guy," pointing toward Askew. "I've been watching him, he seems to be paying at lot of attention to everything going on."

Oscar turned back to the men and saw what Matt meant. Askew was standing on the rear bumper of one of the trucks, watching the other men locking the doors. "He's new but my foreman who's been with me for a while, vouched for him. I've been watching him, he's a hard worker, but I'll keep an eye on him." White called to his men, "Let's gather around." While they took off their gloves and headed toward him, Dominic walked over to Matt.

"You know we didn't need your help."

"I'm not here because I wanted to be, just doing what Vinnie asked." He studied the frown on Dominic's face. "What's wrong?"

"I don't like this. The same two cars have been parked down the street at that party store."

Cusmano took a step back, "Show me."

Dominic moved back to the bank of small windows where he had been standing earlier, "Over there," pointing to the small strip center on Little Mack where a party store and pizza place occupied the far end.

As Matt checked it out, he turned back to Dominic, "Did you tell Oscar?"

"That dumb shit doesn't listen to anything I have to say. I told him this was taking too long."

"Yeah, but did you point out the suspicious cars across the street?"

"No, I started to when he told me not to tell him how to do their job."

Matt was about to panic, "Oscar," He was heading over to where White was giving his men their final instruction. "Oscar, I need to go over something with you, it's important."

*\*\*\**

Agent Downey stood alongside of Chief Mathews, "Chief, we need to change our positions."

Mathews looked over at the head DEA agent wondering what he was thinking. "Chief, I've got a straight view to the front of the warehouse. If I can see it that clear, anyone inside can see us too." Mathews looked over at the building and recognized exactly what Downey meant.

"Detective, I think we've got to move down the street."

Spano watched Mathews who started walking down the path toward the pizza place. He followed his boss as Lieutenant Jackson walked next to the Chief. Agent Downey got into a car with Hollis and they pulled out of the lot. Spano caught up to the Chief, "Detective, I think you need to also move your car, once you've parked it down the street head back here. We can take position in either the pizza place or party store."

The officers and agents moved from their location across from the warehouse and Detective Spano contacted Harper to let her know what they were planning. It made sense to both of them. "Joe, did the Chief or Downey give you any indication of our next move?"

"No but I'm thinking the DEA is running this and we're just frosting on the cake."

\*\*\*

Matt Cusmano moved along the bank of windows in front of the warehouse where Dominic said he saw two suspicious vehicles parked for too long. Matt watched one of the vehicles that Dom pointed out earlier now pulling out of the lot. It headed down the street out of view, then a heavy set man came out of the pizza place carrying a couple boxes. He got into the other vehicle with a lady. "Dom, they must have been waiting for an order, they're going now with a couple pizzas."

Dominic was a few feet from him and kept staring out the window, "I still don't like it, what kind of pizza takes an hour to make?"

"Maybe they're in there eating first and ordered something to go but they're gone now. Let's not create a problem, Dominic." Matt thought maybe the man was paranoid but then again he knew he couldn't be caught up in anything like this. "Dominic, looks like we're about done here, do you know if there's a back door or another way out?"

"Yeah, but we can't get the trucks out of it. There's a small door along the back, I think that it hasn't been opened for over a year. Probably brush has grown over the exit."

"I'm not thinking about the trucks; maybe if we send the trucks out of the front overhead doors, you and I can sneak out the back. If someone is watching they'd be interested in the trucks and what we're moving. I can't get seen in here." Matt knew that Dominic wouldn't be too keen on him sliding out of the back alone but might be okay if he's included.

Dom seemed to be looking at the back of the building, "I like that idea, one thing though; we don't have a car or transportation from there."

Matt headed toward the back door. Oscar saw him going into the back of the warehouse; he called out, "What's going on?"

Looking back, he didn't want to alert Oscar to what he was thinking, "Just checking out our option." Once he got to the door, he saw a rusted bolt at both the top and bottom of the metal door. "Dom; how long since anyone came in or out of this?"

Dominic followed him, "Been at least a year, maybe two, we used to do mechanical work here on our trucks before Vinnie bought that place downtown."

Matt worked on the bolt and struggled to slide the top pin across the bracket that held the bolt, as he did that it made a screeching sound. He bent down and tried to do the same thing on the bottom bolt, it was stuck. Kicking at it with his heel it still didn't move. "Dominic, see if you can find a hammer or anything to use."

Dominic headed back into the main part of the warehouse and Oscar approached, "What in the hell are you two up to?"

"Just looking at options, you got a job to do, go do it."

"You make me nervous, I know you're up to something, give it up."

Dominic not only didn't like Oscar but hated anyone telling him what to do; the blow to the side of Oscar's head was swift sending the man crashing to the pavement. Dominic stood straddling Oscar who was bleeding profusely from the side of his face, "Think you still need to know what's going on, dick head!"

The men that finished loading the last truck were standing near the action and saw what happened. Their concern grew that this job was falling apart. Askew knew that there was a team assigned to watch him and the DEA agent, and he figured by now they must be outside. He had to do something but wasn't sure if it would blow the pending action. He called out, "We can't be fighting each other. What's this about?"

Dominic sneered and took a step toward him but Matt was quick to jump into action, "You guys are right, just a personal thing, we're all okay and everything is fine." Dom turned back toward Oscar that lay bleeding on the floor. Matt tried to push between Dominic and where Oscar laid bleeding; "Dominic, you can't do this; it will blow the whole operation." Dominic shoved past Matt pushing into him as he headed back to the rear door. Matt helped Oscar up; he was wobbly but wanted revenge, "Not now, we'll settle this later, I promise." Oscar had a gash from his cheek to his forehead, "Let's take care of that nasty cut." Matt saw one of the men bringing a clean cloth and another of them had a first aid kit. "Where'd you get that?"

"From the glove box in one of the trucks." They worked on

stopping the bleeding. Askew wanted to see where Dominic headed to, he knew something must have gone wrong, but what? Watching from the corner of his eyes while putting a bandage on Oscar's cut, Askew could see Dominic working on a door in the back of the warehouse. He needed to get this information to the task force, but how?

# CHAPTER TWENTY-NINE

**The news from the doctor's at the DMC wasn't looking good;** Nancy Frederickson was holding her husband's hand as Doctor Guzzardo went over the diagnosis. "Detective, it clearly shows that you've suffered a pulmonary contusion. I'd like to send you downstairs for a second CT scan to determine the severity of the injury. You have bruising of the lungs and the potential of excessive blood accumulating in your lung tissues."

Frederickson was still calm and asked, "Okay doc, where do we go from here?"

"Like I said, we'll send you back downstairs for a CT scan to determine if it was caused by a rib fracture or that bone chip. We also have to check if you have damage to any capillaries."

Nancy was shaken with the news but wanted to keep a positive outlook, if not for her, but for her husband. "Doctor, what is the prognosis if you determine that Don has suffered one of these conditions?"

"One of the major conditions is that the excess fluid can potentially lead to inadequate oxygen levels. Also your husband could have suffered a tear or cut in his lung tissue."

The detective called out, "Hey guys, I'm still here, I can hear you."

Nancy looked over at her husband; she started to laugh when she saw the smile on his face, "Sorry, hon, just thinking ahead." Doctor Guzzardo also smiled; he thought they were obviously a great couple.

"The good news, Detective, is that we know what caused your problem, blunt trauma from the vehicle collision; that rules out many other problems. If it's a small contusion, it may have little or no lasting effects on your health as long as we know more about a possible bone chip."

Frederickson shifted in the bed, how he hated lying flat and now wanted to sit up to be more involved in this conversation, "If it's more serious, doctor?"

"Detective, no need to go there now. The good news is you don't have any other symptoms."

"Like what?"

"You're not coughing up blood, and once we get a look at the CT scan we can make solid plans for your recovery."

"Thanks, doctor," Nancy added while still holding her husband's hand. "When are you going to arrange the CT scan?"

"I'm headed downstairs right now and will get everything going; hopefully they'll come up here in the next few minutes and take you downstairs. I cleared it with your security team." Doctor Guzzardo stood at the side of the bed and put his hand on Frederickson's shoulder, "Detective you have the best possible team here taking care of you; we'll get you back on your feet real soon."

"Thanks, doc." Once he left the room Nancy looked over at her husband. He smiled, "Sweetie, I'm sure everything will be okay. We've been through many things worse than this." She knew he was right, they were still holding hands and the two officers that stood at the far end of the room watched the touching moment.

***

The situation along Little Mack and Twelve Mile was entering the third hour and both the DEA and Detroit Police were concerned at how long the men had been inside the warehouse. The St. Clair Shores Police Chief had arrived with two local officers and they were positioned about three-hundred yards down the street with Chief Mathews. Agent Downey filled the new arrivals in on the situation, "Chief, we wanted to bring your team into the action with it taking place in your area of responsibility. Chief Mathews and his detectives are also here in a supportive role."

The Shores Chief looked over at Mathews, "Guess we're here to get coffee and donuts for the DEA." Both of them laughed, knowing that every Federal Agency surmised that local cops were inferior to them. While the three men stood off to the side, Mathews' phone buzzed.

"Yes, Detective," He listened as Downey leaned in trying to hear what's happening. "Thanks, Harper." Mathews looked over at Downey who was just a few inches away by now. "My support team had an update." Mathews didn't add anything else.

"Shit, Chief, what the hell's going on?"

"Oh sorry, thought you must have already had the information." The St. Clair Shores Chief, Harmon Glass, liked what had just happened; he'd known Mathews for a while and appreciated what he just did. "That was Detective Harper; she and Baker are along the side of the warehouse and Baker said he's heard a lot of noise along the back of the building."

"What kind of noise?"

"Sounds like someone pounding on the back walls."

Downey was concerned, as to what was going on inside. He decided to contact his agents that were on the other side of the building. They confirmed the noise too. Turning toward Mathews, Downey suggested, "Do we know if there's an exit in the back of the building?"

"It's easy to find out," Mathews contacted Detective Harper, "I need you to check the back of the warehouse out for any rear exits." While the three men waited for an answer, Harper headed around the back of the building.

The brush was over three feet tall in many places and mosquitoes and bugs made her feel like she entered a jungle. Once she got to the far corner of the warehouse, she saw that the weeds and growth were even taller. Harper called her partner, "Tom, head back here." Following the path that Harper had made he got to the spot where she stood.

"Wow, how'd you get through that crap?"

"It wasn't easy, but look at that," pointing to the path ahead. He could see that everything along the back of the building was pressed up against the outer wall and much thicker than what he'd already pressed through. "You got anything to get through that?" He nodded his head; she knew they'd have to improvise.

Mathews and Downey waited to hear what the detectives discovered when the St. Clair Shores Chief, Glass, stated, "If either of you thought enough about where you're located, you'd have asked me for help. My team has access to the building plans for the warehouse. They're on the way down here right now."

Downey looked over at him, "Why didn't you tell us earlier?"

"Why didn't you ask?" Mathews knew that Glass didn't like being second fiddle but Downey had relegated him to third or worse. "Agent, whether you admit it or not, this is still in my jurisdiction."

Mathews knew how he felt, "That's great, Chief; I'll let my detectives know." He called Harper to give her the information.

Amy Harper was pleased that they didn't have to negotiate the terrain, "Glad you called Chief, Baker was about to cut his way through the brush with his Swiss Army Knife." Mathews laughed out loud.

"Okay Detective, keep your position, we can't let anyone of them escape out the back. We'll get some tools to cut through that mess." Mathews was pleased that his team was in place to stop anyone from sliding out of the warehouse.

Glass immediately jumped in, "Chief, I've got men closer than you can get your guys here, how about I call to get the tools we'll need."

"Good plan, Chief, we're running with your plan." Downey was the one now feeling like the third wheel.

\*\*\*

Matt Cusmano knew he had his hands full with both Dominic and Oscar at odds with each other and now Oscar would want revenge. Matt wanted out of this situation but was afraid that it was close to impossible. His best option might be to call his uncle. Once he made sure that Dominic spent his time with the back door and Oscar was being treated by his men, Matt tried calling, Vinnie's secretary answered the call, "Sorry, Matt, he's out."

Matt knew he needed help but didn't want to go against his Uncle's orders, "Any idea where I can get to him, maybe his cell."

"No, he didn't take it with him. Matt, he was meeting with a couple men in the office before he left. I thought he was worried about something but he didn't say anything to me."

Matt slid the cell phone back in his pocket. He saw Dominic wrestling with the bottom bolt on the metal door, "Any progress, Dom?"

"This SOB is rusted shut. Look around for any type of penetrating oil, maybe there's a can of WD40 or even brake fluid."

"Okay, I'm on it." He walked toward the center of the warehouse and was met by Jimmy Askew.

"What's going on?"

Matt was surprised, *who was this common laborer asking him what's going on.* "You need to take care of finishing locking the trucks and helping Oscar." Matt turned away and headed back to the bank of windows at the front of the warehouse. He didn't see any of the vehicles across the street that Dominic was concerned about. He thought about just heading to his car and getting out of there.

Just then a voice came from behind and startled him, "Anything out there?" Matt turned quickly, it was Dominic standing right behind him and he was gripping a metal bar. "I thought you were looking for something to help ease the rust."

Matt looked down at the metal bar that Dominic had his fingers wrapped around. He was breathing hard and Matt felt the tingling of nerves start creeping up his spine, "I looked at everything on the work bench and nothing was there to help so then I thought I'd check the action outside."

"So see anything?" Dominic was still gripping the metal bar and Matt didn't like the look in his eyes.

Matt stuttered, "No, no the parking lot across the street is clear, just another car came in and picked up a pizza," he stepped back and was almost up against the wall, "Dom, I'd feel a lot better if you put that bar down."

Dominic looked down at the chunk of metal and smiled, it was an evil smile, one that sent chills up and down Matt's spine. Dominic sneered, slapping the bar in his right hand, "Okay Senator, whatever you want."

\*\*\*

Nancy Frederickson sat at the edge of the large chair in her husband's room, waiting for him to return from the additional test that Doctor Guzzardo performed. She felt it seemed like hours since they had taken him downstairs. Two of the officers guarding him followed the hospital personnel while they wheeled the detective to the X-ray lab. Another set of officers remained outside the room; protecting his wife and making sure no one entered or rigged up something in there. Nancy heard a commotion outside and jumped up as the nurse pushed her husband's gurney into the room aided by one of the officers. She rushed to his side, "Honey, I'm so glad you're back, what did they tell you?"

The detective smiled at her, "Nancy, Doctor Guzzardo said he'd be up here once they've had time to review the pictures." She held his hand as the nurse who was helping, along with another orderly from the staff, pulled the sheet back making sure that they kept Frederickson lying flat on his back. She watched them pulling the sheets slowly and getting him into the bed which took a minute. Once he was positioned and the nurse ran her normal routine of blood pressure and temperature checks, everyone left the couple alone for a few minutes, even the officers assigned to him stepped out.

She leaned over the bed, kissing him on the forehead, "Don, are you okay?"

His answer was sarcastic, "Yeah, you know, I'm really fine now." Once he said that he wished he hadn't been so short with his wife, taking hold of her hand, he turned his head, "Nancy, you know, whatever the results I know I'll be okay, as long as I have you." It was a touching moment for the two of them, one of many that they've had since the terrible crash on the Interstate.

A knock was heard at the door and Doctor Guzzardo peeked in, "You both decent?"

Frederickson quickly called back, "Wait doc, I'm showing Nancy my dance moves," Nancy laughed, pleased that he hadn't lost his sense of humor.

"Well Detective, after reviewing your X-rays, it might take a few weeks, but I'm sure you'll be spinning on the dance floor soon." He was holding three X-rays in his right hand and smiling; a smile that both Nancy and Don took as a good sign.

# CHAPTER THIRTY

**Chief Glass spread the detailed building plans across the front** hood of a car while Mathews, Downey and Hollis peered over the diagram. "You can see from this blueprint that there's one steel door along the back wall, it looks to be ten feet from the north side of the building."

Agent Downey looked over at Chief Mathews, "Where did you say your two detectives were located?"

Mathews immediately pointed to the drawing, "Detective Harper's last call said they were at the north corner of the back of the warehouse. She and Detective Baker were waiting for further orders. One of the many problems is the brush back there is ten feet high."

Chief Glass, nodded, "That's a problem; we have sickles that can help cut through the brush but obviously we can't use any power equipment." He was looking down again at the blueprints; "Although this shows only one door in the back, that's kind of unusual."

Agent Downey had a puzzled look, He looked up at Glass, "Why?"

Glass was still looking at the drawings, "The Fire Department has a requirement that should have made the contractor put more exits in case of an emergency. With three bay doors and a small entrance door in front, plus one other exit in back does not meet standards. There should be at least another one along the other side."

Downey studied the blueprint; "You thinking this might not be the final plans?"

"It's the one on file; my people didn't find another set."

"Then we've got to go on what we have," Downey turned toward Chief Mathews, "Any suggestions?"

"Let me call Detective Harper." Mathews talked to his team and questioned the possibility of a second exit, "Harper, could there be another door along the side?"

"Chief, neither Baker nor I saw the existence of a side door, did the DEA agents on the other side check, there could be one there."

"Thanks, Detective," Mathews asked Downey, "See if your guys can check the other side of the warehouse, maybe there's an exit on that side." The Police Chief was in deep thought, *how did this surveillance of their murder suspect turn into a stakeout at a warehouse in St. Clair Shores? Who was Oscar White?* He turned toward Downey, "I'm not sure what's happened but our suspect is obviously now involved in something much bigger. Maybe the key to your drug trade case."

Downey agreed, "Chief, we've maybe underestimated him. I've got our team back at headquarters checking all of the suspects' pasts. We only know that Dominic Parma is a known thug and that White has been in prison in the past but nothing for years since."

Mathews was concerned that they may have put Detective Askew in a situation that may explode into something they weren't in control of. If Oscar White killed Andy Jones, maybe he's behind much more, but exactly what was uncertain.

***

Tension grew thick inside the warehouse as Dominic Parma still stood in front of Matt while gripping the metal bar. "Dominic, I'm not sure what you're thinking about right now, but I want you to put that down!" Pointing to the bar that Dominic's fingers were wrapped around.

"What, you worried, Senator?"

Matt was staring at him as the guys that had loaded the trucks noticed what was going on. "I'm not a Senator; you know that, we need to complete this assignment."

Jimmy Askew knew he had to do something, he was aware that one of the men in the crew had to be the DEA's undercover person, but which one? Yelling out, "Hey, we got Mr. White's bleeding taken care of, what are we supposed to do now?"

The interruption caused Dominic to turn his attention to the action behind him. He took a few steps toward Askew, "You guys need to lock the trucks up and get ready to move out." While he was doing that, Matt quickly moved from the front wall and away from Dominic. Askew was hoping that he could help control the situation without blowing his assignment. Whatever the issue; this all appeared to be falling apart and Askew knew when criminals start turning on each other, chaos ensued.

Matt was now standing close to where Oscar stood. He wanted to make sure he was okay, he leaned closer, whispering, "Dominic's totally out of control, we need to act; and act now!"

Oscar was looking back to where Dominic had moved to, hoping he didn't hear Matt. The trucks were all locked up and ready to go. Oscar whispered back to Matt; "I'm okay, what's the plan?"

"Oscar, Dominic thinks we're being watched but I don't see anyone out there now."

Dominic was impatient and on the brink of exploding. "So what's it going to be," he yelled out.

Oscar answered as he headed back to the trucks, "Okay, I'm going to send one of the trucks out and once they are down the road I'll have them report back to us. If someone is out there, we'll know right away."

Matt liked the plan but still wished he wasn't in the building. Matt knew the back door was rusted shut." *He couldn't be caught up in this or anything that looks criminal. He was thinking about finding a hiding spot once the first truck pulled out.*

Oscar didn't want to be involved either, and turned to whisper to a surprised Matt when he said, "You know I'm here for the same reason you're here. I owe Vinnie my allegiance and would do anything he asked. That doesn't include going to jail." Calling out to the men standing by the truck, he pointed to Askew. "We need you to take the first truck out. Call me once you're on your way making sure the coast is clear."

Dominic seemed to like that, "Good thinking," making a point to reiterate the message, "Make sure you call back right away if something goes wrong."

Askew wanted to make sure they continued to think he's just a common laborer, "Like what?"

"You stupid or something," Dominic had a scary look on his face, "You'd know if you have a problem, like maybe you're being followed or stopped for no reason."

Askew wished he could take a swing at the big man, "Okay, I got it, and I'm not stupid, just wanted to make sure I knew what you want." Askew turned toward Oscar, "Mr. White, where's my destination?"

Oscar handed Askew a small folded map with an address off of M-25 showing a building in Port Huron. "Here's the key to the building where you're to take it; once you get there make sure you lock the place back up. We'll be sending the second truck, then the third in half hour times behind you." While Askew looked at the map, Oscar put his hand on Jimmy's shoulder, "Remember kid, this is important, call me when you're down the street and check back in every half hour."

Askew appreciated Oscar's approach versus Dominic's, who was still staring at him. He would rather had stayed at the warehouse keeping tabs on the men inside when the foreman walked over, "Hey kid, just do what the boss asked. It will be okay." He winked at Askew, and walked back to the other trucks.

Jimmy Askew knew for sure that the DEA's undercover agent was White's foreman. "I'll be fine Mr. White. Which truck do you want me to take?"

Oscar looked over at Askew then back to Dominic, "The keys I gave you fit truck number five," he pointed to the larger ice cream truck at the far end of the stalls. "Once you pull out of here, turn left on Little Mack to Twelve Mile. You head back west on Twelve Mile to I-94 and take it all the way to the end. The warehouse is just off the road past the Blue Water Bridge on the right side, I highlighted it on the map."

Askew got into the truck and headed out of the opened bay door that Dominic pulled up. Once he turned onto Little Mack, Oscar, Dominic and Matt continued to stand by the bank of windows watching until he disappeared out of view. Oscar held his cell phone and watched the screen as if it would detonate any time. 'Ring, Ring,' everyone jumped. "Yeah?"

"Mr. White, no problems, I'm on Twelve Mile headed west, should be to I-94 in a few minutes."

"You see anything out of the ordinary?"

"No, not too much traffic considering a lot of work traffic still out here."

"Thanks kid". Oscar looked at his watch, it was just after six; it would be dusk in a couple of hours. "Jimmy call when you're on the Interstate." Oscar turned to the others who all had the same questioning look on their face, "It's all good; he's on Twelve Mile headed to the Interstate." He saw Dominic who seemed to punch the air around him with clenched fist and Matt looked relieved. Oscar turned back to the rest of the crew, "Okay guys, let's get truck number two on the road."

# CHAPTER THIRTY-ONE

**Agent Downey had been on his phone for a while and** Chief Mathews thought he had a look of surprise, one that could be a bad sign. He was mumbling something to the person on the other end. Once he hung up he shook his head.

"What the hell was that about?"

"Chief, my investigator came up with the connection we didn't expect involving Representative Matt Cusmano. Now I know why he's here, he's related to one of the men in the Eastern Market."

Mathews waited for the other shoe to fall, "Who is it?"

"His uncle is Vinnie La Russo, the owner of a local trucking company at the Eastern Market. Chief, that was one of the businesses in the building that Agent Hollis saw Dominic Parma coming out of."

Mathews nodded, "Vinnie La Russo, you're sure he's related to him?"

"Yeah, didn't connect them because of different last names, so many Italian last names like that, I didn't put it together."

The fact that their murder suspect may be working for the owner of a trucking company had Mathews wondering, *they never did find Castellanos, only knew he was connected to the Greektown owner. How was this all going to play out, he wasn't sure.*

Downey informed Mathews, "Chief, we're sending agents to the Eastern Market; I want to keep an eye on this La Russo guy, like I said he's been on our radar for a while."

Mathews asked, "How's he related to the State Rep, is he Vinnie's son?"

"No, the State Rep's mom is Vinnie's sister. She went back to her maiden name after an ugly divorce and officially changed her last name but kept both boys with their dad's name."

As they were talking, Hollis yelled out. "One of the bay doors is opening, and a truck has pulled out." They turned their attention to the large ice cream truck that slowly moved down Little Mack and stopped at the corner of Twelve Mile before turning.

Downey shouted, "Let it go, they may be watching," he turned to Hollis, "Get your vehicle and follow it." Hollis trotted to his car and Mathews started to say something when Detective Spano called out.

"It's Askew," Spano was waving his arms, "Detective Askew is driving the truck."

That changed everything, Mathews motioned as Hollis slowed down in front of them. "Agent, its Detective Askew driving the ice cream truck. If he's alone I'll bet he'll pull over just past the intersection. If he continues that means he's got a passenger, maybe with a weapon." Hollis appreciated the information. He continued down Little Mack to Twelve Mile Road. Mathews, Spano and Downey were wondering if another truck would soon be leaving the warehouse. They kept their attention on the large bay doors waiting for something else to happen.

Detective Harper called, not knowing about the truck that just pulled out, "Chief, do we have any other exits to the warehouse?"

"Detective, we're still checking blueprints; however, Askew just drove one of the trucks out of the warehouse and he's headed down Twelve Mile Road, presumably toward the Interstate."

"Do you want us back up in front?"

"No, we can't take a chance on one of the men inside escaping out of the back or somewhere else in case another exit exists." Mathews waited for Agent Hollis to contact them with the location of the first truck that left the warehouse. "Harper, hang-on while I get an update," he held the cell phone as Agent Downey was talking to Hollis. Downey gave him a thumbs up sign, Mathews lifted the phone, "Harper, we've got one of the trucks thanks to Askew." He quickly turned to Spano, "Head along the far side of the building and relieve Harper, I want her up here with me."

Detective Spano wanted to stay in play in front of the warehouse but knew Harper was in charge of the SIU team and it made sense that she'd be with the Chief. He skirted down the street past the buildings and crossed out of view from the front of the warehouse.

Once he was along the side of the building he saw Baker and waved to him. Baker wondered what had transpired. "Something happen?" Baker asked.

"Chief Mathews wants Harper at the command area; I'll run this part of the operation with you." Spano informed Harper and she trotted to where the Chief and Agent Downey stood.

\*\*\*

Dominic started pacing in the warehouse as Oscar White and Matt Cusmano listened to the second call from Jimmy Askew, Oscar was pleased, repeating what Askew had stated, "He's headed west to the Interstate, coast is clear, I'm sending the second truck out." Dominic watched as Oscar gave the driver the same instructions that he gave to Askew. "Make sure you call every half-hour." The two remaining trucks were still parked along the interior wall where they were loaded earlier.

While Oscar continued talking to the driver, Matt walked back up front to the bank of windows, he looked out for a few minutes, took a deep breath and turned to Oscar, "Everything's good here, I'm going to grab my car and head out." He had his keys in his right hand and turned toward the front door.

Dominic stepped in front of him, "Not so fast, Senator, this job ain't done until that third truck is safely on the road."

Matt backed up, looking at Dominic when Oscar immediately moved in, "We're good here, Dominic, we don't need him, the trucks are loaded and the second one will be on the road in a minute."

Turning to Oscar, Dominic shouted, "You ain't in charge," he was still holding the metal pipe, that he pointed again at Matt earlier, "You neither, Senator. You go when I say you can go." Dominic gripped the steel pipe and had a scary look on his face.

Matt moved back, he grabbed his cell phone, "I'm calling Vinnie; he's in charge not you." Matt started to dial when Dominic charged swinging the metal rod like a baseball bat. Matt ducked and fell to his knees, and Oscar hit the pavement ducking when the swish from the pipe just missed taking his head off. Dominic stood his ground looking like a warrior in battle when suddenly from out of nowhere someone tackled him from behind sending him crashing down to the cement in a thud. Oscar's foreman had charged the big man from behind shoving his face into the cement and pulling his arms up behind as if he was going to handcuff him. Dominic was out cold and Oscar crawled over to help his foreman, who was still on top, with his knees in Dominic's back.

Oscar called out, "Matt, find something to tie him up." Matt hurried to the far wall and rummaged through the workbench in the building when the second driver ran over holding a long rope. "Where'd you get that?"

Pointing back to one of the vehicles, "In the truck, it was on the front seat. I'm not sure what it's for, unless it might be used to secure the cargo."

Oscar panicked, "When he comes to, there will be a hell of a struggle. He's like a bull, we got to tie him down, and make sure it's secure."

Matt knew he was right, "This guy's off his rocker; we need to call Vinnie and let him know what's going on." Chaos was the last thing these guys needed, but now their simple operation at the warehouse was in jeopardy, not from any outside source but from one of their own.

***

Agent Hollis spotted where Askew had stopped in the parking lot of the Medical Center on Twelve Mile. The large ice cream truck was easy to spot. Hollis pulled into the south side of the building where Detective Askew was waving to him. They were now parked next to each other and Askew jumped out of the ice cream truck, "We've got to get back there," Askew was talking fast, "The crew inside is starting to get pretty edgy, this Dominic guy is just a little off his rocker." He took a deep breath, "Hollis, they think they spotted you guys and ordered me to call back every half-hour to make sure the coast is clear."

Hollis asked, "Does this truck have GPS?"

Askew was standing next to the opened driver's door, "I checked that right away before I pulled over, no GPS on board. Like I said, I'm supposed to call back every half hour to report in. Hollis, there's four of them in the warehouse beside your undercover agent, Oscar White, another driver, Dominic Parma and a guy that Dominic keeps calling Senator."

Hollis realized that Askew didn't know that they had the guy's identification, "Yeah, we spotted him and Detective Spano sent the photo he took into downtown; he's not a Senator but the State Representative for this district, his name is Matt Cusmano."

"Well Parma is losing it; he decked Oscar White before I was about to leave and then he threatened this Cusmano guy that Dominic keeps calling Senator. We need to get in there before someone gets killed." Hollis called the new information back in to Agent Downey. Armed with these details, Downey and Chief Mathews agreed that they needed to act, and act soon.

Askew gave them solid details about the men inside and the layout was critical, when he talked to Mathews, the Chief could hear the urgent tone in his voice, "Chief, the trucks are loaded with crates of cocaine; worth enough to build a third world country."

Agent Hollis and Askew followed the instructions they were given, locking up the truck and headed back to where the teams were positioned across from the warehouse. The Chief and DEA were planning their move on the men inside. Once Detective Askew got back to the command area, he sketched out the details for them with locations of the trucks and everything else that was inside the building. He told them, "I didn't see any weapons but everyone inside knew that this Dominic guy had a history of violence." Chief Mathews figured that Oscar White and this Dominic guy must have a gun but so far they weren't flashing them. With Askew's details about the struggle between White and Dominic, everyone figured that they probably had a history, one that may had led to the fight inside the warehouse.

# CHAPTER THIRTY-TWO

**Action inside the warehouse was frantic; Oscar and his** foreman tied Dominic up with the rope as they pulled the big man to one of the poles that was a few feet away. Dominic was still out cold, but they knew that wouldn't last long, Oscar wrapped the rope around his waist and to the pole; then he pulled the remaining rope around Dominic's arms. Oscar's foreman helped them and Matt searched Dominic, finding a pistol in his jacket and looked over at Oscar, "He's crazy as shit, if he had a gun the whole time why was he swinging that damn pipe?"

Oscar nodded, "You said it; he's crazy. Guess he thought the lead pipe was more intimidating; whatever, glad he didn't go for the gun."

It didn't take much longer until Dominic came to, his head wobbled from side to side, opening his eyes he glared at Oscar, yelling, "You're a dead man, you hear me, you're dead!" He fought against the ropes to no avail but kept screaming at them.

Oscar and Matt knew that they needed to do something, Oscar suggested. "We need to figure out what to do with him." They were all huddled together deciding what to do next when the bay doors exploded with a black Suburban crashing through the middle door sending dust and shards of wood flying through the air. Chief Mathews and Detective Harper, along with Agent Downey, rushed into the building where the truck created a massive hole. Agent Hollis and Detective Spano charged with guns drawn and Detective Askew was right behind them; "Everyone down on the ground!" DEA agents swarmed the men who were spread out on the ground, handcuffed. Mathews looked over at the man who was tied to a pole, "What happened here?"

The DEA's undercover agent laughed, pointing to the man tied to the pole, "That's Dominic Parma, and these two," motioning to Oscar White and Matt Cusmano, "They did us a big favor, they are the ones that helped tie Parma up, he's nuts." Agents straddled White and Detective Harper pulled Matt Cusmano to his feet, his arms cuffed behind his back. "You're both under arrest, you have the right to remain silent, and anything you say or do…"

Matt had a panicked look on his face and blurted out, "I've been held here at gun point against my will; I don't have anything to do with these guys."

Mathews laughed, "Save it buddy! We've got you on video driving up and getting out on your own. I don't think this is going to help with your re-election campaign." The others chuckled as Cusmano dropped his head. "Get them out of here," Mathews ordered.

Agent Downey walked over to Askew, "Great job, Detective. You played your part well." Askew nodded as they headed over to the other two trucks still lined up along the wall. "Here's your evidence, boss," Askew looked over to Chief Mathews, pulling open the back of one of the trucks filled with crates. "There has to be over a hundred crates in each truck with over fifty pounds of drugs in each one."

Detective Harper was proud of Askew and the role he played, she knew that Detective Frederickson would be happy that the SIU team performed well under fire. She moved over to the detective, as Spano approached. She smiled and put her arm around Askew, "You did great!" The three of them saw Chief Mathews who was watching, he had the look of pride on his face in his team.

Askew turned to Harper, "Thanks, I just did what you and the rest of the team would have done." Mathews kept watching them as he was standing off to the side. Detective Spano gave Askew a fist bump and smiled, knowing that when the Chief put Amy Harper in charge it was a good choice.

Agent Downey motioned to Mathews, "Chief, now that we have these guys we have to get the head of the organization." Both men knew there was more work to do; with the connection of Dominic Parma to La Russo Trucking, the next move will be at the Eastern Market.

Mathews wanted to make sure they didn't overlook anything; "I don't want anyone to touch anything that's inside these trucks, we'll get our video guys here to record all of it." The two teams of agents and detectives had performed well together. Mathews conferred with Detective Harper, the two of them stood off to the side discussing their next move. "I'd like to stay out in front of this investigation."

"Chief, I'll get our SIU team to start a twenty-four hour stake-out at the Market and La Russo's home in Grosse Pointe."

"I agree, Detective, make sure you keep me in the loop." He left the warehouse feeling pretty proud of their performance.

Harper motioned to Spano and Askew. "We need to get Johnson and Allen to take the first shift at the Eastern Market across from La Russo Trucking."

Spano agreed, "You know that they never found anything suspicious when they inspected Castellanos Trucking lot the other day. Maybe they'll have better luck at the Market." She spotted Tom Baker standing off to the side, waving him to join them, "Tom, you need to be involved in this too."

Baker was pleased that he was involved especially with the Chief running the case. "Glad to be of assistance, but you guys did all the work."

Spano wasn't sure how Baker fit into this case but sensed that Harper knew him from before. "It's always a team effort, glad you were here to help."

The officers and DEA agents headed to their headquarters to plan the next stage in the operation. Baker walked with Harper back to their car as Spano took Askew with him. Everything was falling into place. Detective Harper was pleased with the results of the situation at the warehouse but now wondered how Oscar White and La Russo Trucking was connected to Andy Jones' murder? *Could Andy have suspected the trucking company's involvement in this?* Tom Baker knew that something was bothering Harper, but he wasn't sure what it was.

*** *

Detectives were positioned outside the two story building off of Gratiot and Riopelle Streets in the Eastern Market. Their orders were to keep tabs on anyone entering or leaving the trucking company's offices. Although it was now dark, they had a clear view of the entrance. Most of the businesses were closed and they needed to be in place but not stand out. Detective Harper made sure that Allen and Johnson kept tabs on anyone walking around the building and they'd advise her if anything came up.

The Detroit Police sent a team from the North Precinct at Chief Mathews' request. The North Captain dispatched Detectives Charles Ventimigilio and Bob Thomas to handle the stakeout. The Captain felt that Ventimigilio had surprised him with his action at the DMC, so he deserved the opportunity to be involved in the case. Their assignment was to watch Vinnie La Russo's home in Grosse Pointe. The home was a large three story white colonial off of Lake Shore Drive in a gated community facing the river. The officers parked their car in the bank parking lot with a clear view of the entrance to the subdivision. They were furnished with Vinnie's vehicle description and plate number. They knew the stake out would last into the early hours. The two men sat in their unmarked vehicle and Charles looked at his partner, "Thomas, I need to take a short stroll, my legs are killing me.

"Okay, but keep an eye on the front gate across the street. Don't be long." He watched Charles standing next to the car, shaking his legs, then pacing along the side of the car. Thomas turned his attention to the gate and he didn't see Charles duck into the large clump of shrubs a few feet away.

Ventimigilio grabbed his cell phone, and although he got a voice mail announcement, he left a message. "Vinnie, you better lay low, they got your guys at the warehouse and they're out here on a stakeout of your place." He quickly hung up and resumed to pace back toward the vehicle.

Thomas saw him in the rear view mirror, "What the hell are you doing, get your ass back in the car." Thomas shook his head, *why did the Captain stick me with this dumb shit.* They continued watching the entrance, "Charles, you were gone long enough to get us something to eat.

"There isn't anything around here, do you want me to go get us something?"

"What will you use, can't take the car, what if La Russo pulls out."

Charles gave him a look of disgust, "Listen Thomas, I don't like being stuck with you any more than you want to be with me." He settled back in the passenger seat, smiling to himself, what a stroke that the Captain sent him on the stakeout. He's done everything possible to help Vinnie.

# CHAPTER THIRTY-THREE

**Nancy Frederickson was standing in her husband's room when** Chief Mathews walked in. "Chief, I'm surprised to see you, he's downstairs; they're taking another round of X-rays." She was surprised when he moved next to her, giving Nancy a big hug.

"I should have come by a few more times but we've been consumed with the case."

"I know he'll be happy to see you but I'm not sure how long it will be before they bring him back up."

"What's the latest news?"

"Doctor Guzzardo ran some test yesterday and brought us some good news. They feared that Don had a Pulmonary Contusion, but the test showed that the breast bone is only fractured. He'll make a full recovery in less than a month."

"That's truly good news."

They continued talking when one of the officers cleared his throat, "Sir, they're bringing him back in."

Mathews stood off to the side as the orderly and nurse pulled the gurney up to the side of the bed. He watched them slowly pulling the bottom sheets, so that they could keep the detective lying flat. Frederickson didn't see the Chief who was standing near the windows. Once he was positioned back in the bed Nancy leaned over him, "Don, the Chief is here to see you."

Mathews understood that Frederickson had to be flat on his back and didn't see him, "Well, Detective, I'm glad to hear your good news. Nancy said that the doctors are confident that you'll have a full recovery."

"Yes, sir, they said it will be a few weeks but I'll be as good as new."

"That truly is good news. You need to take care of yourself and do everything that the doctors tell you. The team is in good hands with Detective Harper right now."

"Chief, I'm sure Harper's doing a great job, I'm proud of her and the rest of the team. How's the investigation going?"

"We're making good progress but you need to take care of yourself right now. I just wanted to check on you myself." Frederickson wished that the Chief had given him some details on the case but guessed that wasn't something he wanted to do.

Nancy moved in, "Chief, we're so glad that you stopped by, I know that you're busy." She patted her husband on the shoulder.

"Thanks, Chief, if there's anything that I can do just let me know." Mathews bent over him and picked up his right hand, "Detective, you're an important part of our organization, take your time getting better. I'll stop by again." The two men had a bond, one of deep respect. Mathews said good-by to Nancy and headed out of the room.

"Don, it was nice of Mathews to come up to see you, I'm sure he's very busy." She fussed with the covers and fluffed his pillow. Deep down Nancy knew that her husband wanted to be involved in the investigation, not lying here flat on his back. She didn't see the tear trickle down his cheek.

\*\*\*

Detective Spano and Agent Hollis took the lead in questioning the men captured at the warehouse. Hollis and another agent had Dominic Parma in one Interrogation Room and Spano, along with Detective Allen, took Oscar White. They had questioned Cusmano first and when he continued to deny knowing anything, Spano said, "Guess this Dominic keeps calling you Senator. Well, Senator, you're going to be charged with obstruction of justice among other things." He didn't budge from his denials of any knowledge of what was being conducted in the warehouse.

They decided to put the State Representative on ice for a while as they questioned the other two men. It was obvious that he wasn't going to give them anything. He kept yelling that he's innocent, "I was only there because I was to check on that old warehouse. It's in my district and I wanted to demolish it. Those guys in there took me hostage when I showed up." He, of course, said he had no idea what was in the trucks.

Detective Allen had talked to the other driver that was captured but claimed he didn't know anything. Askew confirmed, "He's just one of the warehouse guys." They sent him to the tombs while they continued questioning the main suspects.

Spano leaned across the table from White, "Oscar, it's in your best interest that you come clean. We've got solid DNA evidence that you were involved in killing Andy Jones, you're guilty of murder. You'll going to go away for a long time."

Oscar looked up at Spano, "I'll wait for my attorney."

"It may be a long time till he gets here, this is a capital murder case. The first one to give us the details will get the best deal, the District Attorney is already upstairs talking to the Police Chief." Oscar didn't flinch. Spano turned to Detective Allen, "Maybe you better go see what those other two guys have to say." Allen left the room and Detective Spano slid back in his chair and grabbed a magazine that he brought with him. He read the material for what may have seemed like an hour to Oscar.

The silence finally got to Oscar, "I know that neither of those other guys are going to give you anything, you're wasting your time in here, cop," Oscar sneered back at Spano. Neither man budged.

Agent Hollis was having real problems with Dominic; he kicked and tried to punch anyone close. They had to cuff Dominic to the table. It took three men to subdue him; he was out of control, yelling and threatening everyone. "You need to get me out of here and do it fast. I've got friends that will have all of your badges."

Hollis laughed, "Apparently your dumber than we were told, I'm not a cop. We're both with the Drug Enforcement Agency. Don't think you have any pull there, pal."

Parma wanted to pound on the table but the restraints kept his hands only a few inches above the table so he couldn't make any noise regardless how hard he tried. "You're the dumb shit, buddy, I've got people, we'll find your home, your family, and they'll all pay for this."

Hollis smiled, "Thanks, we've got all that on tape so threatening a Federal Officer will only add to your problems." The two agents kicked back from the table, waiting for any word from Detective Spano.

The interrogation went on for over an hour as Spano and Hollis played their suspects against each other. Oscar asked again,

"Where's my lawyer?"

"Like I said, he's been called, traffic is a mess, especially with part of the freeway still closed." Allen had left the room many times, going back and forth to confer with Hollis, but nothing they said or did got them closer to getting Oscar to talk. It was getting late when the two detectives kept trying to shake one of the suspects loose. Detective Allen opened the door to the room where Oscar White was being questioned. "Detective, you might want to come out here for a minute, the agents said that they've made progress and are getting names and places." Spano jumped up and smiled, "First one to the table gets the deal."

"Wait, what kind of deal?"

"The District Attorney said you're all facing multiple charges, including drug smuggling and murder."

"Like I said, I didn't kill anyone."

Spano pounded on the table, "Well someone did, and we've got your finger prints on a drug packet taken off the body of a dead undercover officer. That makes you the primary suspect."

"What officer? I'm telling you I didn't kill anyone."

"You or someone in your organization picked up a couple guys to work for you; one of them was Andy Jones. You picked him up to do a job and after that you killed them and dumped their bodies in a field off of Jefferson."

Oscar was quiet for a minute, his breathing was short and he kept wiggling his fingers, "I said I didn't kill anyone. I don't know how you have my fingerprints on something found there, but I didn't do it." Oscar shifted in the chair and for the first time had a look of fear in his eyes.

Spano thought he saw an opportunity, "You know who did it then, either way, Oscar, you're an accomplice to murder and facing life in prison for killing an undercover Police Officer."

"What if I knew something, maybe give you information to help you find the real killer?"

"We've been screwing with you too long already, either you know something or we'll see what Dominic has to say." Spano turned and whispered to Allen, but made sure he said it loud enough for Oscar to hear. "Did you get everything that Cusmano said written down?"

Oscar shouted, "I want to know what you can offer me. I'll

need protection."

"No promises, not until I hear what you have to say. We've already got some details and unless you have something new, we can't help you."

"I know who killed your guy."

Spano told Allen to make sure they had everything on tape before Oscar started to give them his information. Oscar White gave them everything they needed to confirm the events and added another name to the list of suspects, the name was Mario La Russo, Vinnie's nephew. Once they felt like they made great progress with White, Spano and Hollis kept on asking him more questions. Oscar White was sweating and wanted something to eat, "You'll get a hot meal and something to drink once you finish telling us everything."

***

Chief Mathews was meeting in his office with Agent Downey and Detective Harper who were filling him in on their stakeout at La Russo's home and business. Harper detailed, "Chief, the officers watching La Russo's home in Grosse Pointe stated that no one had entered or left the residence. A second team has taken over the watch and will keep us advised of any activity from the scene. We're not sure he's even in there because he didn't become a potential suspect until we captured the guys at the warehouse."

Downey chimed in, "We've had the same results at La Russo's business at the Eastern Market. My men saw a young blond enter the building around eight this morning, we're assuming that she's a secretary. They're running a photo of her from the picture that my agents took. We should have the results from the Federal data base." As the group were discussing the events, there was a knock at the Chief's office door.

Lieutenant Jackson soon peeked her head inside, "Sorry to interrupt, I didn't want to call on the intercom, Chief. Detective Spano is outside and said he has important information."

"Send him in, Lieutenant." Everyone turned looking at the door.

Spano stepped into the large office, "Sorry to barge in but Detective Harper said if we had anything new to let her know right away."

Harper figured that he'd call but was pleased that they had some news, "Yes, what is it?"

"Our team, along with the DEA, has been interrogating the three suspects all night, Parma, Cusmano and White. Although Agent Hollis has been instrumental in this, he wanted to continue with Detective Allen gathering more details. We've all concentrated on Oscar White because it was his fingerprints that were recovered from the murder of Detective Andy Jones." Harper moved closer as Spano continued to give them the update. "We've been at White for hours and finally broke him." This was indeed a big break. "He's admitted to being there when Jones was killed, but is telling us that he didn't do it. He said Dominic Parma and Mario La Russo were the ones who are responsible for killing Jones."

Mathews hadn't heard the name Mario La Russo mentioned before during their investigation. He asked, "How does this Mario fit in? Guess he's related to Vinnie, the owner of the trucking company."

Spano looked over at Detective Harper, she motioned for him to continue. "White said that Mario is the nephew of Vinnie, kind of his right hand man. Either way, this Mario guy went with Parma and White to move some drugs, the drugs we captured at the warehouse. They picked up three men, one of them Andy Jones, to handle transporting the drugs."

Downey was puzzled, "Why did they need to pick up some men when they obviously had men of their own?"

"According to White, they planned to kill the three guys as soon as they completed the job. They didn't trust anyone so they couldn't use their own workers." Detective Harper looked very solemn, hearing again about her friend Andy Jones being killed in an undercover operation was hard for her to hear but, thankfully, no one noticed as Detective Spano continued, "White said he and Mario dumped the bodies in the field off of Jefferson. He's admitted that, but said he didn't kill any of the guys but giving us Mario as the killer."

"Good work, Detective," Chief Mathews said. 'Yes, yes,' both

Downey and Harper agreed. "Where is he now?" the Chief asked.

"We're still questioning him in the holding cells downstairs, Askew has him writing everything down and we've got it all on tape."

The Chief questioned, "Can he give us enough to put Vinnie La Russo away?"

"Yes Sir, he's giving us dates and places and we're sending the details to the FBI, just as you directed Chief." Mathews nodded, and Spano continued, "Mr. Sikorski from the Bureau said he's sending agents to confirm everything as we speak. I do have one more surprise; Oscar White revealed that he has details that connects Vinnie La Russo to Castellanos, and at some point they were partners."

That last revelation was great news to everyone. The Chief and Agent Downey, who was standing, looked back at Detective Spano when Amy Harper interrupted, "Joe, does he know where Castellanos is or whatever happened to him?"

"He hasn't any details on that except that there were many times that he was asked to take men to Castellanos trucking lot in the past to move trucks that most likely were filled with drugs and other contraband." The link of Vinnie La Russo and Castellanos was a missing piece of the puzzle from the Detroit Police Department's investigation last year. Spano added, "Chief, we haven't gotten anywhere with Dominic Parma or the Representative. Cusmano still claims he doesn't have anything to do with this and was just there checking on a building in his district to be demolished. He claims that they took him as a hostage when he went inside. Regarding Parma, Chief, excuse the cliché, but he's a little off his rocker. We've had to restrain him and he tried to kick and bite anyone that comes close."

Downey laughed, "Of course, Cusmano didn't know what was in there, especially with drug money probably paying for his election." Everyone laughed; they knew it wasn't the first time a local politician would be linked to criminal activities, and probably not the last.

Mathews asked Downey, "Did your agents see anyone else besides the secretary coming or going from the trucking office."

"No, they've been checking both the entrance and back exit, but other than the secretary and people going in and out of the restaurant downstairs, no one has gone into the office upstairs." Downey changed the subject, "Chief, our investigation into the drug smuggling encompasses the suspects moving product across the river. That's why Inspector Hershel from the RCMP joined me the other day in your office."

Mathews nodded, "I understand, what do you suggest?"

"I feel we need to bring his team into the scenario. His people have been tracking potential shipments that have crossed the Ambassador Bridge somehow. They need to know how these men are smuggling drugs across the border."

Mathews liked that his detectives were involved playing a key role with both the DEA and FBI, now with the addition of the Canadian authorities, it gave his team additional International experience. "I agree, this will help everyone not only in this case but for future events." Everyone was pleased with the progress and they had their assignments to continue the investigation. They all knew that there was a lot of work to go and none of them were ready to celebrate, at least not yet.

Harper cautioned, "We've got another issue gentlemen. With the revelation that Mario La Russo, Vinnie's nephew is the one who killed Andy Jones, we'll need to get a warrant for his arrest, as well as start searching for him too."

She was obviously right, Mathews knew that, "Detective, I want the SIU team to make that your number one objective. I know that Vinnie's capture is vital but since you and Detective Baker have been working on the murder of Officer Andy Jones, I think you should head this part of the investigation."

Harper was pleased with his confidence, "Chief, thanks for the opportunity, our team will make you proud." Downey liked the way that Mathews operated.

The Chief turned to Agent Downey, "I've got detectives from the North Precinct watching Vinnie La Russo's and another team staking out the Eastern Market, they've been working with your agents at both locations. I think we can concentrate on La Russo as Harper tracks down this Mario guy."

Downey agreed, "We've got a solid plan, Chief."

# CHAPTER THIRTY-FOUR

**The FBI was now armed with the details from Chief Mathews** and Agent Downey. They were coordinating efforts with the DEA and following up with the Canadian authorities. The Bureau was preparing Federal search warrants for both the home and business owned by Vinnie La Russo. Meanwhile, Detroit detectives and federal agents kept their stakeout at both places. With the FBI joining the investigation, the Border Patrol was called upon to double their efforts along the coast of both countries. Authorities were concerned, the Director stated, "We're not sure if any of the smuggling of drugs is taking place from boats crossing the short distance from Windsor to Detroit." He knew with only a short two mile span from the Canadian shoreline to Downtown, paired with two bridges and a couple of ferry services operating, that it left many avenues for potential smuggling. It also stretched the agencies involved with limited manpower to keep tabs on International traffic crossings. Bulletins were sent to Marine City and Algonac border stations, as well as, to all personnel on both the Blue Water and Ambassador Bridges.

Vinnie La Russo's home was located off of Jefferson, sometimes called Lake Shore Drive, in St. Clair Shores, and right on the river, potentially giving him easy access to travel by boat anywhere along the long coastline. Mathews reminded his team, "Detectives, it was critical getting the Canadians' and Border Patrol's from both countries involved." He outlined their assignment, "Their orders are to check every potential boat and their passengers from Downtown north to Port Huron, and south all the way to Cleveland."

Detectives Harper and Baker, along with Agent Hollis, reviewed the written statements that Spano had Oscar White complete. She read it aloud, "Hollis, White has said three different times that it was Mario who killed Andy and the other man that was found in the field."

Hollis agreed, "My only concern is that it makes it pretty easy for White to blame one of the guys that isn't talking and the other one that we don't have in custody."

She studied it one more time, "Detective Spano hasn't promised him anything yet, so if we find evidence to the contrary we can pursue more charges against him." Harper read the statement before her another time. "Hollis, it really doesn't matter, he wrote in his own words that once they completed moving the trucks he and Mario had two of the guys in a vehicle and Oscar kept them listening to him when Mario killed both of them. He's as guilty as if he pulled the trigger."

Baker agreed, "You're right. He signed his own confession to the murder." The two of them were pleased with the action of all the detectives and agents on the case. Tom turned to Harper, "So what's the plan?"

"Tom, so far we don't know if either Mario or Vinnie are aware that we've captured his men. If neither don't show soon, I'm assuming that they've been warned. We need to act and act fast."

"I agree, what do you want me to do?"

"I'll contact your Captain and advise him that you're being re-assigned permanently to the SIU."

Baker looked stunned, "Can you do that?"

"Yeah, with Chief Mathews' approval. I also called Detective Frederickson at the hospital and he agreed; he knows that he'll be out for a while and we'll need another person in the department. I cleared it with the Chief. Tom, you're a good detective, Spano and the rest of the team like the idea and you will be a great asset to the team. I'm telling the guys when we get upstairs."

Tom Baker had a smile on his face, "You're something you know, really something."

She just winked back at him.


\*\*\*


Inspector Hershel had just hung-up with Chief Mathews and he smiled, calling out to his aide, "Snyder, get in here!"

A tall young man opened the door and looked puzzled, "Eh,

Inspector did you call me?"

"Yeah, the Americans need our help," the grin on Hershel's face was priceless. "Call the team together, and get Tremblay on the phone."

The young man stood in the doorway, "Tremblay, you want Tremblay?"

Hershel gave him an exhausted stare, "Yes, Tremblay. We're going to be in charge of the investigation on both bridges and all the ferry crossings. Tremblay's Border Guards will be critical to the effort." Snyder left the room, surprised because he always figured that Hershel and Tremblay didn't like each other; probably because Hershel always referred to the man as a real 'hoser'.

The call to the Chief Inspector of Border Crossing Units from Hershel's office came as a surprise. Max Tremblay always knew that the old man didn't like him, let alone respect his men who handled the crossings between the U.S and Canadian Borders linking Michigan and Ontario. "Tremblay here, what's up?"

"Max, we've got an assignment that you're going to enjoy."

Tremblay thought, *the old man never gave him anything that was beneficial to his team before, why this all of a sudden.* "Okay Hershel, what plum assignment are you trying to stick me with?"

"Max, old friend, I don't know what's bothering you, but the American FBI and DEA are asking us to help them. Do you believe that Max, the FBI needs our help."

Now Max wondered; what's Hershel talking about, could there be a terrorist action that he never received a bulletin on? He fumbled through papers on his desk and when he didn't find anything revealing, finally he asked, "What's this all about?"

Hershel detailed the prospects of smugglers bringing drugs across the border and that the FBI and DEA had suspects in custody. He gave Tremblay names and all the information he had. "Max, they also think that one of their suspects may try to escape across the Lake to our side by boat. The guy lives on the shoreline in Michigan and they want us to be on the lookout along with their Border Patrol."

Max was pretty excited, "Sure, give me everything you've got." The two men worked out the details of their involvement in the FBI case and for the first time in years may have forged a real partnership.

\*\*\*

Detectives Harper and Baker laid out their plans in the search for Mario La Russo. Because the DEA and police had a stakeout at the office at the Eastern Market, no need to go there. "Tom, maybe we're making a mistake thinking these suspects don't know that we've discovered the drugs at the warehouse and captured all their men."

He thought for a second, "You don't think we have a leak, do you?"

"I'm worried, we've got too many agencies involved and there's no way to control the flow of information. Our only option is to check the officers from our organization. Do you know any of the people from the North Precinct that have been working the stakeout?"

Baker nodded, "No but I have an easy way to check." She watched him dialing. "Hey Manny, it's Tom, Tom Baker, I need some information." She listened as he seemed to be talking to someone from the street. Baker used street slang and promised some cash for the information. Once he hung up, Tom turned to Detective Harper. "Well, I got two names, the Chief isn't going to like this."

"Tom, the Chief has proven in the past that if we've got a personnel issue, he wants to know. If anyone is on the wrong side of the law, especially if it's an officer, he'll come down hard on them. He'll want to do the same thing with the other agencies."

He knew she was right, "Yeah, the names I have are two officers from the North Precinct," handing her the note with the two names.

Amy Harper looked at it, then back up at Baker, he thought she studied them for a long time, "Do you know either of these guys?"

"No, not really, haven't heard either name before but I'm sure their Captain will want to be involved."

"You're right," looking back over to Baker, "I'll call the Chief, once he's talked to the Captain from the North; I bet he'll want us to go get them."

# CHAPTER THIRTY-FIVE

**Amy Harper was surprised when she heard the voice on the** other end of the line, "Detective Frederickson, I didn't expect to hear from you." Once she said that, she wished that it was something that could be taken back.

"I know Harper, the Chief probably doesn't want me to worry about the case, but I just wanted to say hello. The doctors have run thousands of tests, and given me a clean, or almost, clean bill of health."

"How's Nancy? When I talked to her yesterday she said the doctor was pleased with the test results and you'll be back as good as new in a few weeks."

Frederickson laughed, "Good as new, that makes me about seventy-five percent of normal. Nancy's doing great, been here every second. I finally got her to go home and get the mail and just do some normal things. Harper, what's going on in the case?"

Detective Harper cleared her throat, "Pretty good, we've got some leads that the team is working on. The Chief has let Spano and me run with our ideas."

"Okay, that's the standard line, about the same thing I got from the Chief the last time he stopped by. Amy, what the hell's really going on with the case? Who's responsible for ramming and almost killing me?"

"Sorry Boss, the Chief gave us all orders not to discuss the investigation with you. He's concerned that the stress wouldn't be good for your recovery." Harper knew that telling Frederickson that would be like stabbing him in the heart.

"Sure, you've done what you were ordered to, now either tell me what's going on, or I'll break doctor's orders and get out of this bed and head down there now."

Amy Harper laughed out loud, maybe the best laugh she's had in the last few days, "Same old Frederickson, I believe you'll do it."

"You know I will. Now fill me in, please."

Detective Harper gave him the full details from the person who they're sure rammed him on the Interstate to the events in St. Clair Shores at the warehouse. After he'd been brought up to speed, she asked, "Detective, I need to know if I'm doing the right things?"

"Amy, I'm very proud of you and the whole team; you're on the right track and I wouldn't change a thing. Glad you've added Baker to the group. I won't be back for a long time unless these doctors give in and let me out of bed."

Harper was pleased with Frederickson's vote of confidence, "You're approval means a lot to me, Boss."

"Amy, keep up the good work; I promise I won't let anyone know that you filled me in, hush is the mode."

"I appreciate that. Once we get more details I'll let you know. Tell Nancy I said hi."

"I will, Spano was here, I think it was yesterday or maybe the day before, they all run together. Take care, Harper."

"Thanks." Once she hung up, a feeling of euphoria came over her. Maybe just hearing from Frederickson that he agreed with her, or it was just talking to him, but nonetheless, she felt invigorated.

***

Chief Mathews got off the phone with Chief Inspector Hershel and was pleased with the efforts that the Inspector outlined. He paged Jackson, "Lieutenant, have we gotten an update from Detective Harper?"

"No sir, but I just got off the phone with her. She needed to talk to you about something but I told her you were on the line with Hershel."

"Did she leave you a message?"

"No, honestly I think she seemed almost out of breath, she asked me to contact her as soon as you were free."

"Lieutenant please call her!" He wondered what was new, *she would have left a message if her team captured either Vinnie or Mario La Russo, wouldn't she?* Once she was on the line he quickly asked, "Detective, what do you have for me?"

"Chief, we've got a problem," she stopped for a second, "We've discovered that there is evidence that the North Precinct probably has a mole!" She stopped talking, figuring that he'd jump in right away, after a few seconds of silence, she continued, "Detective Baker and I have the names of two men in the North, Detective Charles Ventimigilio, and Officer Horacio Isaac, that have suspicious backgrounds."

"Where'd you get this?"

"Baker and I were concerned that neither Mario or Vinnie have surfaced since last night, so we started checking around. Baker has an informant that gave us details showing both men in the North having ties to La Russo." She looked over at Baker who was sitting in the passenger seat with a solemn look on his face.

"Why the North Precinct, how do they fit into the investigation?"

She picked up a sound of doubt in his voice, "The North is the only other Precinct that has been involved in our case, carrying out stakeouts at both Vinnie's home and the Eastern Market. We aren't in any position to check the other agencies involved, so we concentrated on the only other unit from our force that is on the case."

There was momentary silence, "I'm guessing you've started this internal check just because both suspects haven't been seen?"

"Yes sir, it just seemed unusual that the owner of the trucking company and his nephew haven't appeared at their homes or place of business. That is why we started thinking they've been warned."

"This all makes sense, Detective. You're right, you can't check the DEA or FBI personnel so checking our officers is your only option. What exactly have you found out about Ventimigilio and Isaac?"

She took a deep breath, "I'd suggest someone have a financial check of both men completed, but Baker's informant assured us that Ventimigilio has close contact to Vinnie La Russo and his trucking business. We're got some dates and places that he's worked off the books for La Russo."

"And Isaac?"

"He's another one of Vinnie La Russo's nephews."

Chief Mathews had to ask, "Detective who else have you told about this?"

"No one, sir, once we had some solid information, I called you right away."

She heard the Chief calling for Jackson to come in, "How in the hell did we miss that?" She hoped he was hollering to himself, then Harper thought she heard a sudden thud. He barked back on the phone, "Harper hold on," She heard him talking, "Jackson, call Captain Oliver in the North, I want him here right now." It was silent again for a second, "Harper, I want you and Baker to get down here right now." The next thing she heard was the dial tone.

Baker waited, "What did he say?"

"He hung up. We're to head to his office right now. Give me the siren, it's in the glove box." After he handed it to her, she turned it on and headed across town to headquarters. The two detectives sat without saying a word to each other as Harper turned onto Michigan Avenue heading to Police Headquarters. Baker wanted to say something but feared that whatever he said, it would be wrong.

# CHAPTER THIRTY-SIX

**The Meeting in Chief Mathews' office was tense, Detectives** Harper and Baker sat outside the large room waiting for Captain Oliver to arrive. After they filled the Chief in on their information he told them that he'd like to go over it all with the Captain before they all talked. Harper understood; it would be weird that a Captain would have two detectives accuse his men of wrongdoing. Lieutenant Jackson brought both of them a bottle of water, "I understand that this has been a whirlwind for you. You both need to know how pleased the Chief has been with your performance."

Harper looked up at her, "Thanks, it's great to know that the Chief has promoted many females to a higher position, we all are proud of your work in this position."

Jackson nodded, "Thanks, Detective." Just then the double doors opened and Captain Oliver walked in; he looked over at Lieutenant Jackson who was standing next to two other people. Jackson saw the puzzled look on Oliver's face. "Captain, the Chief is waiting to talk to you." She escorted him to the door and pushed it opened for Oliver. "Captain, can I get you a coffee or bottle of water?"

"No, thank you, Lieutenant." Captain Oliver moved into the office not exactly sure why the Chief ordered him to headquarters.

Chief Mathews was sitting behind his desk and on the phone, he waved to Captain Oliver, and he sat across the desk where Mathews pointed for him to be seated. Once the Chief completed his call, he stood and reached out to shake Oliver's hand, "Sorry about being on the phone but things keep developing faster than expected." He moved from behind his desk and sat next to Oliver in the other guest chair. That didn't surprise Oliver because the Chief was known to consider himself as one of the officers on the force; because he was a humble person, everyone from the Mayor to every officer highly respected him. "Captain, sorry for the hurried meeting but we've had developments in our investigation that only you and I can handle, at least at first blush." Oliver tilted his head, not sure what that meant. "I know you must have seen the two SIU Detectives outside, they're out there at my request." That comment only added to the anticipation Captain Oliver had been feeling.

Oliver shifted in his chair, turning to face Mathews, "Chief, I hope that you know I'm always at your disposal and anything either I, or my team, can do for you, we'll be ready and willing to carry it out."

"Captain, I appreciate that and I know that your commitment to my office is solid. That's not the reason I asked you to come here today. We've both got a problem." Mathews stopped for a second, "Captain, what do you know about two of your people, Detective Ventimigilio and Officer Isaac."

Oliver cleared his throat, "Oh no, what have they done?"

"So far we're not sure, however, that's why we need your input."

"Ventimigilio has always been on the edge. If I could check the personnel records he's been cited at least twice during my two years in the North Precinct; once for roughing up a suspect and the second time was when he and another officer couldn't be found while on a stakeout."

"How is he still on the force?"

"On the first case that I remember, he was suspended until an investigation was completed. He was partially cleared, although he lost a rank level, demoted from Detective First Class. I could supply you with the findings if needed." Then Captain Oliver held his hand up, "Chief, it's kind of odd that you're asking about Ventimigilio; just this week he was visiting the DMC and tells my guys that there's a suspicious man in the lobby. He called it in and we were able to remove the guy. I was thinking that he was coming around."

The Chief could tell that Oliver was on edge, "Captain, neither man's actions reflect on your leadership; however, news has come to my attention that leads to both suspects being tied to people involved in the murder of Officer Andy Jones." Oliver listened, "I'm going to call Detectives Harper and Baker in; they can cover what they have." The Chief buzzed Lieutenant Jackson, "Could you send the two detectives in."

Once they entered the Chief's office Detective Harper took the lead. "Captain, Detective Baker and I are concerned that the two suspects we've been looking for have seemed to disappear. We ran a check with a solid informant that revealed that Officer Isaac is a nephew to Vinnie La Russo, a key suspect in our case. To our surprise, our information also links Detective Ventimigilio to La Russo. He has been seen in La Russo's office many times and even worked off the books for him."

Chief Mathews continued, "I told Harper that this was her investigation. When I put my Special Investigative Unit in charge, I'm confident that what they come up with is accurate."

Oliver had turned his chair to face the two detectives, "Can I ask who your informant is?"

Mathews quickly jumped in, "Detectives, if that would compromise this case we'll understand."

Tom Baker said, "I don't have a problem with answering that. Chief, I've been working with former Detective Curtis, he retired from the Third Precinct. He's opened a P.I. office and has been a solid resource for me over the past years. I called him because his office is on Gratiot, just past the Eastern Market."

Captain Oliver looked back to the Chief, "I know Curtis, and he's a solid guy. How about Isaac?"

Harper quickly answered, "Guilt by association. We don't have anything concrete on him but if he's heard anything on our case he'd be sure to pass it along to his uncle." They all agreed that it made good sense, although none of them had details pinpointing Isaac to the case, that it would be best to keep him out of the loop, unless Ventimigilio is giving Isaac information to pass along.

Captain Oliver asked the Chief, "How do you want me to proceed?"

Mathews pointed to Harper, "Detective, where do you want to go next?"

Baker was surprised to hear the Chief bounce it back Harper. She said, "I want both of them here now! Neither man can know that we have the other one in custody. It's critical that we put them in separate areas. I'm sure once the Chief has talked to them, he'll turn it over to Internal Affairs."

Captain Oliver suggested that he have both men brought in under the guise of an Internal Affairs' investigation, thus taking their guns, badges and phones. He was about to make a call when he suddenly stopped, "Oh shit, Ventimigilio was one of the detectives on the stakeout at La Russo's home in Grosse Pointe."

Baker spun around, "No wonder we can't find La Russo; he's been warned." Everyone in the room knew that was what must have happened.

Mathews told Captain Oliver, "Make the calls, we need to get both of them out of uniform and out of circulation." Turning to Detective Harper, "Get everything you can from them." The plans were set, everyone headed to their assignments. This case was growing wider with every day.

***

Detective Spano and Agent Hollis continued talking to Oscar White, extracting every nugget of information possible to help the case. Once they completed the details, they decided to turn their attention to Dominic Parma one more time. "I'm thinking we hit him with facts, pounding away with what we know might just shake him."

Agent Hollis agreed, "With both of us coming at him, it could trip him up into telling us something more to help us find Vinnie." Both men headed back downstairs to the cells in the lower level of the headquarters building.

When they opened the door the officer standing guard was glad to see them, "He's been screaming for the last two hours, this guy is nuts; I checked to make sure he couldn't hurt himself but it took two of us just to make sure he was secured to the table."

"He still hasn't had anything to eat or drink?"

"No, we tried once. I took a tray with juice and a sandwich on it and when I got close the whole damn thing ended up being thrown back at me."

Spano shook his head, "Sorry kid, I know he's scary, but why would he refuse to eat?" Spano and Hollis made their way down the short hall and everything was quiet; they looked at each other, kind of surprised that maybe he'd settled down. Opening the steel door, they saw the man slumped over the table, "We need a Medic in here!" Hollis tried pulling Dominic back off the table and Spano tried to feel for a pulse.

The young officer ran down the hallway, "An EMT is coming." The emergency tech wasn't far behind, Spano and Hollis had Dominic on the floor, and he was still unresponsive.

The EMT knelt down and proceeded to work feverishly trying to get a pulse from the man lying on the floor. There were now three of them doing everything possible to revive Dominic Parma but nothing was working. The young lady said, "Looks like he had a seizure of some sort, swallowed his tongue." A man continued feverishly working on Dominic as Spano and Hollis watched wondering how did this happen. A second EMT tech rushed down the hall with oxygen as the first man was making an incision into Dominic's throat, Once completed, he inserted a small tube that resembled a straw and blew into it. Watching his chest he told the other tech, a tall blond, "We don't know how long he's been down, there's no pulse or heart beat."

She looked up at the detectives and asked, "When was the last time anyone had contact with him?"

They both looked over at the young officer, "Maybe twenty minutes to half-hour ago."

It was hopeless; she looked back up, "Your suspect, Dominic Parma, is dead." The two detectives looked at each other, speechless.

# CHAPTER THIRTY-SEVEN

**The news of Dominic Parma's death quickly got back to** Mathews and Detective Harper. Spano and Agent Hollis called the Chief and Agent Downey, making sure they had the details. The Chief was stunned, "If this guy was so violent and restrained," he mumbled, "How could this have happened?"

Harper was concerned that the media would relate this to police excessive force, "Chief, the emergency techs clearly stated that he had a seizure and swallowed his tongue." Turning to Baker, she wondered, "Was there any indication in our records that he had a medical issue?" It almost seemed that she was mumbling.

Mathews turned his head, waiting for some news they hadn't received yet, "Detective, I'm not sure what you are thinking, however, at some point this will have to be released to the media and the general public will be clamoring for an explanation. In today's concern about excessive police force, I understand that it will be a story."

She was shaking her head, "Chief, he was restrained but couldn't do anything to hurt himself; it just had to have been a medical emergency. Spano said the officers standing guard heard him yelling and swearing but that's what he's done ever since we brought him in."

Mathews nodded, "There will have to be an investigation. Once the Medical Examiner has cause of death we might have a better answer." Although they seemed flustered, they still had Oscar White and his statements plus they hadn't really questioned Matt Cusmano fully. Mathews stated, "We've got to get something from that State Rep.; we know he's involved deeper and we can use White's statements to move him to talk." The Chief suggested, "Harper, why don't you get Spano and Askew working on this because I'll need you here once the officers from the North Precinct arrive; she nodded and they both left to arrange the assignment. Captain Oliver was busy having both Ventimigilio and Isaac brought downtown and the Chief wanted them questioned as soon as possible. Mathews looked at Harper and Baker, "I think one or both knows the whereabouts of our last two suspects."

The teams of investigators had their work cut out for them, two suspects on the loose, two still in custody and one dead. Now the question about involvement from officers in the North Precinct again haunted the department. Chief Mathews paced in his office, waiting for the men from the North to arrive. Lieutenant Jackson buzzed the Chief, "I've got two officers from the North Precinct up here with Captain Oliver."

"Send them in, Lieutenant." Mathews wanted to stay calm but was having trouble containing his anger. Once the men entered he stood and pointed to the conference table, "Sit over there." Everyone knew this wasn't going to be a general conversation. Ventimigilio sat on the right side of the table and Oliver sat next to him.

Isaac stood for a minute looking at his Captain, then sat across from both of them. "Captain, I still don't know why you need me here?"

Oliver wasn't pleased but didn't want to upstage the Chief, "Officer, this is simple, the Chief asked us to be seated and that's what we're going to do, got it!" All three men sat at the large mahogany conference table as Oliver took a deep breath.

It was quiet in the room as Mathews fumbled with papers on his desk, purposely stalling. There was another knock on his door and Detectives Harper and Baker entered. "You can join us at the conference table," Mathews stated and followed both of them. Everyone was seated; Baker remembered being here just a few days ago under similar circumstances. Mathews had a folder in front of him, and he knew that Captain Oliver had taken both men's badges and weapons, "Officer Isaac, what do you know about a man named Vinnie La Russo?"

Isaac shifted in his seat, "Not sure what you mean."

"It's simple, do you know Mr. La Russo?"

He looked over at Oliver then back to Ventimigilio, "Yes, kind of, well I mean he's my uncle on my mother's side."

"Thanks," Mathews turned to Ventimigilio, "Charles, how about you, do you know Mr. La Russo?"

Ventimigilio was smug, "Yeah, I've seen his name all over town on those trucks." The man leaned back in the large conference chair and raised his eyebrows, "I'm sure everyone has."

That was not the approach that Mathews wanted to hear, he now had a scowl on his face and asked, "How many times have you worked for La Russo or his company in the past year, and Detective, don't screw with me or I'll have your ass right here and now."

That smug smirk was gone and Ventimigilio's hands started to shake, "All off the job, sir."

"Not what I asked, how many?"

"I'm not sure, maybe a half a dozen."

"Does that count the day at the DMC when you were an accomplice to the murder of a suspect we had in custody?" Now the room was silent, Ventimigilio was denying ever being involved with La Russo or his organization unless it was manual loading or unloading trucks. "I don't want to hear that crap, we've got you on surveillance at the hospital talking to Dominic Parma, one of La Russo's men. Parma gave us everything."

Charles broke down and was in tears, "I didn't know what they were doing; they just wanted me to tell them a room number." He was sobbing and had to know that it was over now.

"Just a room number? Minutes after your visit to the DMC, our suspect is found dead in his room, now Dominic said you're the one who did it." The Chief used the dead man's name to pry the story out of Detective Ventimigilio.

"No, I didn't do nothing. They had me divert attention from the guards. Maybe so they could set up the person who killed your suspect."

"Then who was the killer, if not you?"

"Some nurse that Mario knows, she was hired to take care of it." Harper moved behind Charles and Captain Oliver stood next to her.

"Get up," Oliver said, cuffing Charles to the shock of Isaac who still sat on the other side of the table in fear. "You're a disgrace to the uniform. You'll write all this down when we get downstairs."

The Chief held his hand up, "Wait Captain, one of these two is going to save themselves a few years in prison by telling us where Mario or Vinnie La Russo are hiding. "First one to speak gets the break."

"I don't know," cried Isaac; "it's Charles that warned Vinnie last night." They all turned toward Charles.

"So the ball's in your court. Ventimigilio, either tell us what you know or you go down for two murders."

"Murder! I didn't kill anyone."

"Maybe not with your own hands but you're an accomplice to both murders and will do life for them." Mathews stood, "Detective, take him away; we'll get the answers from either Dominic Parma or Oscar White."

Charles Ventimigilio knew they had Vinnie's men, and most likely both of them had been coerced into talking, especially Oscar. He quickly stated, "Wait, I didn't do anything, Dominic's your guy, he's crazy, wanted to blow the whole hospital up, I just passed on a room number."

"No, you didn't do anything, just warned La Russo and now he's escaped. Help us find him and you'll spend less time in prison. I promise we'll put you in the general population and when they find out that you were a police officer, well you know what's next."

Ventimigilio knew the Chief wasn't kidding. He'd heard about what prisoners do to ex-cops, "Chief, I did call Vinnie when I was involved on the stakeout. I left him a message that his guys were caught. I never really talked to him. I'm sure he's planning on using his boat to escape."

"So where would he go?"

"I know he's got a cabin off of Lake Huron, on the Canadian side."

Just then Isaac jumped in, "I know where it is. I've been there as a kid with my mom." He turned to Captain Oliver, "I can't go to prison, I didn't do anything; I'm just related to the guy."

Oliver turned toward the Chief; Mathews looked at Isaac, "Okay, this is your last opportunity to prove what you know. If you get us to the cabin and we find La Russo it will help us, help you with the District Attorney."

Isaac jumped up from his seat, "I'll do it; I'll do anything not to go to jail."

# CHAPTER THIRTY-EIGHT

**Chief Mathews was pleased with the results from the** interrogation of Ventimigilio and Isaac in his office. Once they had lined out the details, he gave Detectives Harper and Baker instructions for planning the raid in Canada. "Detective Harper, I'll need to contact Inspector Hershel with the RCMP, we'll want to arrange a combined force to accomplish this. You'll need to get Officer Isaac's information with a map and take it with you and Baker and I'm sure that the Inspector will want his Canadian team to be in charge of the search, That's reasonable due to it being in their jurisdiction. Whatever we do, we need to keep Isaac from contacting anyone, just in case he decides to change his mind and tell his uncle we're coming."

Harper understood, "I'm going to have Baker assigned to controlling him and getting all the details we need before putting him in the tombs downstairs."

Mathews agreed, "Once we've captured Vinnie La Russo, and hopefully, Mario and have them in custody, they'll all stand trial here for everything."

Harper was happy that the Chief intended for her and Baker to be involved with the Canadian team. She was also impressed on how the Chief handled the interrogation of Isaac and Ventimigilio. "Chief, I've got the map where Isaac has penciled in the location of the cabins. He said that it is huge and has three out buildings. I'm sure it's well stocked with weapons too."

"Harper, whatever it takes, I want both of them brought in alive. If it's true that Vinnie La Russo had a relationship with Castellanos, he more than likely was also connected to the drug cartel in Greektown. Detective, I think our investigation points out that he's responsible for Detective Frederickson's car crash."

She hadn't thought about that, "You're right sir." That made her think about Frederickson, *I need to go see him*, she mumbled to herself.

The Chief picked up the phone, "Lieutenant Jackson, call

Inspector Hershel and you might as well call Agent Downey with the DEA," he turned to Harper, "I'm sure the DEA will want to join the party. I'll handle everything with Director Sikorski and the FBI later."

Once the plans were set, she asked, "Chief, changing the subject, when can we get Andy Jones' body released to his mom? I know she's been grieving and I'd like to tell her the truth about her son."

"Real soon, I'd like to capture these guys before doing that. It would be nice to tell her we have the men in custody for killing her son. Detective, the department will pick up all expenses and she'll get any benefits that Andy had coming." Mathews smiled at his detective, "You know it's important to remember friends and your request is one that reminds all of us about the importance of our families. They, too, serve with us."

Harper was pleased with his answer, "When Andy's mom has the funeral planned, I'd like to attend."

"Sure, and Detective, I'll be there with you. It would sure be nice if we've captured everyone involved in her son's murder and in custody when the funeral takes place."

As Detective Harper left his office, Lieutenant Jackson put a call through, "Chief, it's the DMC. The doctor wanted to give you some information on their autopsy on the body of Dominic Parma."

"Put her through," He hoped Doctor Nagappala, the head of Pathology, had an answer on her team's autopsy. "Yes, Doctor, I appreciate your fast work."

"I wish they were all this easy. Your prisoner suffered a seizure; during our autopsy we found that he had an epileptic event that is most commonly associated with people that have SUDEP, sudden, unexpected, nontraumatic death. There was nothing your officers did or could have done to stop this from happening. Our postmortem report will detail all of this for your department."

"Thanks, doctor, this is a great relief. Do you have anything further on our heart attack patient?"

"We should have something for you later today."

Once he hung up, he leaned back in his chair, relieved that he'd have details backed up by the DMC investigation when this was released to the press.

\*\*\*

The call to Inspector Hershel in Windsor, from Chief Mathews, came as a pleasant surprise. Hershel started getting his team of Sergeants and Inspectors ready to carry out the combined raid with the Michigan officers. He told his aide, "This will be a full assault at the cabin." Once he had everyone filled in on the plan, he contacted his Deputy Commissioner to detail the facts of the investigation. As the Senior Inspector in Ontario, Hershel was well thought of by his Commander, and the Commissioner in Ottawa was pleased that Hershel had a solid relationship with his American counterpart. The joint task force wanted to take action as soon as possible so that the suspects didn't have time to move their location. An APB was sent to every airport and train station on both sides of the border, just in case the two men tried to get out of the area.

Hershel studied the map that Mathews faxed to him. He knew that Grand Bend, Ontario was a beautiful tourist site on the east coast of Lake Huron. With two Blue Flag Marinas and Pinery Provincial Park, it offered many possible escapes routes for the suspects. "We've got to have the Coast Guard secure every water exit preventing an escape once we've started our search. I've contacted the Commissioner and he'll give us both aerial and Coast Guard support."

The aide told Hershel, "Sir, Tremblay's on the phone."

"Tremblay, it's on, just like I told you earlier. The Americans have good Intel that their suspects are in a secluded cabin just outside of Grand Bend. The Commissioner has given us approval to head the search and will give us full support."

Tremblay was still surprised that Hershel was willing to share the investigation, "Okay, when are we planning on moving?"

"I promised the Detroit Police Chief that we'll take a couple of their detectives along with us."

Tremblay was surprised that Hershel was willing to share the case, even with him, let alone the Americans. He asked, "We're still going to be in charge, Eh?"

"It's our case, we'll handle the search and apprehension of the suspects. The Americans will get to try them in their courts first then we get our trial on drug smuggling." Both men were pleased with the prospects of improving their perception to officials in Ottawa. "This can only result in positives for us," Hershel reminded him. Tremblay knew he was right.

\*\*\*

Detective Harper had the SIU team gathered detailing the Chief's plans, "Baker will take control of our suspect, Officer Isaac. He's given us the potential location of a cabin that Vinnie La Russo owns in Grand Bend, Ontario. I have a map and we've sent a copy to the Canadian team. The Chief has our team joining with officials from the RCMP. Their Chief Inspector is going to handle the search because it's in their territory." All the detectives wanted to be involved but understood that the Canadians should be handling it. With Grand Bend being a Canadian tourist city, they can't have the Americans rushing in, even though it was an escaped US citizen that they were chasing.

They studied the map that she had spread across the conference table. Detective Askew turned to Harper, "Do we know how far Grand Bend is from Port Huron?"

Detective Spano chimed in, "Guess it would depend on highway or boat travel." It was easy to see that you could cross the Blue Water Bridge and take Highway twenty-one north to Grand Bend. "Looks like about sixty miles," he said. "However by boat you end up in Canadian waters the majority of the trip, although it looks like it would be about the same distance."

Harper told the group, "I'm waiting to hear from Inspector Hershel. I'm sure they'll plan a three prong approach and the Coast Guard should block the port at Grand Bend; thus no one can escape by boat. Hopefully, we'll have air support via a helicopter helping in wooded areas. I'm sure that Hershel will want to set up road blocks as we start our search."

The team was surprised how Harper described this. Tom Baker pointed to the map, "Sounds pretty thorough, General." Harper looked back at him and everyone laughed.

"Guess I'm just excited," she put her head down but had a huge smile on her face.

"No, I'm truly impressed." The others nodded, agreeing with him.

Mindy peeked into the room, "Detective Harper, there's an Inspector Hershel on the phone for you."

"Thanks, can you send it to the Conference Room?" When it came through, Askew hit the monitor and they all stood as Hershel appeared on the screen. "Inspector, I've got my team here and we're just looking at the map of the area."

Hershel was impressed with both the technology employed by the police, and the leadership that the lead Detective displayed. "Detective Harper, our teams are readied and will deploy at eighteen hundred hours. Your Chief told us that you and your Detective Baker would be accompanying us. I was thinking that you could meet us in Sarnia, and we can head to Grand Bend together."

Harper looked at Spano, then Baker, "I just got off the phone with Chief Mathews. He agreed that your team is to be in charge of handling the search for our two suspects and we'll take custody of them once they're captured, so meeting in Grand Bend makes more sense; let's set our rendezvous place."

# CHAPTER THIRTY-NINE

**Chief Inspector Hershel stood along the driver's side of his** vehicle waiting for Detectives Harper and Baker to arrive. His GMC Suburban was parked in front of the Oakwood Resort on the Bluewater Highway. He arranged rooms for the members of his team and the two Americans. Tremblay was parked behind him and wondered why the Inspector was upset. He strolled up to Hershel's vehicle, "What time are the Americans supposed to meet us?"

Hershel slowly turned toward him, "This is our case, if they're not here in the next ten minutes I'm leaving." He had just finished with his statement when the black Suburban appeared coming up the long circular driveway. Making sure everyone heard him, "About time!" Hershel waved, as Harper pulled up behind Tremblay's vehicle.

They watched as she got out on the driver's side and two other men climbed out of the vehicle. Hershel had a frown on his face, "I thought that just two of you were joining us."

"That was the original plan but Detective Spano and Baker are key to the investigation, so I decided to bring both of them along, hope that's not a problem?"

Hershel looked down but then said, "Not a problem, but they need to follow my command."

"We're all good with that, so what's the plan, Inspector?"

Max Tremblay had a strange look on his face and whispered to Hershel, "She's cute, very cute," Tremblay softly said, looking back at Hershel. "Now I know why you're mad, she must have set the meeting place."

Hershel had a stern look on his face but didn't answer Tremblay, "Detectives Harper, Spano and Baker, this is Inspector Max Tremblay. Max handles all the Border Crossings from Michigan and New York into Canada." They exchanged handshakes and she introduced her detectives to both men. "I've made room reservations for tonight at the Resort for all of us. I know it will get dark about twenty-one hundred hours."

"Thanks Inspector, we appreciate your thoughtfulness. I was thinking that we have a couple hours of daylight and was hoping we can head to the location of the suspected cabin."

Hershel nodded, "I agree, let's take my vehicle. I have a team that is stationed about a mile from the location. We've set up a road block; they're waiting for our orders." Harper, Spano and Baker jumped in the back seat as Hershel and Tremblay got in the front. Hershel was talking as he pulled out, "The cabin is about fifteen minutes from here; the area is somewhat secluded but my men have checked out the area and we've got men covering the two roads that lead out of the private driveway. Detective, we're concerned that they have a couple boats in the well outside the cabin, so I've radioed that in to our Coast Guard and they're manning a post at the Marina."

Detective Harper figured this was the best time to share her new information, "Inspector, the DEA flew a drone over the area when we got the location of the cabin from La Russo's nephew."

Hershel spun around in his seat, "Just when were you planning on sharing that?"

"When I knew that we'd be heading to the scene. Inspector, I brought the photos to give to you."

He wasn't happy but took the packet that she handed him. "Tremblay, look those over."

Tremblay thought that this combined operation was now in jeopardy, he knew Hershel wasn't fond of someone one upping him. "Hershel, these look good." He studied the photos, "I see that they have three boats and exactly where the cabin is located, if you call that a cabin, it's huge."

Hershel pulled over grabbing the photos, "When did they take these?

"A few hours after we got the location from our informant, this wasn't my idea. The DEA sent a drone in making sure we wouldn't be in a fire fight with a small army."

"Yeah, okay, guess that makes sense," He continued driving to the spot where the RCMP was in position, it took about twenty minutes. They took Highway 83 east to rural route 2. Once they turned on RR 2, the road became gravel and all of them bounced around, "Sorry about the ride."

Harper had been reviewing the information on her lap as Baker studied the roads. "Inspector, how close are your men to the entrance of the suspected cabin?"

"I've got two teams guarding the exits, we should be coming up to the first team soon." Hershel slowed down and pulled to the side of the road, his men were stationed along the side of the road, "Anyone coming in or out?"

"No, Inspector, we haven't seen any action since we arrived."

"Okay, if you spot someone approaching call me right away." Tremblay was interested in making conversation with Detective Harper. Turning in his seat facing the Detectives in the back, he asked, "How many officers will you be using on this case?"

Harper winked at Tom Baker, "Oh, in the field or back at headquarters?"

Tremblay looked puzzled, "I guess both."

"We've got every available officer working the case. Together with the DEA and FBI there must be over a hundred people in on this. I know our Chief also has two or three seaplanes operating from the Port Huron Station."

Hershel burst out laughing, "You dope; she's screwing with you." Suddenly his phone rang, "Yes, yes, how soon after we left?" Pulling the vehicle to the side of the road, Hershel quickly asked, "Did anyone see a spot to pull off this road, maybe into the woods?"

Harper answered, "I saw an opening back about a quarter mile."

Hershel spun the steering wheel around heading back in the other direction, "My men said two vehicles are headed our way, they just passed their checkpoint. One was a black Lincoln MKX, Michigan plates; the other vehicle is a panel van, also with Michigan plates."

"There it is," Harper was pointing to an opening in the trees to the right, Hershel pulled his vehicle onto the dirt track between large trees and behind thick shrubs, and stopped. Harper and Baker pulled their weapons and jumped out of the vehicle. Baker pulled a tall tree down toward the back of the Suburban, it was bushy with a thin trunk and covered the back of their vehicle. The three detectives were joined by Hershel and Tremblay. Harper noted, "This looks like a four wheeler trail."

"Yeah, either that or for snowmobiles," Hershel added. The five of them hid in the brush waiting for the vehicles to pass their location. Hershel was mad, "If we had more time we could try to stop them." The sound of gravel hitting the undercarriage of cars was close, then the MKX appeared, dirt covered and driving too fast on the gravel path. "Looks like one man inside."

Harper had her cell phone aimed and took photos, one after the other. The van came behind with at least two men in the front, "Can't tell if anyone else is in there besides the two guys up front." She snapped more photos, "I think I got a good shot of the driver of the Lincoln." Baker moved toward the road, peeking out to see how far the vehicles had passed. Harper said, "I got a real good photo of the driver in the Lincoln,"

Hershel looked over her shoulder, "Any idea who it is?"

Amy Harper nodded, "I'm pretty sure it's Mario La Russo. I'll send it to the team back in Detroit for confirmation."

While she was doing that, Hershel made a call, when he finished, he looked at the others, "Our men at the checkpoint said that just the two vehicles passed. They said that they could see at least four guys in the van." Tremblay was shaking his head, Hershel pounded on the hood of his vehicle, "How in the hell did our guys let them through?"

Tremblay nodded, then added, "Looks like they're planning for a battle." This was a concern for both the Canadians and detectives, one that they feared would most certainly escalate the action.

\*\*\*

Chief Mathews and Agent Downey reviewed the message from Detective Harper, "Chief, I think we'll need more men up there." The prospect of Vinnie La Russo arming his cabin with more men to protect him was one that neither agency hoped would happen. Downey continued, "Chief, I'll call Ottawa, maybe the Commissioner will approve us sending a Black Hawk from Selfridge."

While Downey was making his call, Mathews decided to send

Harper a message, updating her on what they were doing to support them. He thought he'd text her versus calling, thinking, *he didn't know if she was trying to keep in a silent mode.* The Chief was now concerned that the team in Grand Bend didn't have enough fire power in the event that this became a gun battle, one that neither the Chief, nor Downey, planned for. His other concern was that maybe Vinnie had been warned.

Downey ended his call, "Chief, the Commissioner feels their team can handle the situation, however, he has given us approval for extra personnel to support our detectives."

"Great, I just texted Harper but haven't heard back, I'd like to send two more detectives."

Downey understood, "I was thinking that I'd send Hollis with two other agents. That would bring us to six American officers on the strike team." Both men were in agreement, protecting their people was critical and capturing the suspects looked like it would be more difficult than originally expected.

Mathews phone chirped, he checked it, "It's from Harper, she sent their coordinates. She said Inspector Hershel turned around and headed back down the road to where his team has set up a checkpoint."

Downey asked, "Why didn't Hershel's team grab the new arrivals on the gravel road before they had a chance to get to the cabin?" Both men seemed puzzled and were hoping for the answer to that question.

Mathews looked over at him, "That's a good thought, I'll ask Harper; maybe she knows more." They agreed to wait until she called back.

# FORTY

**Inspector Hershel pulled his vehicle up to the team of his** officers stationed along the gravel road leading to the suspected hold out of Vinnie La Russo. He didn't mince words, "I need full details, why the hell did those vehicles get by you?"

One of the sergeants immediately answered, "Inspector, we had moved our vehicles off the road and were off the path and none of us heard cars heading our way. By the time any of us had time to react, the first car, a black Lincoln was upon us."

"You were to keep everyone else from passing, sergeant, we'll talk about this more later. What can you add for us?"

The sergeant had a pale look on his face and cleared his throat, "Sir, the first vehicle just had a driver in it but the van that followed had four men riding in it. We couldn't see much more but we know that we've got five more people to concentrate on."

"Sergeant, we'll have to change our plans, we'll have more officers from Windsor coming tonight and I've approved more people from the Detroit Police and DEA to join our efforts. They're on the way now." Turning to Tremblay, "Max, how many men do you have at the Bridge?"

Tremblay check his I-pad, "We've got five Sergeants at the Blue Water Bridge in Port Huron and I have two more that could be en route from the ferry crossing in Wallaceburg."

Hershel looked over at Detective Harper, "What did you hear from your Chief."

"He's dispatched Detective Askew and Agent Hollis from the DEA to join us. Their riding with two more agents from the DEA, and I gave them our location." She shifted her stance along the side of the vehicle, then moved closer to Hershel. "I want to have our people handle securing the road leading to the cabin now."

"Detective, I understand your concern, but our men are capable of doing that."

Looking the Inspector straight in the eyes, "I would think so, this isn't a request but I'd appreciate your approval."

Hershel took a deep breath and nodded, waving to one of his

men to approach. "Sergeant, the detective and I want to know exactly what happened when the two vehicles came down the road."

The Sergeant looked down at his feet before saying anything, "Inspector, we were making sure our vehicles couldn't be seen from the road and I guess we were talking, we didn't see them approach. It was too late to do anything." The young man knew that wasn't what the Inspector wanted to hear, but he knew he'd have to tell the truth.

"Sergeant, this may be a long siege, we need everyone alerted to the pending action. I'll talk to the men but I want you to know, this is on all of you, we can't fail due to lack of following orders." The man walked away with his head down.

Harper knew it was tough for the Inspector to scold his men, especially in front of her, "Detective, I'll agree having our men join your guys in securing the road once your other people arrive."

"I'd appreciate that, together we can better serve the assignment." Hershel reached out and the two of them shook hands, "You're good people, Detective."

"You too, Inspector, you too."

***

It was close to twenty-one hundred, when both teams were up to full strength and had set their new check point on the gravel road. The dusk made it much more difficult to see anything in the wooded area. Detective Harper had filled Spano and Askew in on the situation as Hollis and the second agent leaned in. Inspector Hershel and Tremblay walked over to the group, "Detective, what do you suggest to do now?"

Spano was surprised to hear the Canadian Inspector ask Harper that question. "Inspector, as I see it we've got a couple of issues. It's too dark to make a rush on the cabin and the fog is closing in. However, I think we have the element of surprise if we do go in the dark."

Hershel stood back and watched the interchange between the Americans and could see that all of the men listened to Harper and were in agreement. "Okay, we'll need to review the surveillance photos that the drones took earlier." They all huddled around the map that Hershel spread on the hood of Detective Spano's vehicle. Spano and Hollis took out their cell phones and clicked on the flashlight app so that everyone could make out the details. Hershel pointed to the water's edge and three boats in the water, positioned to take off. "They've got two cigarette boats and a cabin cruiser lowered in the water. Before we do anything we'll need to get the Coast Guard in position in the event that they jump in the boats."

Hollis leaned in, "We've also got two twenty-five-foot Defender class boats just off the shoreline that can move into position to support your teams, Inspector."

"That would be great," he drew a circle around the cabin, "We've got to put people inside the circle before we make our move, thus we'll have everyone trapped. If they can't get out of our contained area, we'll have a better chance of taking them alive."

"I agree," Harper added, "Inspector show me where you want our people to position themselves." They plotted out the terrain around the cabin, setting up the strike force they were planning to use. Each officer was given their order; no one was to fire until Hershel gave the order.

Detective Harper contacted Chief Mathews to update him. "I have full trust in you and your people, Detective," Mathews texted back. "Have Inspector Hershel advise his men that taking Vinnie La Russo alive is critical to our case."

"I already have, sir. We'll keep you informed." Harper knew that Mathews was still manning headquarters with Agent Downey, even though it was close to midnight.

\*\*\*

Vinnie La Russo was happy that Mario handled the assignment and brought the four extra men to help defend their escape. He planned to go over the details with his nephew, "Mario, tomorrow morning right before sun up I think we'll load the boats and head out of here." Vinnie pointed to a map on the table, "I've got a plane that we'll get to right here," pointing to the map, "Mario, it's perfect, it's located near an Indian Reservation that controls the whole area; we don't have to worry about any authorities."

Mario smiled at his uncle, surprised about the details, "Great plan, I knew you had something set up but who's supplying the planes?"

"Castellanos, he's been hiding up there for the past year. I've sent him the money to set it all up. It's funny but he said that the locals don't even know that he's around. Everyone pretty much keeps to themselves. He has a cabin up there; it's beautiful, tucked away not too far from the shoreline. Castellanos said he has a clearing just past his cabin that will allow the plane to land and take off."

Mario looked surprised, "Castellanos? I thought he was dead!"

"Yeah, so did everyone else." Vinnie laughed, a wicked laugh that Mario hadn't heard from his uncle before.

"You kept this to yourself. Didn't you trust me?"

Vinnie put his arm around the younger man, "Mario, it wasn't a case of trust, once the cops got everyone in Greektown last year, Castellanos came to me looking for help. In return for helping him, we got the drug trade that he and Fotopoulos controlled. We've made millions in return for hiding him out."

"I'm surprised, Uncle, but impressed too. You've come up with a solid plan." The young man didn't know if he should try to change the plans but offered, "Since you've got everything all set and we've loaded the boats maybe we should leave tonight."

Vinnie looked back at him, "Mario, if the cops had any idea where we are, we'd already be under siege. This place is a secret, only a couple people know about it and they'd never give it up." Vinnie looked outside and pointed to the boats, "Mario, it's so damn dark out there you couldn't even see your own hands. How about a compromise, how about we'll leave around four in the morning."

Mario gave in, "Sounds good, but if it's okay, I'll make sure everyone's aware. I'd like to load the boats now. I just want to get as far from here as possible." He walked from the large wooden structure to the boat shed where the four men were putting their items in the two cigarette boats. "You guys have everything you need?"

"Yeah, boss, these are two fine rides." The leader, Vlad, wanted to review the plan one more time, "Okay, we're supposed to handle these two sweet boats and run protection for you in the morning until you get to your location on the coast, right?"

Mario nodded, "We figured that two of you will be in each one of these and Vinnie and I would take the cruiser. The idea is that you'll flank us as we head out of the channel. One change though, I want everyone ready to go at three."

Vlad looked back to his men that watched them talking, he nodded, "It's going to be pretty foggy, but we can do it, you can count on us. I know my guys wanted to know about our payoff."

Mario held his hand up, "Vlad, we talked about this. That's why I gave you one-hundred thousand when we left the Eastern Market. You get the other half once we dock at the final destination." Vlad signaled with a thumbs up to his men and shook hands with Mario. Turning, he gave the update to the guys standing next to the first cigarette boat. Mario listened for a few minutes as Vlad gave them the directions. The plans were made, they'd leave the docks no later than four in the morning, but should be ready by three. Mario reminded them, "Guys, we'll have to traverse a dense fog but the channel has markers so we shouldn't have any problems." Mario headed back to the cabin to update Vinnie. Both men gathered their items to put in the cruiser, "Vinnie, I got your suitcase, let's load the cruiser now and make sure we're ready to go."

Pointing to the case that Mario was holding, "That's the most important thing, it's full of hundred dollar bills. We'll have to pay people in New Brunswick in cash once we get to the rendezvous point that Castellanos has set up."

"I'm guessing Castellanos is going with us?"

"Yeah, I had him open an account at the same bank in the Bahamas. The fed's don't have any way to trace it. We've got enough to last all three of us for a very long time." Both men laughed, they knew that they had a perfect plan. They headed to the docks carrying everything to the cruiser. Vinnie told Mario, "Leave that money case in the cabin, we'll check it in the morning."

# FORTY-ONE

**Detective Harper and Inspector Hershel had covered the new** plan with both teams, "We'll all go at twenty-three hundred hours," Hershel told the group that was gathered around him. "We'll have the element of surprise on our side." They huddled around the map that Harper brought from surveillance photos that she had shared with the Canadian team. Hershel continued, "You can see the main cabin is about thirty to forty feet in front of the boat docks. We'll need to separate the men that we saw coming in earlier from the boats as soon as possible. We can't let them get into the channel. Detective Harper and her teams will take the right side of the cabin. I'll take another team to the left side," turning to his partner, "Tremblay you and your team will go for the boats. That's going to be critical to our success."

Tremblay asked, "I understand that it is important, I've issued the grenades to my men."

"Good Max, blow the boats up if you have to, but we can't let them get into the channel."

Max understood, "We can't take a chance on innocent civilians getting involved."

Detective Harper made her pitch to the teams, "It's very important that we take both key suspects alive, they have details on the drug traffic trade that both countries need to gather to stop it." She then motioned to Detectives Baker and Spano, "Tom you come with me and Joe you take position with Inspector Hershel." Once she completed instructing them, Hershel motioned to his men, assigning a Sergeant to each group. Harper pointed to Agent Hollis, "Hollis, why don't you split your men to each of the three groups." He agreed and separated the agents, assigning them to the teams that were going over individual assignments.

It was dark but the cover of midnight and fog could give them the element of surprise they hoped for. It was a two hundred yard trek through the brush and wooded area but the three teams were ready. Hershel and Harper gave everyone the signal and they made their way to the edge of the clearing. Hershel ordered them, "Remember, I don't want anyone to attack until I give the order." The key players were in Tremblay's team. Once they dismantled the boats, the suspects would be surrounded. Trying to be as quiet as possible, the joint task force moved closer to the docks and Tremblay raised his hand, holding them until he had Hershel's order to charge. There it was, one beep on the radio and Tremblay waved his men to move in. This was going to be a silent charge until they were close enough to take the boats. Suddenly they ran into immediate gun fire. Everyone heard the rapid gun fire that rose out of the darkness sending a quick ending to the silence. It was coming from one of the cigarette boats, "I'm hit," was heard from the charging team that was already trying to defend their attacking position.

The sounds of the attack were on, everyone in the charging group figured that Tremblay and his men had started to carry out the orders. Detective Harper and her team now aimed at the one light that showed in the cabin, sending a volley of bullets into the building. Hershel and his men did the same thing moving in from the west side in a simultaneous attack. Surprisingly, there wasn't return gunfire from the cabin. Harper and Baker were now along the side of the building and held their fire looking for a response. She called Hershel on the radio, "Inspector, what's the situation on the other side?"

"We've blown out the window on this side but no one has returned fire here."

"I've got the same situation." They both could here bullets flying from the shoreline where Tremblay and his team were attacking the three boats. Hershel was sure he heard a motor, "Detective, I think they're all at the shore, maybe we need to re-enforce Tremblay's team."

"Agreed, let's leave part of our men here and head to the boats." Harper grabbed Hollis who had joined her, "We'll head to the docks; Baker, you and the two sergeants take the cabin from this side." She headed to the docks and Hershel did the same thing on the other side of the cabin. Harper was crawling through the wet grass avoiding the gun fire that was overhead as Hollis followed. The gun fire from the shore was loud and rapid, turning to Hollis, "They've got automatic weapons; Tremblay needs our help."

They made the trek further to the west and could see the bow of the cabin cruiser. It was still in the water but someone was firing back at them from the rear deck. They heard the engines roar and the sound was too close to be anyone else but their suspects. She made a circling motion to her team with her index finger, they separated firing back at the cruiser in front of them. She continued to crawl toward the front of the cruiser, yelling out, "You're surrounded, give up."

There was still gun fire returned at them as their team approached. Detective Harper rolled over, "Hollis, we've got to get to those cigarette boats." They were making headway when the sound of an engine roared from the shore. She thought that she could see the hull of one of the speedboats lift out of the water, sending a wall of water over the docks. There was more gun fire from the eastern side of her position and she heard the second cigarette boat's engine roar to life. It, too took off and she was puzzled, *where was Tremblay and his team?* Suddenly silence from the cabin was broken when rapid fire sounded like it came from inside. *She wasn't sure what direction should she go to?*

Radioing back to Detective Baker, "What's going on there?" There wasn't an answer. The sounds of gun fire that had suddenly erupted from the cabin and continued attacks from the shoreline had all three teams in multiple battles. Their surprise move wasn't a surprise after all. How did the men at the cabin know they were coming? With the darkness, it was hard to tell who was shooting at whom.

Both cigarette boats left the docks and were plowing through the quiet water of the narrow channel. Mario was at the helm of the first cigarette boat and Vladimir was lying on the rear deck firing at anything that wasn't in the second cigarette boat. Vinnie was grabbing onto the seat, being thrashed back and forth as the speedboat sent a wash over the other boats moored in the channel. The buoy ahead stated 'no wake' as Mario pulled the throttle back racing up to over seventy miles per hour, not even half the speed capability of the high powered machine. The second cigarette boat followed about twenty feet behind, bobbing in the wake of the first boat, trying to make its way into the Marina ahead.

The gunfire at the docks was now limited to the attack on the cabin cruiser. Harper radioed back to the cabin again but didn't have any success raising Baker. She heard Inspector Tremblay who must have been to her left side.

Tremblay shouted, "I called the escaped boats in to the two cutters in the Marina, they're going to block the entrance to Lake Huron." Harper waved back, acknowledging the move.

Detective Harper and Agent Hollis were now at the shoreline and joined Tremblay who was in the middle of a firestorm with at least two men still aboard the cruiser. "I've got a man down, he's been treated by one of my guys, but will be okay," Tremblay then said, "We've got at least two shooters on the cruiser," then he pointed to the boat, "One of them is at the helm, most likely behind a reinforcement of some sort."

"Any idea who we've got in there?"

"Pretty sure it isn't either of your main suspects. I'm sure it looked like Mario was on the cigarette boat."

"Any idea on Vinnie La Russo?"

"No, I can't say that he's been spotted yet."

Once she thought that her two suspects were getting away, Harper didn't want to waste time firing on the cruiser. Harper and Hollis spent a magazine of bullets aimed at the position that Tremblay pointed to, then Hollis hurled a small grenade at the front of the cruiser, the blast was enormous; the front of the boat rose ten feet in the air with a blaze shooting out across the dock and a man's screams pierced the night's darkness.

The cruiser was engulfed in flames as they all approached from the rear and Tremblay made his way to the bow. The fire was now out of control and spread across the boat to the wooden dock. The cruiser was sinking and they could see one man slumped on the top deck. He was surrounded by flames that leaped at him from both sides. Agent Hollis jumped on the sinking ship, grabbing the man who was out cold, and pulling him to the rear that was still out of the water. Harper leaned over the side and helped to pull the body to the dock that was quickly being eaten by the encroaching flames. "Jump, Hollis," she yelled. He leaped over the side as they dragged the man to the grass. Tremblay was now at her side and Harper pointed to the cabin, "We've still got gunfire coming from back there, we need to help Hershel and Baker out." The body they pulled off the cruiser wasn't either suspect, as expected. The man was dead.

All three of them turned and ran along the wet grass to where they heard muffled gunfire and Tremblay radioed Hershel, "What's the situation?"

"We've taken a direct hit, whomever is in there has grenades and I know at least one of our men are down, maybe two." Harper and Hollis got there first and joined Hershel at his position.

"Where's Baker?" she asked.

"Not sure, we were heading to the side of the cabin when the person holed up in there tossed a grenade at us. I saw Baker and my Sergeant hit the dirt but then a volley of bullets made me hit the deck. I haven't seen them since."

Harper had a lump in her throat, "Were they hit?"

"Not sure, detective, but we've got to get this guy before trying to see what happened."

She knew he was right, "I'm going in from the left, Hollis you go to the right, Inspector cover us." Before he could answer both of them made their way to the side of the cabin. Tremblay arrived and both he and Hershel took aim, firing at the side of the cabin protecting the approaching team members. Hollis tossed a grenade into the opened window and debris flew everywhere and the wall collapsed. Hershel and Tremblay followed, now with guns drawn but no one was now firing back at any of them. Detective Harper slowed in the grass, a man's body was lying face down in a puddle; it was Baker. She slid to his side and called his name, "Tom, Tom you okay?" He didn't answer. She ran her hand over his side and it was wet, *is that blood or dew, please let it be dew*, she thought.

Hollis made it to her side, "We got the guy inside," he saw she was holding Baker, "Is he okay?"

"Doesn't look good." Hollis turned on his cell phone and pressed the flashlight app, Harper rolled Baker over, his face was covered in blood and she could see what looked like a gash along the side of his head. "We need to stop the bleeding."

Hollis looked around and ran back to the side of the cabin, he returned with a large piece of material. "Where'd you get that?"

"Off the dead guy in the cabin, don't think he's going to need it anymore." They both wiped at the obvious wound to Baker and Harper cradled his head as Hollis tried to revive him.

Inspector Hershel was now at their side. He didn't say anything when Spano crawled next to Harper. "Amy, let me get in there."

She continued to cradle Baker's head as Spano and Hollis worked on him. "Harper, he's been shot, looks like a chest wound." Spano tore Baker's shirt and Hollis kept his flashlight on the man lying in the grass. "I've got a pulse," Baker was struggling to take breaths as the team crowded around him trying to see how they can help.

# FORTY-TWO

**The cigarette boat churned its way through the Marina and** now spotted the two cutters closing in, blocking the opening to Lake Huron. The cutters had their guns aimed at the first cigarette boat when the second boat appeared, gaining speed and aimed directly at the hull of one of the cutters. Yells from the bridge could be heard, "Shit, they're going to ram us!" The sailors were informed that key suspects were most likely on board and it was critical not to let them make it into the Lake. The order came to fire at the two charging boats, but the cigarette boats were now clipping at over one-hundred miles per hour and were on top of the two cutters in seconds. The first boat crashed directly into the crease that the two cutters created when they were nose to nose and the second cigarette boat followed. The composite fiberglass hull and windshield of the first boat ripped a gaping hole in the cutter. Both cutters took damage to their hulls and were taking in water. The two speed boats made their way past the rock formation protecting the channel and disappeared into Lake Huron.

One of the cutter captain's radioed back to Inspector Tremblay, "You didn't tell us that these guys are riding with Jason Bourne; they crashed right through us. We've got serious damage and can't pursue them."

Tremblay relayed the details to Hershel. "I'll need to call this into the American cutters stationed in the Lake." The call to the eighty-seven foot coastal patrol boat sounded the alert. The USCGC Barracuda was positioned along the northern coast of Lake Huron in Canadian waters. The RCMP Commander in Ottawa gave the boat clearance to operate in the waters because the Canadians only had the two boats that were stationed at the Marina, and after the crash, were out of commission. Another Canadian cutter was positioned too far away to get into the chase with the time they were given. The USCGC also had another cutter that took action heading south along the Lake toward Port Huron. Everyone agreed that it made more sense that the suspects would head north but they had to make sure all areas were covered. Once Tremblay got confirmation that the Barracuda was taking action, he turned his attention back to the situation at the cabin.

Mario, standing at the wheel, continued to keep the throttle wide open as the two cigarette boats cut through the dark waters of Lake Huron, heading to their destination. The white water that splashed up along the sides of the boat were the only things that they could make out. They checked the depth finders insuring that they were in deep enough waters and tried to stay as close to the shoreline as possible. The cigarette boats were traveling at close to one-hundred-fifty miles per hour, faster than any chase boat could catch up to. "Vinnie, you okay?" Mario hollered.

The man had fallen at least twice, once when they collided with the cutters in the Marina. "No. I'm not okay, what the hell, you're crazy. I thought we planned to let the other boat hit the cutters first."

Mario was pissed, "I got your ass out of there, and that's all you say, who should have gone first. They had their guns aimed at us, either charge through or be killed. If I didn't suggest that we stay on the boats, we'd been captured back there."

Vinnie was surprised at the way Mario came back at him, he'd never done that before. "Hey, remember this is my plan, I'm in charge."

That's how it had been his whole life, Mario was finally done, "You selfish old son of a bitch. I saved your life back there and all you care about is who's the boss. Well right now, I'm the boss; you better hope I don't toss your ass overboard." Mario ordered the second cigarette boat to peel off and head toward the Blue Water Bridge. He messaged them, "You'll need to stay south along the American side; we can't have the Coast Guard chasing just one boat."

\*\*\*

Inspector Hershel called in to the back-up team in Sarnia, "We need a medivac, we have one critical injury with at least two men down." They answered with an affirmative, and confirmed that a chopper would be there in ten minutes. "Detective Harper," Hershel said, "I've got a doctor in a chopper on the way; how's he doing?"

Harper was still cradling Baker's head and Spano answered, "We've got a pulse and he's breathing. I've got his face to stop bleeding with the medical items that Hollis found in the cabin. He's still losing a lot of blood from the chest wound."

Tremblay made his way back to the group on the ground, "I got the details to the American group and they'll take up the chase in the Lake. How's our guy doing?"

Spano answered, "Not sure, how about the Sergeant that was shot?"

"They've got him stable, hopefully more of a flesh wound."

Hershel came running to the group, "Max, we've got a chopper coming in from Sarnia, they'll get our men to the hospital." Hershel hardly finished his statement when the sound of the approaching helicopter came into their area. Looking up, "Max, try to signal to them."

The chopper flooded the ground with bright lights and slowly lowered into the clearing along the side of the large cabin. Two medics jumped out and ran to where Harper and Spano were tending to Tom Baker. "We'll take care of him," one of the medics quickly stated. They crouched over him, immediately inserting an I.V. into Baker's right arm getting important fluids into him. Harper continued to stay on her knees as they worked on him. "You did a good job," the medic said aloud to no one in particular, "He's stable, lost a lot of blood but we've got some on board." They slid a stretcher under Baker and carried him to the chopper.

Tremblay yelled, "I got one more guy that's injured, can he jump on?"

"Yeah, anyone else coming with us?"

"No," Harper called back, "We've got two people that escaped. Just take good care of them." Spano was surprised that she didn't want to go but happy that she decided to continue to lead the team. They watched the chopper lift off and disappear into the dark skies. Harper turned to Hershel, seemingly with a new resolve, "Okay Inspector, what's next?"

\*\*\*

Vinnie wasn't happy with Mario but realized that his nephew might feel the same way right now. "We've got to make it to the spot that Castellanos has set up for us, it's supposed to be marked but it's so damn dark and foggy, I don't know if we will find it." He waited for Mario to answer.

Vlad, who had paid attention to the argument that the two men had, jumped in to the conversation. "We got to radio the other boat to let them know the final plan."

When he said that, Vinnie turned to the back of the boat, almost forgetting about Vlad being on board. "You're right, come on up here and we'll call them." Vlad made his way to where Vinnie was holding onto the seat. The boat continued charging through the water at enormous speeds heading along the shore just north of MacGregor Point. They both went into the cabin to see the map that Vinnie held showing the rocky shores with a memo from Castellanos warning that the waters could be treacherous. Vinnie decided to tell Mario, "If you want to review this with Vlad, I'll come up and hold the wheel."

"Okay, that sounds good, come on up here," slowing down, he held the wheel with one hand waiting for Vinnie to make his way to the helm. When they were close, Mario reached out grabbing his shoulders, "Here, grab the wheel."

Vinnie grabbed the wheel and must have wondered if Mario was really going to help steady him or really toss him overboard. "Got it," Vinnie said. Mario stepped back letting Vinnie get behind the wheel and plopping into the seat.

"Keep it steady, don't slow down too much, we need to get to our destination." Mario slid into the cabin to where Vlad was holding the map. "Vlad, you'll need to contact them once we're clear on this." They set the plan, and Vlad was okay with everything. He was holding onto the railing with one hand and the map with the other. He took the first step up when Mario clubbed him from behind, with the butt of his gun, knocking the big man to the cabin floor. Vlad hit the bottom with a thud and Mario put a bullet in the back of his head. "That's your meeting spot." Vinnie heard the gun shot and wondered where his pistol was, looking over to where he had been holding onto the seat he saw it, lying on the deck. Mario appeared out of the cabin, "I know we planned to get rid of him, so I thought this was a good time." Vinnie had a strange look on his face that told Mario something was wrong. "You okay?"

"I'm not sure, you're the one holding the gun."

"What, are you talking about? That crap from before? It was just a ploy to get Vlad off guard. Hey, we're in this together, but remember we're a team. Now we don't have to share the money with any of them." Both men laughed.

Vinnie asked, "What about the other cigarette boat, they'll expect us to meet at Point Clark, like we told them."

"Yeah, about that, the map I gave them will send them directly into one of the small islands that juts out into the Lake. They don't know how treacherous the rocky waters heading to the Bridge are. At best they'll go aground, or if we're lucky they'll crash. Either way, they don't know our final destination. We're on our way." Mario took over the reins of the boat and opened the throttle to full speed.

*** 

The situation back at the cabin was dire, two men being transported to the hospital, the suspects escaping into the vastness of Lake Huron and not having any idea where they were headed to. Harper stood next to Inspector Hershel, listening to him getting the details from the Captain at the air station. "Okay, Captain, how many will it hold?" Once he completed the call, he turned to Harper. "We've got a CH-146 Griffon Chopper on the way. It's a tactical transport that can take all of us, hopefully, following the course that the cigarette boats took." It wasn't much, but now it was their only option. The cigarette boat had a huge lead and because the cutter chasing it hadn't any success in finding where it headed to, things started looking bleak.

"How long before it gets here?"

"No more than ten minutes."

Agent Hollis and Detective Spano had completed searching the cabin but, unfortunately, didn't find anything showing where the suspects might be headed. Spano said, "I can't believe that there isn't anything here that tells us what their plans were."

Tremblay added, "Guess it could have helped if we captured one of these guys. They might have given up the plans." He turned back to the dock where the cabin cruiser had sunk, only the shattered hull still visible. Then he looked over at the cabin with the side wall blown out. We got two of them, but there were four thugs along with the two suspects. Maybe one of those other thugs is still hiding. They looked at each other, the sound of the chopper overhead got their attention. Tremblay turned to his sergeant, "Spread out and search this place one more time."

The chopper landed and Hershel and Harper ran to the opened door followed by Hollis and Spano. Tremblay yelled out, "I'll handle things here, I'll call you with an update if we find anything."

# FORTY-THREE

**The cutter, Barracuda, continued its search along the choppy** waters of Lake Huron with no results. They checked with the second cutter that patrolled the southern area of the Lake going toward the Blue Water Bridge. The Captain radioed, "Have you had any sightings heading your way"

"Negative, the only things we've seen is a steel hauler making its way down to Lake Erie. We circled it to make sure they didn't pick up any passengers but their Captain said they hadn't seen anything in the water."

The cutters were at a disadvantage, the cigarette boat had a top speed that was three times that of the cutter and although the Barracuda had a small chopper that it deployed in the search, they didn't see even a wake from either of the cigarette boats that it chased. To top it off, they were chasing two boats, with no idea which one held the key suspects. Could they have split up? Once they were aboard the CH-146 Chopper, Inspector Hershel contacted the American cutter that was headed north along the Canadian Coast. "Captain, this is Inspector Hershel with the RCMP, can you give our chopper's pilot your location?"

"Roger that, Inspector."

The pilot radioed the information back through everyone's headphones, "Looks like we're chasing a ghost, folks. We have a couple issues, first we're chasing two boats that have top speeds of one-hundred-fifty miles per hour, and Lake Huron has the longest shoreline of any of the Great Lakes." Detective Harper shook her head, it wasn't anything she wanted to hear, however, it was the reality of the situation. He continued, "I've contacted the two cutters, neither have sighted your suspects. The Barracuda has decided to move closer to the shoreline and just passed Point Clark, that's where the shore turns further to the east."

"Captain, this is Detective Harper, what do you suggest?"

"Our best bet is to follow the cutter's path but skirt closer to the Canadian shoreline."

Harper and Spano had the same thought, "Why?" She asked.

"Detective, your side of the Lake has more towns and cities that might report seeing something suspicious. Our side is dotted with small villages and many Indian Reservations. There are great hiding spots in Canada versus in Michigan." That made sense to all of them.

"Okay Captain, let's do it your way, we need to find these guys." The chopper flew along the Canadian coast as low as possible hoping to catch sight of one of the escaped cigarette boats. The Captain had his lights on, illuminating the surface below. The only thing they could see was black murky water and occasionally rocks that jutted into the surf. They had been airborne for thirty minutes without any results. Still no news from the Cutter and the DEA had added surveillance drones from Selfridge Air National Guard. Harper and Spano sat peering out into the dark hoping to spot something.

Hershel got a radio call and everyone turned to see what it was about. "Thanks, you did a great job getting them there. We're on the move, heading along the coast, Tremblay is still at the cabin and hoping to find anything that would help us in our search. " He turned and saw Harper and Spano along with Hollis listening for some news, hopefully positive. "Detective Harper, your man Baker is at McLaren Hospital in Port Huron, he's in the Trauma Unit. The ER team has him stabilized and he'll be in surgery soon. His Vitals look good." They all gave a thumbs up and Spano patted Harper on the back.

She breathed a sigh of relief, then asked, "How is your Sergeant, Inspector?"

"He'll be fine, already in a room. Thanks for asking."

"Spano, once we catch these guys, I want to head to McLaren Hospital in Port Huron." He knew what she meant and understood.

The chopper kept searching along the Eastern Canadian coast of the Lake. It was flying about five hundred feet above the surface of the water and kept their floodlight focused on the area below. Harper and Spano were happy that Baker's condition was looking good. Spano said, "Harper, we'll get them," as he smiled at her.

"Just glad that Baker's okay. My fault that he's involved."

"No I don't think so, I bet if you asked him, even now he'll tell you the same thing, that's right where he wanted to be. Harper, let's go get them bastards." She finally smiled back at him and gently punched him in the shoulder.

\*\*\*

Mario held on to the wheel tightly when Vinnie asked, "What are you planning to do with the body down there," pointing to the cabin below.

"Can't dump it out here, it will leave a trail for them to follow."

They continued running at a high speed, and Vinnie looked at his map, "Mario, there should be a few small islands coming up soon. From what Castellanos mapped out, we should stay to the right side because our landing area is not far from the last island."

Mario slowed down, concerned about the waters depth so close to the shoreline, he checked the depth finder, "Vinnie, keep your eye on this for me, it reads fifty feet, then went down to thirty. We can't be below fifteen feet. This is almost too shallow."

Vinnie studied the screen, "You're sure we need to be on the right side?"

"Yeah, I'm looking right now, you should see three islands in a row; the last one is the biggest."

Mario was down to fifteen miles per hour, not leaving a wake when the second island came into view. He tried to use the flood lights on the front of the boat but only one worked, he figured that the other one was damaged in the collision with the cutters in the Marina. "Okay, here's the second island."

It was very small and then another came into view, "Vinnie look at the map, here's the third little island. This one is much bigger." Vinnie was still positioned next to Mario and had the map in one hand while checking the depth finder. "Okay, Castellanos said he'll put a marker on the rocks, we need to watch for it."

"How in the hell we gonna see anything in this darkness. What exactly are we looking for?"

Looking down again at the map, Vinnie said, "He put a bright red hockey stick standing up in a pile of flat rocks. That's where we need to look for a cleared spot to hook up to." They floated past piles of rocks but neither man saw the marker that they searched for. They were at the end of the last of the three small islands when Vinnie yelled, "There, over there, looks like a totem pole but I'm sure the top is a hockey stick."

Mario shook his head, "How are we to be sure that's it. Christ, you said there are Indian Reservations along the coast, maybe it's their sign."

Vinnie looked back at him, "What? You think the Indians in Canada worship hockey gods. It's the damn marker. There should be a little cove to pull into." They had floated about a hundred yards past what might have been their marker when Vinnie hollered, "The cove, that's it, right here."

Mario shut the motor down, "Vinnie, grab something to pull us to the shore." Mario climbed to the back and had ropes in his hand, hoping to have something to tie up to.

"I got some rope, can you use this?"

Mario looked at what Vinnie was holding, "That's perfect! I'll just hop over the side," holding the rope in one hand he jumped for the shoreline, glad that Castellanos must have cleared the sharp rocks because he slid off the moss covered rocks into the shallow water. Still holding the rope, he got to his feet and pulled the boat.

"You okay?" Vinnie asked.

"Yeah, I thought you said he had something for us to tie up to. I don't see anything like that." He pulled the rope tight, holding the cigarette boat in place while looking for a spot to tie the boat up. "I don't see anything, I'm going to try to see if something will work on the shore." Mario pulled the rope and tied the end to a small tree. "It won't go anywhere, hopefully we won't need it again." The boat lodged in the cove.

Vinnie slid his leg over the side and hopped out, into the shallow water. "If we're at the right spot, the cabin should be close to the shoreline." The two men climbed up and over the rocky ledge, making their way along the shore. Vinnie stumbled, "Shit, it's still so dark, I can't see anything. We better be careful, we don't know what's ahead. We don't know if we're in the right spot, we don't want to alert someone if we're in the wrong field." Walking a little farther Vinnie turned to Mario, "I'm pretty sure this is Castellanos' place. He sent me a photo, the cabin is over there," pointing to the small wood structure that stood out in the darkness with a yellow light glowing from the front of the building, "He has a barn around the back, the plane should be parked in there."

Mario had burrs on his legs and was pretty tired, "I could use some sleep and something to eat."

"Yeah, me too," Vinnie was still sore from all the bumping around in the cigarette boat. He knew he would have bruises everywhere.

They made it from the path to the front of the cabin. It was dark inside but the hue from the yellow bulb allowed them to see into the front room. Vinnie walked to the bank of windows on the front porch, he tapped on the window, looking back at Mario, "I don't want to get shot; I bet not many people come to the porch." He called out, "Nick, it's Vinnie and Mario."

They stood on the porch for a few minutes and finally saw lights come on from inside. The man inside opened the door a slither, it was Castellanos, "What the hell are you doing here at this time? I didn't expect you for hours!" Pushing open the door wider, he stood in the doorway in his boxer shorts, shaking his head, "It's still the middle of the night."

Mario was standing behind Vinnie and let out a loud laugh, "Nick, you look pretty good for a dead guy." They both laughed and then Mario and Castellanos hugged. Mario stepped back, "Nick, why didn't you let me know that you were okay. Christ, you missed a heck of a funeral." They both laughed again.

Castellanos turned to Vinnie, who looked pretty ragged, "Okay, why are you here so damn early, and don't give me a bunch of crap."

Vinnie nodded, "Let's get inside and I'll tell you the whole thing." They moved into the small room and Castellanos turned on a lamp. "You guys want some coffee?"

"Hell, yes," Mario plopped into a big chair and kicked off his shoes. His socks and pant legs were wet and shoes were soaked. "You got something I could put these into, like a dryer."

"No, I just hang clothes outside, there's a couple of hooks on the back porch." Pointing to the back door, he continued heading into the kitchen to put the coffee on. "Vinnie, come on in here, I want to hear this story."

Vinnie followed both of them and thought that getting his

shoes and socks off was also a good idea. Once all three of them were sitting at the kitchen table and Castellanos brought them some dry clothes and poured them a cup of coffee, Vinnie started to tell him what happened. "We had everything all set, Mario brought a crew from the Market to help with our escape in case we needed them. Then I got word from one of our guys. Thank goodness for cops on the take; a guy in the Third Precinct calls and says the cops had joined a task force with the Canadian police and planned a surprise raid on the cabin. We were lucky, Mario had the guys get everything ready right after the call and we were on the cigarette boats ready to pull out when they attacked."

Castellano looked over at Mario, "So I guess you shot your way out?"

"Kind of, actually one of the guys was still in the cabin and he held down the cops for enough time for us to get the boats going and out to the Marina. I know we could hear gun shots and an explosion when we were headed down the channel."

"But you obviously got away, bet those cigarette boats helped."

Mario smiled, "You bet, one-hundred-fifty mph, we flew out of there. Had a James Bond moment in the Marina but it worked out okay."

"What did you do with the boats?"

"Just one boat and I tied it to a tree by the Lake. Vinnie said you'd have a spot but I couldn't find it."

Castellanos turned to Vinnie, "Okay, how close are they, and you better level with me."

"I'm not sure, we probably need to get out of here as soon as possible. Mario had the guys in the other cigarette boat head across to the U.S. side of the Lake and we followed the route you and I planned."

Castellanos suggested, "Mario, we'll ditch the boat in the Lake. We can sink it and take off in the plane."

While they were talking, Vinnie got up and went in the front room, he quickly returned, "Mario, where's that suitcase?"

Mario looked down on the floor, "Guess we left it in the boat, we can get it later."

Vinnie shook his head, "I'd feel a lot better if we had it now."

Mario shrugged, "I got no pants, shoes or socks on, it ain't going nowhere."

Castellanos turned to Vinnie, "Let's wait till later, it will get a little lighter soon. Mario, I'll go with you, it's kind of tricky down there. Vinnie, how much time do we got before we need to get out of here?"

Vinnie thought about the suitcase that was loaded with cash. "Okay, but I'm thinking, they'll figure this out soon, we need to take off as soon as it's light enough to do so."

"Okay, Mario and I will push the plane out of the barn after we get that suitcase. It gets light a little before six, we'll go then."

"How big is this plane?" Mario asked.

"It's a Cessna 172, can seat four people. I didn't know who Vinnie was bringing with him. It's one of the most popular light aircraft, it will get us to wherever we need to get."

"I didn't know you were a pilot?"

"I wasn't when we bought it. Took lessons, I've logged a hundred flying hours, we'll be fine, Mario."

"Yeah, that's what they told the people on the Titanic."

# FORTY-FOUR

**The pilot of the chopper continued skirting the shoreline when** he suddenly banked to the right and went lower, much lower. The co-pilot asked, "What is it, Captain?" surveying the surface.

"Over there," pointing down to a building on the shoreline. "There's a cabin with a pretty big barn out in the middle of nowhere." He went back up to five thousand feet. "Why would someone have such a big barn and no sign of crops anywhere. We need to check that out." He radioed back to his passengers who were already looking out the sides, "I've spotted a cabin that looks suspicious, thought we should check it out." The sky was getting a little brighter with the sun coming up over the ridge. They had been searching for well over an hour and it was close to five-thirty. The pilot dipped down over the field one more time, and his passengers peered out hoping for a positive sign of their suspects.

The CH-146 was a tactical helicopter that the Canadian military employed. It was multi-use, equipped with aerial firepower, reconnaissance and rescue ability. The Captain knew he could accomplish almost anything the crew wanted. "There, over there," called Spano. Everyone looked out to the left, "It's a boat tied up to the shore, not a dock insight. Is that the cigarette boat?"

"Yes," Inspector Hershel quickly answered, "That's it."

The pilot lifted back up turning out farther into the Lake, "You've got to decide, if we make another pass and they're down there, it will signal that we're close."

There was a lot of conversation from his passengers, "Captain, can we set down close enough that we'll be able to hike to the cabin without too much trouble."

He answered, "Let me make another pass farther inland." He made a wide bank back to the east and there was a hint of excitement in the chopper. Harper had moved to the edge of her seat and pressed the headphones tighter, wanting to make sure she heard every word that the Captain was saying. They were now over a wooded lot and soon climbed over a ridge that opened their view to the field where the cabin and barn in question were located. The Captain came back on, "I'm afraid the chopper is going to warn them so I'm going to peel off," he banked back to the ridge and then asked, "What's the plan?"

Inspector Hershel immediately said, "We can't let them get back to that damn boat, Captain, can you sink it?"

Detective Harper cautioned, "Won't that tell them we're here. Maybe you should set us down first."

The Captain came back, "Detective, I can blow the boat up at any time, it could be in the water and I can still do it. I'll drop you all off in the field far enough from the cabin so you can make a protective approach. Then I'll take care of that boat."

It was agreed. "Hershel made sure everyone was well armed; the chopper had a variety of rifles and small arms and each person was issued a grenade. Harper reiterated, "Captain, we need to take these guys alive if possible."

"Understandable, Detective, we'll do our best. We need to be ready for anything."

***

Mario ran to the barn where Vinnie and Castellanos were loading their items in the small plane, "There's a helicopter out there. I thought I heard it and then the sound went away, but I'm sure it's back and sounds closer."

"You sure?" Vinnie said, "I didn't hear anything." They peeked out of the barn and all three looked across the horizon but nothing was in view and none of them heard the sound of a chopper.

"I'm sure there's one out there. How long before we can take off?" Mario was in a panic.

"We're ready, just finished gassing up the plane, we need to push it out to the field." Nick Castellanos and Mario started to push the plane as Vinnie pushed open the double wide barn doors. They stopped for a second, "Wait, I think heard it," Castellanos said. He stood in the opened barn doors, "You're right, it's a chopper, sounds pretty close." They continued pushing the plane and made it outside when he yelled, "What the hell was that?" A loud explosion followed by a flame burst from the sky came from near the shoreline. It was followed by a sudden eruption with a blaze rising high in the dark sky. "They've blown up the boat."

The small plane was just outside of the doorway of the barn and Vinnie hollered, "How far do we need to push this before you can take off?"

"We need to get it a few feet further," as Vinnie and Mario continued to push, Castellanos climbed in. He was working on the dials and levers and he called out, "Clear away from the front," the blades of the plane's prop sputtered and spun as smoke from the engines bellowed out.

Mario asked, "How fast can you go? Can we outrun that chopper?"

"Yeah, once we get up, the engines will gave us a maximum speed of one-hundred-eighty mph."

Vinnie grabbed the handle and climbed in followed by Mario, "Let's get the hell out of here."

The chopper appeared out of the sky heading right for the front of the barn and was swooping lower. Mario's eyes were as big as a saucer and he yelled, "They're going to blow us up." He pushed opened the door and jumped out, running as fast as he could, Vinnie followed. The engines were still reviving up and Castellanos jumped out and decided to run. The propellers continued to spin and the plane started to roll in a circle.

When Castellanos caught up to the two of them he shouted, "Christ, Vinnie, you've got the military coming after you." The sound of the explosion this time was much closer and deafening, all three of them fell to the ground as the plane and barn went up in flames. Shards of lumber fell from the sky landing on top of them. Castellanos got to his feet, a little wobbly and started running for the woods. The other two were scrambling to their feet and took off running in different directions.

Detectives Harper and Spano were now running at full speed when they saw the plane and barn going up in smoke, Joe saw one of the men running and charged toward him. "I got this one," Spano called out. It was like watching a slow motion replay in football as he leaped from the ground tackling Castellanos. Once he had him on the ground he pulled the man's arms back and cuffed him. Not sure who he had, but he knew the guy wasn't going anywhere now.

Looking up, Spano could see Detective Harper and Agent Hollis giving chase to two others that ran from the barn. Harper was gaining on her guy and Hollis made sure his guy wasn't getting too far into the woods. The agent shot once, bringing the runner down, like a deer in the field. Hollis made it to his guy and rolled him over, "Vinnie La Russo, you're under arrest."

"You shot me, I need a doctor."

"Yeah, you'll get one but not too soon. It's only a leg wound." Pulling Vinnie to his feet, Hollis saw Spano dragging Castellanos with him. They both looked out and saw Harper who was now almost at the cabin. The guy she chased was on the steps when she grabbed his jacket and spun him around and they both ended up on the ground. Spano was now just a few feet away and saw her put an elbow in the guys back and then a knee to his crotch. 'Ouch, Spano thought.'

Pulling her guy to his feet, he was doubled over and couldn't stand straight. "Mario La Russo, you're under arrest."

Inspector Hershel had caught up to his three American partners who each had one of the suspects in cuffs. Vinnie was yelling, "You can't arrest us, cop, we're in Canada, out of your jurisdiction."

Hershel laughed, "He's right, detective, Mr. La Russo, you're all under arrest and in the custody of the Royal Canadian Mounted Police. I'm Chief Inspector Hershel, and you'll be charged with drug smuggling and terrorist activity in Canada."

The look on Vinnie's face was priceless, "Terrorists, we ain't terrorists."

Harper loved it, the fear on Vinnie's face was worth everything. She turned to the Inspector, "Once you've arraigned them, could the United States take this scum into custody, we'd like to charge them with capital murder of a Detroit Police Officer."

Vinnie sneered, "You ain't got nothing, cop."

"Oh yeah, guess your old friends, Oscar White and State Rep Matt Cusmano think everything they knew could help us with that. It was surprising how quick they were willing to make a deal."

As they secured their prisoners, the chopper circled and landed in the open field a hundred yards from the cabin. The pilot and co-pilot climbed out, "Guess these are your guys? Didn't want to get too close to that bonfire," pointing at the blaze from the plane and barn.

Hershel shook his head, "Yeah, good work, Captain. But I have to say, when you veered down it scared me too."

"Great work, Captain," Harper said. "We couldn't have done it without you."

\*\*\*

When the call came into headquarters Chief Mathews and Agent Downey gave out a cheer. Lieutenant Jackson smiled and was happy that the SIU team captured the key suspects. Mathews looked at Jackson. "Lieutenant, we need to contact the rest of the team and the Mayor. After that, why don't you head home, you deserve the day off."

"Thank you sir. I'll take care of everything." She didn't know why, but she shook his hand, "Glad to be working for you."

"Glad to have you on our team, Lieutenant."

Mathews turned to Downey, "We'll have some negotiations to complete with the Canadian Commander in Ottawa, but I don't see any problems, do you?"

"No, I think everything will be just fine."

\*\*\*

Harper kept her promise, she had the chopper drop her off in Port Huron to check on Baker. He had just been out of surgery and smiled when she came into his room. "I must be dying if you're here to see me."

"She gently touched his hand. "You better not be dying or I'll have to kill you." They both laughed, Baker held her hand as they sat silently.

# FORTY-FIVE

**It was a cool fall day as Detectives Harper and Spano made** their way into the Chief's office. They were greeted by Lieutenant Jackson. She immediately got up and shook both of their hands, "Good job, Detective's, I know everyone on the force is proud of you."

They smiled and thanked her. "It was nice that the Chief gave us a day off. I'm not sure why but he said we're to report here before going upstairs."

Jackson smiled at both of them, "Yes, he wanted to talk to both of you before today's press conference." Jackson led them into the Chief's office and closed the doors as she walked out.

Mathews was all smiles; he held up the morning Free Press, pointing to the headlines. '*Combined Canadian and Detroit Police capture Murder Suspects*!' He handed it to Detective Harper, "Great job, Detectives, I can't tell you how much this all means to the city. The press has been clamoring for answers to their questions and I've been able to hold them off until this morning. We'll all go downstairs, our Mayor, as well as the Mayor of Windsor, will be there. I think he's bringing Inspector Hershel with him. Remember this was a joint task force so Hershel will probably want to say something too. Would either of you want to speak?"

"No thanks, Chief," Harper said. "We couldn't have succeeded without the Canadians' help. Inspector Hershel and Tremblay were great and the Captain of the helicopter was awesome. Chief, he crippled both the cigarette boat and plane for us so catching these guys was pretty easy."

Spano chuckled, "Yeah, but you should have seen Harper take down Mario. She tossed him around like a rag doll." They all laughed, even Harper, who turned to Spano, "Oh, the Lions are looking for a free safety, I might give it a try out." It was great to be able to enjoy the moment.

Mathews leaned back and picked up something off his desk. "I'd like to do this before the press conference, I promised Carole Newton with Channel 7 and exclusive with both of you later on."

He held two small boxes in his right hand while talking, "Detective Harper, your leadership of the SIU team in this case and during Detective Frederickson's absence has been remarkable. Everyone upstairs and on the force are proud of how you handled yourself, and so am I. It is indeed my pleasure to award you a well-deserved promotion from Sergeant to the rank of Lieutenant." He pinned a single gold bar on each of her uniform lapels.

A tear ran down her cheek with a huge smile on her face. "Chief, I appreciate this but really the whole team was involved in the case."

"I agree, Lieutenant." The sound of him saying Lieutenant almost made her turn around looking for someone else. "I have a few more awards to hand out." Detective Spano, you've been promoted to the rank of Sergeant, First Class." He handed Joe the arm badges to apply to his uniform. "Joe, you and Amy did us proud. This was an International case and the way you both worked with the Canadian authorities and our own DEA was exemplary."

Harper turned to Spano, "Congratulations, Joe, you earned this."

"You, too, Lieutenant." They both had a broad smiles on their face.

Mathews nodded in approval. "Guess now you know why I asked you to wear your uniforms. Hard to pin this hardware on your golf shirt." They all laughed. "Spano, Lieutenant Jackson has a Sergeant jacket out there for you. I wanted both of you dressed showing your new rank for the press conference."

After handshakes they both started to walk out of the office and Harper stopped, "Joe, I need to ask the Chief something," she doubled back knocking on the door.

"Yes?" The doors opened wide and Harper stood there, "I hope you don't mind Sir, but I have two requestsc."

"What is it?'

"Andy Jones' mother has been waiting to bury her son. The Medical Examiner said they held his body at your request. I'd like to help Andy's mom bury him."

"Absolutely, Lieutenant Harper, that was an oversight on my part. Not only can we release his body but we need to tell her about her son's heroic activities as an undercover officer. The department will pay for his funeral, a full honor guard will be present and I'd be proud to stand at her side with you. What's the other request?"

"Baker sir, he did a great job and deserves a promotion."

"I agree, his name has already been submitted to the review board for his role and promotional considerations are in the works.

"Thank you, sir."

The Chief added, "Harper, you better call Andy Jones mom and give her the news. I'd rather you tell her, can't let her see it on the television. I know you'll give Carole Newton some details about Andy for her article. Let Ms. Jones know she'll get anything Andy had coming including death benefit and insurance monies." Harper nodded, "See you outside in an hour with the press; bring the whole team down, will you."

"Will do, sir." She walked out of the office, head held high and broad smile on her face. Spano was waiting at the elevators for her. "Thanks Joe, you're a good partner."

"You too, Lieutenant."


\*\*\*


It was close to one in the afternoon and the DMC hospital staff was surprised to see four police vehicles and an entourage of officers, including the Chief of Police, arrive at the main door. The group made its way up to the second floor where two officers stood guard in front of one of the rooms. They stood straight, not exactly sure what was happening. Chief Mathews quietly asked, "Is the Detective and his wife in there?"

"Yes, sir, they're just now watching the press conference."

"The station said it was being telecast as a tape delay for the noon news. We'd like to go in if it's okay?

The two officers didn't quite know what to do, "Yes, sir," They pulled the door opened.

Mathews motioned for Harper and Spano to go in first. Amy walked in followed by Joe. Nancy was surprised to see them, "Hey, we're just watching all of you on television," Detective Frederickson had a puzzled look on his face. He was pretty much still flat on his back but the doctor had approved the bed to be raised a little allowing him to see everything. He saluted, "I'm very proud of you." Then to his surprise the Chief walked in, followed by Askew, Allen and Johnson. "Who's watching the store if all of you are here?" There was a good round of laughs and Nancy held his hand and had tears in her eyes.

The Chief stepped to the right side of the bed, "Don, I know your team promised that they'd get the guys who did this to you, I'm proud to announce that your entire SIU team was involved in some way or another but we got them." There was a cheer from the group. Doctors and nurses were gathered outside in the hallway, wondering what exactly was going on, but when they heard the cheer they also cheered, not knowing why, but they did.

Frederickson looked at Harper and Spano and realized that they were wearing new hardware. "I guess there's congratulations in order. Congrats Lieutenant Harper and Sergeant Spano." They both smiled back at him.

"Yes, Don, you'd agree your team did an outstanding job and earned the new stripes. Along with that, I'm pleased to announce that you are being promoted to Lieutenant First Class." He held the small box in his hand and looked down at Don. "I don't think they'll look too good on your PJ's." That brought laughter and tears around the room. Nancy leaned over and kissed her husband on the cheek and he was totally speechless. "Don, the doctor said you'll be up and walking by the end of the week. That's truly good news."

Although he had a lump in his throat, Frederickson held his hand up. "Chief, you and the SIU team did a great job, I don't know what to say other than I love you all."

The scene was becoming a mini love fest and Spano broke it up, "Hey you can't do that in here or I'll have to arrest some of you." It was great seeing how they all got along and that there was so much good news to celebrate.

\*\*\*

The procession on Lake Shore Drive in Grosse Pointe was a major event. Police cars blocked the streets as legions of officers lined the entrance to the St. Paul Cemetery off of Moross Road and Country Club Drive. The two black limos pulled behind the hearse and stopped under a beautiful red and orange leafed maple tree. It was a beautiful fall day, close to sixty-five degrees and Mary Ann Jones stepped out of the vehicle, followed by Amy Harper and Chief Mathews. Harper held Mary Ann's hand as they followed the six officers from Andy's unit that rode in the second limo. They would carry Andy's casket to the grave site. It was a solemn event that honored a fallen officer.

White covered chairs were set in a circle around the grave site where Mary Ann Jones and Lieutenant Harper took their seats. Chief Mathews sat in the row behind them along with the members of the SIU team. The pallbearers took seats on both sides of the ladies and the Catholic Priest from St. Paul's stood along the side of the casket. His eulogy was short but personal. He had baptized Andy and been his parish priest until Andy joined the Army and was deployed to Afghanistan. He pointed out that Andy was an alter boy at the small school, then a promising young high school football player. The service was short but very touching. Amy Harper held Mary Ann's hand the entire service and the two had forged a relationship that would help both of them through this rough time.

The police kept everyone back from the grave site and roped off the area, extending protection around the cemetery, however the general public was allowed to line the fence on the side street that gave them a good view of the events. The press was asked to limit photos to a minimum and it appeared that they were doing that. The press was granted special access to Mary Ann Jones before the funeral and Carole Newton planned an evening special report for the six o'clock news. Her report would feature Andy's time in Afghanistan with the Army Special Forces and transition to becoming a Detroit Police Officer. Chief Mathews made the agreement with Channel 7 and Carole, with the news teams keeping their coverage to both the military and service of her son as a police officer. No details or aspects of the pending criminal case were to be mentioned.

Leaves fell almost on cue as taps were played by the military band from Selfridge ANG and officers stood saluting. Tears welled in the eyes of friends and fellow police personnel, but no one noticed a tall man that was standing along the gated area. He seemed to be paying special attention to the female Police Lieutenant that sat with Mary Ann Jones. He seemed to be taking photos with his cell phone while holding today's newspaper rolled under his arm. The headline told the story of the newly promoted Lieutenant Amy Harper, with her picture plastered all over the front page. He watched intently, knowing that one day he'd settle the score.

## *The Author*

Tony and his wife, Kathy,along the Detroit skyline.

bbbbbbcbb

# About the Author

Tony Aued is the author of two acclaimed series, The Blair Adams FBI Thriller series, which has earned best-selling awards for the first two novels, *The Package* and *Abduction*, and his new Murder Mystery series that is anchored by *Murder in Greektown*. The new series introduces the main character, Detroit Detectives Don Frederickson, and Amy Harper. It is set in Metro Detroit.

His four book FBI Thrillers are a departure from many other FBI novels with the lead character, Blair Adams, a twenty-three year old female taking center stage. The series has been extremely popular with fans and has been compared to other character based sequels like, Alex Cross, by authors like James Patterson.

Readers describe Aued's writing style similar to that of David Baldacci and James Patterson. Aued said that he enjoys bringing his readers into the life of his characters with the twist and turns that each of them take. The novels have received acclaim from the Macomb Daily, Times Herald, Advisor and Shelby Source.

Tony is a retired teacher who also enjoyed a corporate career that took him throughout the southeastern United States. He enjoys talking to writers groups, book clubs and making presentations at local libraries.

He and his wife, Kathy, have two children and a grandchild. He currently lives in Michigan with their dog, Baxter.

# Special Thanks

To my friends Don Frederickson, Brian Sikorski, Joe Spano, Beena Nagappala, Russell Chavey, David Guzzardo and Carole Arnone, I hope you enjoy the roles you played in this novel. Special thanks to the officers in the Shelby Township Police Department for their assistance.

Thanks for allowing me to use your names for my characters.

Made in the USA
Middletown, DE
08 November 2019